In Every
Face
I Meet

SCEPTRE

Also by Justin Cartwright

Interior
Look At It This Way
Masai Dreaming

In Every Face I Meet

JUSTIN CARTWRIGHT

SCEPTRE

First published in 1995 by Hodder and Stoughton
A division of Hodder Headline PLC
A Sceptre Book

10 9 8 7 6 5 4 3 2

British Library Cataloguing in Publication Data

Cartwright, Justin
  In Every Face I Meet
  I. Title
  823.914 [F]

ISBN 0 340 63782 X

Typeset by Palimpsest Book Production Limited,
Polmont, Stirlingshire
Printed and bound in Great Britain by
Mackays of Chatham PLC, Chatham, Kent

Hodder and Stoughton
A division of Hodder Headline PLC
338 Euston Road
London NW1 3BH

For Penny

One ∫

I wander thro' each charter'd street
Near where the charter'd Thames does flow
And mark in every face I meet
Marks of weakness, marks of woe.

In every cry of every man
In every Infant's cry of fear
In every voice, in every ban,
The mind-forg'd manacles I hear.

How the Chimney-sweeper's cry
Every black'ning Church appals;
And the hapless Soldier's sigh
Runs in blood down Palace walls.

But most thro' midnight streets I hear
How the youthful Harlot's curse
Blasts the new born Infant's tear
And blights with plagues the Marriage hearse.

William Blake, 'London'

∫

November 1990

The boom in mozzarella, trade or consumer led?

The freelance writer Julian Capper has failed to come down firmly on either side. He has concluded that the boom, the one-thousand-percent increase in consumption of mozzarella in the last five years, is a product both of promotion by the supermarkets and demand created by holidaymakers returning from package tours to Italy. The situation is complicated by the fact that pizza is becoming ever more popular, and some of the cheese used for pizza is not the authentic mozzarella, which is produced in Campania. Even in Italy, there is debate about real mozzarella, with the claims of regions like Salerno and Calabria discounted by some experts.

Still, it is clear that the supermarkets have promoted mozzarella successfully. British consumers are even trying the traditional buffalo mozzarella. *This cheese is of an immaculate whiteness and is best accompanied by a glass of crisp, Italian white wine.* That is what he has written. He has also pointed out that mozzarella has an affinity with tomatoes, basil and good olive oil. (He has written about olive oil two or three times in the past.)

Julian Capper conjures the delights of eating mozzarella under a vine in places like Aversa, Agerola and Battipaglia. He has never been to these places, nor indeed to Italy, but he can well imagine the fragrance of the hillsides, the warmth of the sun, the cheerfulness of the peasant population, the simple pleasures of milking the family buffalo, the large vats in which the milk is stirred by hand with a wooden paddle, the conviviality of the local trattoria, the distant views of the Bay of Naples – in fact the all-round love of life which you acquire when you purchase a round ball of mozzarella, suspended in lightly salted water.

He writes for a number of trade papers, but *The Grocer* is perhaps the most demanding. He is hurrying to get his article on mozzarella in the post because he is doing jury service. He has to report at the court each morning at ten and may be required for two weeks or more. He has sent off two other articles: one commissioned, to *Travel Trade Gazette* on Romany caravan holidays, and one speculative, to *Software User* (who are not returning his calls at the moment) on spreadsheets and the home office. He is short of money. There is a possibility of a loss of earnings claim from the court, which he can make backed by a letter from his accountant. He has no accountant at the moment because his last accountant's fees were taking nearly a third of his earnings.

There are a number of attractions to spending two weeks as a juror. Although he had never intended to write for trade papers, he has found that a writer can profit from all sorts of experience, even the simple one of discovering the origins of mozzarella. But cheese and Romany holidays are not really in the same league as murder and bank robbery and rape for providing an insight into the workings of society. He knows, of course, that by the time a case reaches court it will have been repackaged (a word he uses frequently in *The Grocer*), but he believes he will be able to see behind the artificiality and the formality to the human issues. He feels that he will be exploring the real world in some way. As a writer he is always on the lookout for the real world. So he has no doubt that he will profit by his time in court.

He has also found the last five or six years lonely. Writing is not as fulfilling as he had imagined it would be when he set out, after leaving the advertising agency, to go freelance. The agency seemed to be concerned only with the patina of life; he regarded his inevitable sacking as a badge of honour. At the time he believed that he would be freed to pursue larger thoughts and nobler activities, which included writing a stage play about the nature of language. But instead of occupying his mind with spacious thoughts, he has found himself brooding on the rudeness of editors, the smallness and lateness of cheques, and the closed shop of national newspapers. Far from writing his play, or even starting a novel, he has become caught in a solitary round of telephoning and proposing stories to unenthusiastic editors, or chasing payment of the few commissions he has been able to secure. He also spends a good deal of time thinking about the business of being a writer rather than writing.

So he is setting a lot of store by his two weeks (or more) of jury service. He is proposing to use the time to think more deeply, to relaunch himself, to use the term which the trade press favours. He hurries to the post office, pressing the back of the manila envelope down hard as though it may still spring open, and pushes his copy into the postbox. He can hear it land, like a pebble thrown into a well. (In Aversa, where they certainly still have wells.)

Yesterday was his first day. They were shown a film about their duties. They keep a surplus of jurors in the huge holding room. These jurors are called at random to the various courts. He was called, but the case could not start for legal reasons. Jurors are not privy to legal argument, but Julian Capper likes to keep himself informed, if possible. They have been assured that they will sit this morning. Although they have not been told the nature of the case, Julian Capper has discovered, by looking at the lists posted in the entrance to the court, that they are sitting in a case of murder. He has established contact with some of the other members of his jury. He has spoken to them and said, 'Sounds as though it is going to be an interesting case.' He hopes to be elected foreman. They don't know – how could they? – the weight he is attaching to this experience. They don't know that for him this experience could mark a turning point in his writing career, an opportunity to break away from writing about the grocery trade to tackle more cosmic issues. He cannot explain to them, and they might resent it if he did, that he feels that he is more responsible for the outcome of the case than they are. He feels as though his life, never mind the defendant's, could turn on this case. The defendant is not just a man on a murder charge, but a character in a drama imbued with personal significance for Julian Capper. It's an exalted feeling.

He has equipped himself with notebooks and plenty of finepoint pens. And he is looking forward to familiarising himself with the ordinary intercourse of daily life. Re-acquainting himself, he thinks, because he has never lost his sense of society around him, even though he has been living a solitary life. He believes that we inhabit a thinking, interconnected universe. (His article on the communications revolution, 'We're All Neighbours Now', comes to mind.) He doubts if the murder they are about to try took place in isolation from society.

They are already gathering in the jury collection room. Julian Capper thinks that if you saw his fellow jurors in the street you would be pressed to decide what brought them together. They have a frayed look. There is nothing urgent about their clothes or their shoes or their haircuts; apparently none of them has very pressing business elsewhere. Julian Capper is certainly in that broad category.

Joyce, their bailiff, is a handsome black woman with glossy hair cut in an executive style. It may be hair extensions. Her eye sockets are deep and her eyes carry no wounds of anxiety or doubt. Life has given the jury more wounds. Many of them carry their possessions in shopping bags. Joyce summons them to Court Four. She is wearing a gown, which twitches and sways as she leads them out of the holding pen and into the corridors beyond. They follow, like schoolchildren, excited and a little nervous although Keith, the personal fitness trainer, is walking with a small group of admirers. He is on his second week and knows the ropes. They are now asked to wait in their own jury room, which is where the deliberations will take place and where Julian Capper hopes to be elected foreman in due course. He feels that his work has equipped him to make order of the facts.

There are six men and six women. One of the women wears a sari. Between her eyes is a deep, red dot. The oldest of the men coughs at regular intervals; his face is dry and deeply engraved. Another small woman checks her handbag constantly. There is a woman in a jogging suit, called Lynne, who sits close to Keith. Keith is wearing a sweatshirt and baggy trousers with a large, white band down the side. One young man wears a blazer and a club tie, responding to some idea of the court's dignity which doesn't appear to be shared by the others. Joyce explains to them that they will be called into court soon. They will be asked to take an oath, but they can opt not to swear on the Bible if they wish. There is a knock on the door and they are called. The court itself is not far away down the green carpet. They file in, to find that the lawyers are already there in their gowns and wigs. Julian Capper thinks it is like walking on to a stage, already lit and with the scenery in place. In the dock is the defendant, and sitting next to him a police officer. The jurors take their place directly opposite the defendant, in two rows.

– *Court rise.*

The clerk of the court and the barristers bow their heads briefly as the judge appears via his personal back door, through the panelling. The judge probably has a lonely life. He has his own chambers and his own servant – and his own entrance – but Julian Capper imagines that he, too, is isolated from human warmth. The jury stands obediently as the judge takes his place. Back there, just before the door closes again, Julian Capper gets a glimpse of some green leather chairs. It's back there that deals are struck, of course.

The judge glances up from his papers as they are sworn in. In his wig and red gown with a black sash, he is an imposing figure, although it is hard to tell what he might look like in a suit or in leisure wear. He looks directly at the jury.

– *Ladies and gentlemen of the jury. Before we start, I would like to tell you that under the jury system it is for you and nobody else to decide the facts. My job is to direct you on points of law, and you are obliged to follow my direction, but I am not here to decide the facts. That is for you. The prosecution will give you an account of the facts of –* he glances at his papers – *of February the fifth earlier this year, and they will attempt to prove beyond a reasonable doubt that the defendant is guilty of murder. The burden of proof rests on them. The defence do not have to prove anything. But they will, of course, give you an account of what happened on that day which will differ greatly from that of the prosecution. Witnesses will be called by both sides. You will be asked to evaluate their evidence. You should wait until you have heard all the evidence before you make up your minds.*

Let me tell you now that you may choose to believe all, or nothing, or a part of what a witness says. You may think a witness is not telling the truth in some particular, but you may still believe some of his or her evidence. In order to convict the accused, you must be sure beyond a reasonable doubt that there was an intention to kill. You must also be sure that the accused was not justified in killing the deceased. There are occasions under our law when one person is entitled to kill another. These are when this person believes, or is entitled to believe at the time, that his life is in danger. Under our law a person is only entitled to use as much force as is necessary under the circumstances. Before we begin, may I thank you in advance for your public service, and may I remind you that if you have any questions of clarification you wish to address to me, notify your bailiff and she will pass them on. This case is likely to last for eight or nine days. Mrs Badenoch, would you like to begin the prosecutions's case?

One of the barristers stands up.

– Thank you my lord.

Julian Capper is poised, his pen is ready. Mrs Badenoch turns to the jury.

Two ∫

Si l'on me presse de dire pourquoi je l'aimais, je sens que cela
ne se peut exprimer qu'en répondant, Parce que c'était lui;
parce que c'était moi.

Michel Eyquem Montaigne, *Essais*

∫

Monday, 5 February 1990

Anthony Northleach stands on the platform waiting for a train. Even now, when English people are growing larger and taller – in fact everybody, all over the world seems to be getting bigger – he is still a good four inches taller than most of the other men waiting. He has a large head, with dark hair which straggles slightly on his collar, suggesting that he doesn't take hair-cutting seriously. A few years ago, some cars were described derisively as gas guzzlers. Being big invites the same ambivalence, as though he is using up too much of the earth's available supplies. At the same time, being big seems to promise honesty and directness. As he waits for the train to announce its arrival with a telegram sent ahead along the rails, he is full of expectation. The skin of his large, raw-boned face, and his broad, slightly flat nose are stretched tight; his body, too big for any useful purpose now, is full to bursting with expectation. He is plumped up with it: for a start, England have beaten France 26–7 in Paris. And also the government in South Africa has announced that Nelson Mandela will be released soon.

Anthony Northleach has never got used to the gust of dead air that precedes a train out of the tunnel. It is a warm, unwelcome breeze which plays over your face, a mineral wind of metals and cables containing a suggestion of geology.

The doors open unwillingly. They shuffle in. Anthony always

performs a stocktaking, scanning the faces of the women for human signs. He reads *The Times* and looks at the swaying faces at the same time. They sway in unison like seaweed as the train speeds – how fast? who could tell? – through the exhausted soil of London. Down the furred arteries of the city.

Some of the women tuck themselves up like hens, plumping themselves out into a little world of their own, small tents of womanhood from which they peep out truculently. Others have those London faces: low expectations, cheerful, easily amused, self-deprecating, open to hurt, strangely unworldly. Lots of black women, but less black men at this time of day. God, the bewildering variety in their faces. The blacks dress with verve. He admires it, although the young men in their hoodies and track suits, who seem to be more numerous by evening, frighten him. Anthony has reached an age when he sometimes feels unprompted stirrings of dread. These boys are dressed to combat a chill wind off Lake Michigan. They all seem to have, as the sports commentators say, upper body strength. He doesn't think of them as English, although of course they are.

As the train gets to speed, the girls concentrate on their reading, some actually mouthing the words, others just moving their lips occasionally in mute emotion. He loves them, he thinks suddenly. God knows how many times he has made this journey accompanied by all these anonymous girls, the plucky ones, the tired ones, the anxious ones, the beautiful ones, the achingly young ones, the plump and the skinny ones. There are Pakistanis, Malays, Chinese, even Japanese, who wear cute little hats like Diane Keaton. How many of them have had sex the night before? How could you know? He reads his paper, folded tight. He wants to read about Nelson Mandela. Mandela will be released soon, certainly no later than next week. Although he has never come right out and said it, Anthony believes that Nelson has been thinking about him, just as he has been thinking about Nelson. There is two-way traffic in these relationships. Souls, if we have them, must be able communicate.

Twenty-seven years in prison. *Free Nelson Mandela.* He likes the song. He likes the way they sang *freeeee* with a quaver, which sets up a complementary quaver in his chest. He isn't musical. Sometimes he regrets it bitterly. It is in the genes or DNA or whatever, like being bald or incapable of doing maths. Somebody like Alfred Brendel doesn't really deserve his fame, just as a monkey which can climb a palm tree with its tail doesn't deserve an Olympic gold medal for parallel bars. He tried to learn to play the guitar, like everyone else, but he didn't get beyond G-seventh and C. His fingers were too pudgy. He is younger than Mick Jagger. Mick must be forty-five, -six. The other Stones have become specimens from palaeontology. He'd never seen faces so wrecked, once when they had all been held up at Charles de Gaulle by fog.

    — They look like Coelacanths, he said.

    — You do say some really, really silly things. Fergus is exhausted, go and get in line for a few boarding passes, Geraldine said.

    — You were looking at them too.

    — Everybody's looking at them, but they aren't making inane remarks.

They got boarding passes in the end, but the Stones were whisked off in a private jet. Anthony thought that they deserved a private jet for 'Satisfaction' alone. He can do a passable imitation of Mick, clapping his hands together and making an outward, circular motion, like a seal begging for a herring, with his knees pressing together. (As a matter of fact, almost everybody of his age can.) Geraldine is becoming businesslike. She is teaching children with learning difficulties and studying for a diploma in psychology.

    — Why's nobody allowed to be plain dim any more? he once asked her.

    — God you can be offensive.

At the same time he is becoming less businesslike, less and less drawn into the strange business of the world. While she is equipping herself with useful jargon, tools to prise open this world, he finds himself reading history, to prise open another world. It's obvious why history holds attractions as you get older: you want to see if there are any spiritual tips which can be applied here and now. So much history seems to have been waged in the name of spiritual values. He passed the Swedenborg Society's large house in Bloomsbury the other day on his way to the magic shop to buy juggling balls for Fergus's birthday. It had a snappy neon sign in the window. It said, in moving red stipples, 'THE DIVINE HUMANITY'. He went in for a pamphlet.

One day he was sitting on the train and he looked at all the faces and thought about the ceaseless activity going on there, the cells doing whatever it is they do, all loosening their hold and losing their tension and so on. All the faces looked to him like candles dripping relentlessly – he thought of that Kubrick film, *Barry Lyndon*, shot in Ireland – and he was saddened for his fellow passengers. The cellular activity has a purpose, but the purpose is non-human. The cells live their own life wherever they find themselves. They – as people in the office like to say – have their own agenda. He is one of the few who have no agenda. Down here deep in the worm tunnels, in the filtered aquarium light, he inspects the faces to see if they know what he knows. They are the faces of his fellow citizens in all their vegetable variety. They are his communicants, a changing congregation every day, admittedly, but his colleagues in this journey which he takes each morning from the car park near New Cross to the office on the edge of Holborn. The parking is a crazy arrangement, set up by the then finance director as a tax dodge to do with company cars – he can no longer remember the details – but he has become used to it.

It was raining when he got into the tube station. Up there it is still raining: some of the recent joiners have rain on their hats and heads and shoulders. A very big fellow sits down next to a small Chinese girl. His raincoat is soaking and she must be getting wet in her little black suit, but she cannot move away. He opens the *Mail*, the sports pages, oblivious: 'SEVE: I'LL BE BACK'. Anthony hopes it is true. Seve has looked bewildered since he got married. He reads about Mandela. Mandela is a prince of the Temba tribe. He was a lawyer before they put him in jail. He is believed to have lost weight inside, although the only pictures of him are on a security camera walking down a corridor. He's been in a private clinic. We need these heroes. Untarnished heroes. Anthony used to admire many people when he was a boy. Even politicians. Now he's become more selective. Now he can't stand Mrs Thatcher with her grating voice and head cocked like a parakeet when she reluctantly has to listen.

Pressed by Geraldine, he will admit that she is a remarkable woman. *–Of course she is. I'm not saying she's not. But so was Lucrezia Borgia.*

– I knew you would say something smart alecky like that.

The other night they were having dinner in Highbury with the Ellingtons. She prides herself, rightly, on her rustic Italian food. They heard a loud rumblerumble in the soil beneath the house. The house shook itself like a dog standing up from sleep, a sort of harmless familiar vibration.

– What's that?

– The tube, said Sarah, *it's only thirteen feet beneath our basement.*

Thirteen feet! For years he had pictured himself near the centre of the earth. At this moment they were probably skimming along just beneath the sewers and the gas mains of Clapham. Maybe we place too much faith in the deadbeats who drive the trains through this netherworld. He saw them coming off work the other day, wearing sandals and trainers and talking about footbal: *Ian Wright stuck it in the back fucking hell fuck me 'e's like a fucking greyhound blackhound dontcher mean fuck off 'e can't do it when it matters no bottle.* A driver not long ago was so drunk he drove his train right through a station and destroyed it. The whole place, gingerbread trellising and gothic windows, came crashing down like a child's train set. No-one was hurt, it was a freight train, but the driver was found walking up the line calling for a taxi.

The large wet man has opened the newspaper right out to read the health section so that the Chinese girl's view is sharply reduced. Until quite recently people were almost phobic about space. No matter how crowded the train, they created a little *cordon sanitaire* around themselves. Not now. Not everybody is so fastidious. Recently one guy actually fell asleep with his head lolling on Anthony's shoulder. He was wearing a double-breasted suit; double-breasted suits, like Anthony's father's, have become popular again, but in a flashy kind of way. They are quite cheap at Next and places like that, although Next seems to be headed down the pan. Like so much else.

He still has a suit, made at his father's insistence in Savile Row. The sleeves are different lengths. His father had some ideas about gentlemanly behaviour he had picked up in the bank. When he joined the bank, it had a string of offices in the colonies. Sometimes Anthony thinks about ordering another suit, although Savile Row prices are absurd: over a thousand pounds for a suit. Parallel universes have sprung up. Some people pay huge sums of money for clothes, others buy American surplus. They dress themselves like GIs on rest and recreation in Saigon, or state policemen in leather jackets or pilots in silk overalls. You can go to the National Theatre and see people in everything from dinner jackets to deliberately torn jeans. Sometimes he and Geraldine dress for a dinner party or drinks and have quite different interpretations of what is expected. She will be wearing leggings and a large sweater and he will be in a suit, or he will be in khaki trousers and a linen jacket, no tie, only to find her in Nicole Farhi. Farhi, the name sounds Persian, or perhaps it is Italian. Names have become richer and more exotic too, but also less easily placed.

Northleach sounds dull these days, too English and yeoman-like. Geraldine's maiden name, Button, which she was happy to relinquish fourteen years ago, is chirpily English. Nobody is certain about anything any more. Anthony sees it as a reflection of the state of the country. Geraldine, with her pretty bunched-up little face, eagerly sniffing the cultural wind, is often confused. She is like a weathervane that turns a little slowly but also more surely than he does. She is nearly forty. Forty in eleven months' time. He hopes it doesn't hit her too hard, as it did Diana Millroy, who tried – how hard? – to jump off Battersea Bridge and is now having an affair with her painter and decorator who beats her, Geraldine says. There is so much tragedy, not even tragedy, more like turbulence, bottled up and dying to gush out, it's like Yellowstone Park, where they went last summer with Jet Tours. A bear as big as a house took their picnic. The look on its face as it chewed carefully – business as usual – amused him. They were safely inside a soft-sprung Chevy from Rent-a-Wreck at the time. They all felt liberated, like people in a road movie: the Northleaches getting their kicks on Route 66.

Forty in less than a year and already he can see her mother appearing, like one of those kids' films where ghostly special-effects figures slip in and out of reality. But then he can hear himself sounding like his father. Sometimes he says meaningless things to Fergus – *Do you have to eat with your elbows on the table? Could we have the television just a little quieter just so we can make conversation occasionally?* – and knows he is just blowing the ancestral conch shell. Worse, he and his friends acknowledge that they are sounding like their fathers. The difference is, their fathers meant it. Nobody knows any more.

The train screeches: metal is discontented stuff. It makes a variety of noises which tell him where they are in the underworld. Even as he reads that Mandela has been forced to summon Winnie to a prison conference about her finances – Winnie likes spending the money that Scandinavians send in – he knows from the metallic protest that they are approaching the river. Winnie is building a big house. She is trying to franchise the Mandela name, like McDonald's.

The train slaps and rattles and groans. At least once a month they are delayed by suicides on the line. What a way to go. With all the gentler ways of killing yourself, one hundred Paracetamol and a glass of whisky for instance, why throw yourself on the line to be cleaved apart by the train? Mike has seen one, an Asian girl in a sari, cut right in half long before the poor fuddled driver could apply the emergency brake. In fact, applying the brake made it worse because they had to move the train back over her body. She was a schizophrenic, it turned out. Some of the passengers, Mike said, complained about having to change trains. Their view was that once she was dead, which was obvious to everyone, there was no point in holding up things as though some new truths would be revealed. The driver took early retirement and counselling. The language of counselling and empowering and parenting and resourcing, which Geraldine is learning, is spreading all over the place. In Rochdale recently it seemed the Satanists were taking hold, but really it was only a misreading of the new grammar by eager carers. This caring talk of dysfunctional families and recovered memory is the new Esperanto for the busy classes.

Swedenborg, as far as he can understand – the pamphlet is heavy going – was trying to reconcile the spiritual and the physical by changing the language to accommodate them both. That's what these people are trying to do too. The language is being overhauled. He doesn't mind. History shows him that everybody puts faith in these creeds and mantras. But the computer language at the office, which a lot of them already speak fluently, is different. It despises traditional language. It's as though the computer folk are saying, *You were conned, sold a pig in a poke. You didn't need it, it's all here.* It makes them happy to discover that their weaknesses at school were no more than a lack of information technology. They don't need to waste time on old-fashioned niceties. Children now have this contemptuous technical edge too. Fergus wants his own computer. Everybody in his class has one. Geraldine says he will learn to program it, which sounds fine and very relevant, but he thinks Fergus will just kill more space creatures. So Fergus has his new vocabulary and Geraldine has hers, and he must make do with the old, creaky one.

There are so few elderly people at this time of day. He's definitely, at forty-one, in the top half of the divide. Now the train stops. Everyone looks up, ready to exchange knowing, weary smiles but immediately it starts again with just a flicker of the lights. His mother says that she is invisible to people under fifty. But people at the office, much younger than his mother, complain of the same thing: *I have become invisible. These young girls just look right through me. They don't see me. When I talk to them, they get a fright.* They complain that the eyes of the young cannot be detained by the sight of people over forty. Older people seem to be cluttering the place up.

The truth is many people have done his mother good turns and shown her kindness since his father died, but she prefers to remember the slights, most of them imagined or exaggerated. This weekend he has to take her car to a new garage. She doesn't trust the mechanic, a Cypriot, who puts old parts in her car instead of new ones. She knows all about this racket. She even knows the word 'scam'. And then she wants to move from the cottage he helped her buy after Freddie died because the neighbours use weedkiller which is giving her bronchial tubes hell.

– *Have you asked them to stop, have you explained?*

– *It would be no use.*

– *How do you know?*

– *I haven't lived seventy-two years without picking up a little understanding of human nature.*

– *I'll speak to them.*

– No, it's no use. Anyway, the sort of people in the village are not what we were expecting. It's full of builders.

She and his father had planned for years to go and live in this village when he retired, but they kept putting it off and then he died just over a year, more like eighteen months, ago. Anthony shouldn't have persuaded her to go. He thought it would take her mind off things, to have the cottage and garden to work on. Geraldine said that he had rushed his mother: *You didn't give her time to come to terms with it. People need to grieve.* He didn't say that stopping her from grieving was exactly what he had had in mind. And because he hadn't allowed her to grieve, he is now on twenty-four-hour standby as plumber and mechanic. It is forty minutes to her cottage, if you can get through East Grinstead.

– I must move from here.

– Where are you going to go?

– I'll find somewhere in town.

It breaks his heart. She wants to go and live in a flat in London among strangers. As well as becoming Mr Fixit, he has also found a shaggy mantle, belonging to the paterfamilias, descending on his shoulders. He is too young for this. Mandela is exactly the same age as his mother, born in 1918. Mandela in the Transkei, his mother in Lucknow. Mandela has apparently refused all kinds of offers from the government to leave the country with as much money as he needs to go and live quietly in Scandinavia or Tanzania. He is a tough old bastard. *The struggle is my life.*

The train is coasting now, the metal components jostling one another as they slow for the station. *And my life is a struggle.*

There is a great picture of Will Carling scoring a try. The photographer has him in midair, with a relaxed look on his face. He seems to be smiling as he hovers with the ball comfortably tucked under his right arm. His left arm is stretched out in anticipation of landing. Anthony believes that sports have special meaning for him. He thinks he has a personal relationship with this team which has just beaten the French 26 to 7, in Paris. *The Times* rugby correspondent says it is as complete a win as could have been wished for. His relationship to the team may be a little like the special relationship which Mrs Thatcher and President Reagan are said to enjoy. Most people of their age are lucky to be invited to Sunday lunch once a month with their children and yet there they were having a great time, enjoying banquets, making speeches, whizzing about in golf carts and commanding planes to strike. Will Carling is smiling for Anthony as he sails over French soil.

Anthony also thinks the news has special significance for him. It is important for him to be kept up to date with what's happening in Romania or what Gorbachev wants in Lithuania. It is certainly more important for him than for Geraldine. She is unmoved unless it is something about Fergie or Diana or an actress having a baby. Or about the problems facing the social services. Then she too assumes a proprietorial air. Sometimes he thinks we are all just trying to fix ourselves in a windy universe, fix ourselves like those plastic magnetised letters that have lodged on their fridge door for some years. Just like every other fridge in every house in England which is home to children. He sees that Mandela is suffering for him. He sees Winnie not as most of the papers are depicting her, as an evil woman, but as an aspect of his own character. Winnie shows him what can happen to human beings under unbearable duress. While Nelson was on Robben Island, serene in the knowledge of his own goodness, she was taking all the flak.

He turns another page. It's Nelson week. His biography is being published. He writes movingly about Robben Island. The beauty of the weather, the distant view of Cape Town, the importance of exams, the difficulties of marriage, the hurt of receiving no letters. When Anthony's mother sees the news, she sees a series of betrayals. Nobody consulted her. Nobody told her that black people and Oriental people and people with funny accents were going to come shouldering their way on to her news. Even newsreaders are black. She has nothing against them, particularly Trevor McDonald, but she feels uneasy that people who don't have good accents are allowed to read the news, never mind the importance given to them on the news. You can't have a country where everybody is valued equally. To her the evening news is a confirmation that the ship is taking on water. Luckily she won't be around to see it go down, but she feels sorry for Fergus. God knows what sort of country he is going to grow up in, an only child.

— *When are you going to have another one?*

– It's not that simple, Ma, as you know.

After Fergus there had been a problem with Geraldine's ovaries. Not irreversible, but so far Fergus is an only child. They stopped talking as though there might be another some years ago. In his heart of hearts Anthony believes he brought on this barrenness by his affair with Francine, which started two nights after Fergus was born and lasted seven blessed months. Francine left the company to work in Australia. Nothing to do with him. When she departed, overland, for Perth, he was saddened. But he was left with a gift, a memory of undimmed sweetness. She had a funny little body and a comic and touching way of talking when they made love. Her legacy is his recollection of this love feast. He treasures it. He remembers and repeats to himself her words, her quirky observations which would probably have driven him mad if she hadn't gone to Western Australia.

– Coconut oil is a feast for bacteria. Your wife's a pillar of society. I've got bad blood. I like bonking too much, it's not healthy.

She thought she was from a doomed substratum. Emigration was her only hope. And study. She had attended many night courses and was a member of the institute, which he isn't. He should really join, but he had let it slip and he would have to pass an exam. In bed she was game for anything. At the office she looked startled and anxious. She was out of her element, like a cowboy in a city suit. Bed was her prairie. But having sex with her did something to his fathering abilities, though the fault was traced to Geraldine's ovaries by a Harley Street specialist. The gynaecologist, who had done some work on unspecified members of the royal family, was a gift of Geraldine's mother. – *Go and see Frinker. He's the top man. He wrote the book.*

It was the only time he had been to Harley Street as a patient, or prospective patient. Harley Street was a frontage of huge waiting rooms containing reproduction Sheraton furniture, Chinese carpets and *Country Life*. The waiting rooms were so grand that there was no space left for the doctors. They had to work in tiny rooms at the back. Mr Frinker, after two visits and some tests, indicted the ovaries and Anthony got off scot-free. Mr Frinker was not medically trained to detect guilt. It is strange, this business of top doctors and surgeons calling themselves Mister. Very English.

The train is slowing again. The lights flicker but it keeps going. He wonders sometimes how much margin of error they have. These carriages have an unreliable note; they are clapped out, ready for scrap. The girls glance up for a moment as if the blank tunnel walls will tell them something. He feels protective towards them. He is like the captain of the *Enterprise*. He and Fergus watch *Star Trek* together. The split infinitive always gives him a small stab. *To boldly go*. If he sees a girl get on with short stocky legs which no amount of dieting can help, he feels deep sympathy. They wouldn't want his sympathy, but he extends it freely to womankind. They have a hard time. Francine was a little short in the leg but it made no difference when she was lying down. Now, eight years later, he feels a stir. Jesus. He read a survey in the *Sunday Times* where it said that sixty per cent of married men and fifty per cent of married women had had an affair of some sort. It also said that ninety per cent would have one if they could be sure of not being found out. Winnie has apparently had lots of affairs while Nelson has been inside.

He has written some lovely letters to Winnie and his daughters. – *Zinzi: On some days the weather on the island is quite beautiful, beyond words*. He was allowed only one visit a year in the early days. His daughters – he seems to have three – have provided him with anxious moments, paying the bills and so on. And now his wife.

The train stops at one of those stations where there is never any activity. The doors open and close with hardly a single person getting on or off. Women are like the geysers bubbling in Yellowstone Park. They register every seismic change and discord in the world. Nelson writes heartbreakingly about small matters on his godforsaken island while his wife is rampaging around Soweto with her bodyguards, the football team. He turns the page; there is Mike Tyson trying to get off the canvas looking like a newborn heifer. James Buster Douglas, a total unknown, has knocked him out. How is it possible? Tyson looks as if a lorry couldn't knock him over, never mind a washed-up forty-year-old fatty. But there he is, struggling to see the world straight. Once they have been knocked out they are never the same again. It's the fear that it could happen a second time. Anthony loves watching boxing although he thinks it should be banned. Nelson likes boxing. Tyson sent him a pair of his gloves a few years ago.

Your own station has a weary familiarity. He thinks it's probably like rabbit runs, marked in some way by the passage of feet and feral scents. He doesn't remember much biology. He doesn't remember anything much from school days. It's all gone down the plughole. He adjusts his feet in readiness. He always feels an ache in the intestine as he gets ready to exit. All the passengers pivot towards the door. It's like the Kirov, he thinks. Matthew Freedman, the lecturer on Geraldine's course, gave them his free tickets. Really, he wanted to take Geraldine. This Freedman imagines he's from a Woody Allen film in New York, but he teaches in Guildford. The Chinese girl, even though she has been moistened, directs a look at the man in the raincoat as he stands up which is, for a moment, full of naked longing. Her eyes, for that moment, show the pupils like small black seeds in the whites. He thinks of black bean sauce at Ley-Ons in Wardour Street where he and Francine used to meet. Francine would eat anything: fishlips, eels, squid. He would usually choose the sweet and sour something or the barbecue pork noodles. Funny how the Chinese say 'barbecue' quickly, as though they cannot cope with all the vowels: *bahkew*. Once she got him to eat some slippery parcels from a bamboo steamer. They tasted like snot. Bogies. – *Don't be disgusting*, she said, sniggering. He was thirty-three then.

The doors open in that mean, grudging way. They shuffle up the stairs on to the escalators. They all stand now, transported upwards to the uncertain light of a February day, released from the brief communion of the journey, like hopeful souls, like baffled pilgrims.

Anthony thinks the trouble started when they moved to a new building. The old one, Dyson Chambers, was, it is true, gothic, a not very fashionable style. Now it's a gothic doss house, having been in the three years since they moved into the new building a gothic printer's, a gothic wholefood restaurant (soon closed down by the health inspectors), a gothic T-shirt factory and, briefly, a gothic soul music shop. Now they are stuck with the £32 per square foot and a fifteen-year lease which, as Alistair said, you couldn't pay anybody to take off your hands.

Anthony adjusted quickly to the new layout, all glass and pastels and uplighters, after the crenellated, curved, nooked and partitioned building with its firedoors and useless passages adorned with extinguishers and canvas safety chutes (which looked like canvas cummerbunds). He liked the new way of living, out in the open, but the speed with which Dyson Chambers went downhill after they vacated, when the lease was up, shocked him. The new building, the Spice Mall, sucked all the life out of Dyson Chambers. Dyson Chambers went on to short lets – 'Easy in, easy out.' The phoney casualness of this offer only emphasised that the building was moribund.

They are just around the corner now, right on Upper Gladstone Street, while Dyson Chambers is tucked away in Priory Street, one of those apologetic side streets full of sandwich bars and cheap printers. The one next to Dyson Chambers, where they used to have the stationery done, was robbed by a man with a gun and a balaclava over his face in broad daylight. He got away with six hundred pounds and fired a shot at – in the direction of, anyway – Leonardo from Venezia Sandwich Bar, who had come out to see what was going on. The bullet went right through the glass leaving a small fractured exit wound just under the words 'Today's special, Turkey and Ham on Ciabatta.' Ciabatta is a new thing, chewy bread from Italy. The bullet ended up in a huge roll of mozzarella that Leonardo buys wholesale. The funny thing is, the man in the balaclava, the shot going off, the money stolen, the ventilated cheese, none of this was taken seriously even by Leonardo. It was a bit of excitement. An aberration. Three months later and the police have still not arrested anyone. Anthony saw Dyson Chambers promiscuously selling itself and he inspected the hole in the glass and the mozzarella and he thought, *Things are on the slide*. It is a deep, elemental movement. Like the earthquake in California, a slippage. Two plates of the earth moving separately. Big things like that and the nature of the universe intrigue him. He finds himself thinking about them with satisfaction. His father used to read bits from the newspaper about politics and international affairs with disdain and relish:

– *Look at this. They never learn. The one thing you can be sure of is that you can't get on the same wavelength as an African. They have different values.*

Just as his father thought politics were addressed to him personally, Anthony can see personal significance in these elemental facts. They are probably the only facts. Continents colliding. Black holes and quarks. They are physical things, of course, but they border on the mystical or religious. Religion is just another way of describing the things we don't understand. But he doesn't know for sure. The Swedenborg Society is unable to provide much help. The Swedenborgians assume too much. He wants to know what we can assume. – *If need be it's a cause for which I am ready to die*, says Nelson. It's a thrilling idea, but how can you think like that if you don't know the fundamentals on which everything is based, if it's based on anything? If it's not based on anything at all, how does Nelson know he's prepared to die for it?

In the old building his desk stood in a small office, which was really a corridor that had long ago been closed, like a disused mine working. Now his desk stands behind a partition in a module, as it is called. He is an associate director, so he has a little space around him with some satellite desks and cupboards. An associate director is not a very big potato. As a director, he would have a solid office, with just one glass window in the door, big enough to suggest openness – the company objectives tell of *an integrated and open approach to the changing shape of company needs, building confidence for the implementation of goals* – but small enough to suggest a certain exalted need for privacy and original thought. Anthony is just at the point where not being made a director would mean he is being passed over. Even now, at forty-one, it is a little late.

Thelma comes into his module with a cup of coffee in a mug which is made of some earthy substance decorated with what look like plasticine flowers. Thelma is a name on the verge of extinction. She is a strange woman; she lives in the YWCA hostel in Lloyd Square and is a keen cook, although she appears to have no one to cook for. She is devoid of relatives of any sort and in the two or three years she has worked here has failed to make any friends. She is quite handsome with a shiny, nun's skin, but she seems to be out of her time. Although he does not have a secretary of his own, he has a share in Thelma. Thelma, he has been told, lives for him. But Thelma lives in a very minor way, begging to be spurned. It is hard to turn down this mute plea for anonymity. One day he realised she reminded him of his mother's old girdles, Playtex with a shiny front panel, which used to lie in a corner of her bedroom like discarded surgical appliances. His mother's bedroom, where she slept alone, was a warm, untidy place, full of cuttings from newspapers and magazines and gardening catalogues which arrived with the change of seasons. She had an immense round jar of powder which spilled on to the dressing table like the pasta pot in the Italian fable. The bed itself stood on stout wooden legs and was always disarrayed. Geraldine likes their bed to be symmetrical, with the covers and the matching floral cushions neatly lined up. He wonders where these forms we carry around come from.

    – *Cook anything nice over the weekend, Thel?*
    – *I am just getting into Thai food. Lemongrass and so on.*
    – *Lemongrass? Is that nice? It sounds like lawn clippings.*
    – *It's a sort of bamboo I think. Lemongrass and coconut milk.*
    – *Very exotic. How do you learn to cook Thai?*
    – *From a book. I'm thinking of going there for my holidays.*
    – *Lovely.*

Why does she want to go there? All those childlike prostitutes and sex bars. It's a man's country. He watches Thelma moving off. Her big, sausagey legs will draw attention to her in Thailand. If she goes. She seems to live now in a world where the distinctions between the real and the imagined are blurring. But then, who doesn't? She makes coffee for Anthony and types at incredible speed and cooks on one ring in the Y. Now she is coming back.

    – *There's a meeting in the small boardroom. Ten o'clock.*
    – *Is that instead of or as well as the twelve o'clock?*
    – *Both, I should think.*

He would like to have a rosewood table, with a lamp on it. He has a desk with a black melamine veneer. On the walls are prints in pastel frames of ice-cream cones, kites and beach chairs. The world has gone pastel. As it has become harsher. The chairman has a panelled room with an oil painting of a horse behind his desk. Anthony once inspected the painting, while waiting for an appointment. It had a tag in silver attached, 'Bolero, by Red Mist out of Ice Dancer'. The chairman said that the horse was being covered now after winning six races and coming fourth in the Oaks. It was a filly.

– *Lovely filly. Once in a lifetime. Actually made some money. When you've got one like that it's a pleasure. Tony we're not making any new directors this year I'm afraid, except for the chap from Hong Kong, but I just wanted to assure you that as soon as the economy turns round we will be. Do you like horses?*

– *I can't say I've had much to do with them. But I like the look of them.*

– *Stupid things really. Not too disappointed, are you? You understand the circumstances, don't you? It hasn't been a good year and it would not look right. Do you know what I'm getting at?*

– *I think so.*

– *Good. The music has stopped for a while and there aren't enough chairs, if you ask me. If I am honest.*

That conversation took place a year ago. Nobody has said any more to him about a directorship. Frank Johnstone-Borwine, the chairman, has become withdrawn. His finances are rocky. He has sold his racehorses. The others find it hard to believe that the wheels have stopped turning. They talk of blips on the graphs and upturns and downturns as if they know that there is some mathematical explanation: *It'll bottom out.* They all have this idea that there is an upward graph. Try telling that to the Aztecs or the Sumerians. Most people live without realising that there is a multiplicity of ways of explaining things. So meetings have taken on a ritual character. They talk about forecasts. They forecast forecasts. The truth is, nobody has a clue. Geraldine also asks him for reassurance. She has noticed his disengagement. Like the others, she wants him to be proactive. Perhaps, he says, when Nelson comes out, things will change. When Nelson comes out Anthony will be made a director and the chairman will buy a new horse and Thelma will go to Thailand, to further her understanding of lemongrass. Thelma is still hoping to get a pay rise so she can leave the YWCA and have a flat of her own where she can entertain properly.

Anthony is touched. She attributes her lack of social success to the cramped living conditions and the improvised cooking. Anthony finds this looking to the future unrealistic. What's the future got? A few years ago his mother started looking backwards exclusively. The accumulated past is more real and vivid to her; it's backing up like water at a dam wall. Thelma comes by again.

– *More coffee?*
– *Yes please.*
– *I'll get you some folders and things.*

Thelma would like him to look businesslike. As they jot down their proposals and forecasts and detailed timescales, she knows he has a tendency to stop listening. He has read that the brain has a mind of its own. It makes its own decisions. He finds it hard to be engaged by these projections. Thelma comes back with a selection of pads, coloured pens and his calculator. She places another cup of coffee in front of him, and seizes the old cup deftly. He gets out the newspaper, he doesn't like the sound of this Richardson in Mrs Mandela's team. The Kray twins had an associate called Richardson. There is a seam of violence in Winnie's life. Like the underclass.

He looks instead at the airborne picture of Will Carling again and sips the coffee. Twenty-six to seven. The French play rugby with their national character on display, particularly prone to recriminations. Like their politicians. Women imagine that men are hiding behind sport in order not to face up to the more important issues which they wish to discuss. Women have become confrontational. The reason is that men now feel guilty about what they really think, so they hide their thoughts. This infuriates women. Mike told him a story the other day: A man (Mike called him 'a bloke') comes into his office. 'I had a bloody funny experience this morning,' he says, 'I went into the buffet and the waitress said to me, "Milk and sugar, sir," and I said, "I'll just nibble your tits." I just blurted it out. Bloody embarrassing.' And the other bloke says, 'Look, I had a bloody funny experience too, my wife comes up to me at breakfast this morning and says, "Milk in your coffee darling," and I said, "You fucking bitch you've ruined my life." I just blurted it out. Bloody embarrassing.'

Thelma appears in the gap between the hanging cupboard and the fax machine.

– *Your mother's on the line. Do you want to speak?*

Thelma is never sure if he is going to have time for his mother.

– *Yeah. Put her on. Hello Ma.*

He wonders what it is; perhaps the chemicals drifting from the farmer's over-medicated fields are worrying her again.

– *Hello Ma. Are you there?*

– *Anthony.*

– *Yes Ma. What's up?*

– *I've just been reading this marvellous account of the life of Evelyn Waugh's first wife. Have you read it?*

– *No, I haven't.*

– *Anyway, darling, I've cut it out for you and I'll send it. Did you get a letter this morning?*

– *Yes. I am just going through my post now.*

– *I won't keep you. I know you're always busy.*

– *Thanks for that. Everything else all right?*

– *Not really, but you're coming round on Sunday, aren't you?*

– *I'm not sure we can. Geraldine's got some conference and I'm in charge of Fergus.*

– *Bring him.*

– *He's got karate. I'll ring you this evening. We'll fix something.*

But he is speaking to a dead phone. He has disappointed her. She is always cutting things out of the paper and sending them to him along with letters and documents she has found. She has a strong interest in literary figures and their love children, sexual difficulties and country houses. They speak to her of a world which she believes she would have liked to know. He will have to get over and see her somehow.

In some ways he shares his mother's wish to have lived in a more richly appointed world. He would prefer a more richly appointed office, for a start. With proper drapery like the casually hanging sheet of silk drawn by Leonardo. He is becoming more interested in art exhibitions. The skill of Leonardo is incredible. And he loves portraits, the gleaming greedy eyes, the little vanities. He finds these surfaces, these plastic folders, these matching pens, the showoff calculators that can do logarithms, the promiscuous green chairs in the meeting room, the light slim phones, the flecked carpet (flecked with what looks like bits of wafer crumbled from the ice-cream prints) demeaning. They are not made by any human agency. The connection with humanity has gone out of them. Design is everywhere. Design is, like computing, a concept which aims to expunge the human frailties and cap off the human gases. Design proclaims that a thing is complete. Leonardo never regarded his paintings as complete – so the catalogue said, and he can believe it. Once a design is finished, a new design is worked up, which gives an idea of the value of design. Design is to art what air-fresheners are to lavatories.

But what is he worrying about? In the old place he sat in a corridor. They are having a meeting about skills. If they improve their skills they will have the edge. They are veering off into metaphysics. 'Skills' has become an anthropological word. The need to improve their skills is a bluff. It's really just a way of continuing the needling and pecking like at school. School was a charnel house of childhood innocence. Every crease, every corner, every fold of your flimsy self was explored and derided. Then you did it yourself to the new boys: *Your mother's got fat tits*. The teachers, too, were always grading and dividing. This non-stop evaluation, which you thought was just part of childhood, turns out to be part of working too. Evaluation is the motive force of our system. It's Darwinian. The Swedenborgians say that only the great Emanuel was able to interpret God's purpose. He had been given the code. A Swede living in frozen Stockholm in 1862 seems an arbitrary choice by God. People will believe anything. Once they persuaded a boy called Trengrove, who was trying for elusive popularity, to burn down the cricket pavilion, which he almost achieved with some white spirit from the art room. He was caned and harboured justified resentments against his former friends. A few years ago he had a nervous breakdown after his wife left him for a man who sold swimming-pool heaters. It is a kind of soap opera. Everyone is getting divorced or being fired or giving birth to children with brain damage. And now his mother, who was accused of having floppy tits by Barton, is living in fear of chemical sprays and builders with turbo-charged four-wheel-drive cars. His mother's breasts were full and widely spaced.

Women's bodies are a source of interest to him. Even Thelma's. He speculates, although he would hate to see it, what Thelma's body looks like. Human bodies are so blatantly designed for sex. Within that broad specification they come in many variations.

Our body which is us, of course, but also a piece of baggage we acquire unasked to lug with us throughout our lives. It deteriorates at its own pace. Anthony finds that the elasticity in his chest is going so that he has unmistakable little puckerings around his nipples now. He must jog or go to the gym. Jogging is big. You see women running in Lycra tights hoping to reshape their backsides. And it does seem to be possible: Geraldine's friend, Leonora, has been working out ferociously for nearly a year. There are cords and pumped-up veins, like Martina Navratilova's, in her arms and legs. The added attaction of her new, boyish shape is offset by the manically enthusiastic way she comports herself. She wears leggings at every opportunity. Her eyes are intense, bulging slightly, and her skin has taken on an unnatural colour, caused by mineral drinks and exposure to the weather on her long safaris through the frosted lanes and windy parks around High Woods. Her husband is on contract in Saudi. He's a surveyor. Before he left for Saudi he had had no work for a year. Before that they were quite prosperous, and put in a swimming pool and a brick barbecue, curved to avoid the breezes and conserve the heat, or something. Anthony cannot remember the engineering principles involved, patiently explained to him by Nigel, who was wearing a lime-green polo shirt which became spattered with flying drops of fat before Leonora put an apron on him. The apron said, 'Nigel Spafford, licensed to grill'. In the corner was the logo of his firm of surveyors, Spafford, Knight and Matthews. They are in liquidation. Underneath the names of the partners was a protractor in gold so that he looked like a Freemason. And now Nigel is in Saudi, much fitter apparently, nothing to drink, and Leonora is working her body. The children are in boarding school, although they are, he guesses, only about Fergus's age, only eight or nine.

This is the way things are going: professional people, semi-professional people, are required to become gypsies. They have to become mobile, like Americans. Restless, like people in a road movie. The bear in Yellowstone eating their picnic serenely. He smiles.

– *You look happy, says Thelma.*

He hasn't seen her come up.

– *I was thinking about a grizzly bear, Thelma.*

– What are you on? Give me some.

But Thelma can't tell jokes or make funny remarks. They come across plaintively. Like Trengrove's attempts at popularity. Life is cruel to some people.

– The meeting's starting late. The board meeting's run over.

– Okay. You'll keep me informed.

The board. He used to long to be on the board and receive the important memos and discuss the long-term finances. The board is another of those devices to divide and rule. He has read a book about the nature of human conversation by a lecturer at Oxford. A don. It says that all human discourse is a Darwinian exercise at feeling out the enemy. There has been a rash of these books about society and management. Now the board is ganging up on the chairman. He is rocky. Anthony remembers him talking about his filly with such affection.

– I brought you some more coffee.

– Thanks, Thel.

– Do you want to see the management committee report?

– Okay.

Why did she say 'I brought you some more coffee'? She is trying to modernise her speech. She likes the words 'mindset' and 'envision'. But she is forever tied to this old-fashioned, bulky self. Her skin is sort of unfinished, with moles and overlarge pores. She is now proposing to introduce her awkward self to the decorous, slight Thais, in her doomed quest for equilibrium. She returns with the report, which he puts on his desk heedlessly. She reproaches him silently; no more than a bat's squeak reaches him, but he is unmoved. He knows what's in it; more incantations.

– Are you going to do the klongs, Thel? he asks to propitiate her.

– I am. They cook on the boats, it's amazing.

– Pretty smelly now, I'm told.

Thelma looks startled.

– Not the cooking, the klongs.

– Oh, probably. But it's a different culture.

She can be relied upon for the banal clincher. He loses sympathy.

– Could you run off twenty copies of the weekly report?

She knows she is being banished. He has a little reserve of cruelty and pettiness. It upsets him that he can be unkind.

Why are we so concerned about our personalities? We treat them like mad relatives locked in the cellar. They can cause us untold trouble. With schizophrenics, what happens is that the relatives in the cellar smash down the door and invade the dinner party upstairs. Human life, he thinks, is all analogy. *It's a cause for which I am prepared to die.* This sounds like a religious fable. He doesn't know. The whole Soviet empire, falling down, proves to have been founded on a fable, Marx's belief that heaven could be built on earth. When they have meetings upstairs they talk about the firm as if it had a heart and a head. A truer analogy would be with Fergus's squeaking and squawking computer games, which have some aspects of reality but are entirely lifeless. Seven years ago, when he joined, he too believed it was a living thing. But he might as well have joined the Scientologists whose temple he sees outside East Grinstead on the way to help his mother.

He turns back to the sports pages. There's Tyson, trying to raise himself off the canvas. With his little effeminate voice and those eyes that have seen a lot, but now are seeing nothing. Mandela was a boxer. Mandela loves Muhammad Ali, who stood up for black people. Strange to think that Mandela admires Ali, strange as being told that Mother Teresa admires Martina Navratilova. Black people always want dramatic, vigorous heroes. He has an affection for Martina, too. She wants to be an American, but that name hangs around her stiffly, with its Eastern European brocaded heaviness.

He doesn't put the newspaper down when Thelma tells him there's a call for him from the bank. The bank is offering all sorts of new services.

– *Don't put them through, Thelma.*

– *It was the bank.*

– *Only put through Mr Spicer, the manager. The rest are selling something.*

Mr Spicer is a Cockney who has been at the bank man and boy. He admits he is looking forward to early retirement. – *It's all gone down the drain. They don't need bodies no more. Just computers.* Mr Spicer's face is becoming comical. His face is poorly fitted together, like Fergus's Mr Potato Head; when he grimaces his nose and cheeks make extravagant independent movements. All

Cockneys become characters when they get older. They specialise in a kind of gloomy cheerfulness. They take pride in their ailments and their antipathies. Out on the streets their sons now give you the finger and scream obscenities for no reason. They are in a frenzy. It could be diet. They always have a drink, something which looks like a hospital sample, in their vans and sporty little cars. Mr Spicer belongs to the previous generation, grateful to have joined the professional classes, always a little humble, and unworthy of the honour.

Anthony's mother sends him notes. He remembers this morning's message. He dreads these communications because they contain messages about the cosmos which he does not wish to receive. He opens the envelope. – *Your father left this in a book he was reading. It was in a book called* Three Bucks Without Hair. *Funny title. Gives me the creeps, I thought you would like the poem.*

On a piece of Croxley writing paper with a rough texture is written:

A Poem for Anthony

A blemish
On your porcelain nose
Your childhood's gone
After my youth.
You are me.
I am you.
Without you
I do not exist.
Your flight has begun.
Stay awhile.
I am you.
And you are me.

Anthony reads it again. His father's handwriting is very neat and precise, although he was a chaotic man. Anthony feels leaden. His father's presumption drags him down: *I am you. You are me.* Did he really feel this? Anthony doesn't feel the same way about Fergus. Fergus comes from another lumberyard of human timber altogether, nothing to do with him. He heard a phrase the other day, 'the crooked timber of humanity'. 'Nothing straight will ever be fashioned from the crooked timber of humanity.' Something like that. It's presumptuous of his father, phoney sentimentality, to refer to his onrushing adolescence this way. It was the semaphore of the sexual tumult that nobody is prepared for. He remembers Mr Dibley's sex lessons, which passed like an express train of forced bonhomie. Man-to-man stuff. All quite straightforward. Masturbation was all right, but not in excess. In excess it made you listless. But Mr Dibley, with his flowered wallpaper ties and hunted eyes which never rested on any individual boy, did not put a figure on it. No bottom line. It was a more open-ended time. Now Anthony reads of the pleasure, the obligation even, of multiple orgasm. He has seen a video where a woman masturbates after rubbing herself with soothing, and fragrant, oils. The voice of a sex expert with very heavy glasses who makes unwelcome appearances in the video from time to time, explains how this is done, lending the whole thing that bogus solemnity which is creeping in all over the place. Television and radio are full of people filled with concern about issues of stunning solemnity.

Stay awhile. I am you. You are me. It was his father who did not stay. After his working life was over he seemed to run out of human fuel. He sputtered and stopped. Anthony's mother is keen to establish some family bonds, which she now perceives. When she leaves this world – poisoned by agricultural spray or run over by a Suzuki jeep – she proposes to go cocooned in family love. The silkworm is spinning an elaborate construction. *Your childhood's gone*. Horses, dogs and cats were older than Anthony when his father wrote that letter. The dog, Toby, was fifteen. When it died soon after, that was the end of childhood. Red Indians, Native Americans as they call them now, bury their pets with them when they die. When Toby died Anthony made an unsuccessful plea for him to be buried alongside Granny in the churchyard.

Thelma, and many other people, have a few half-understood ethnographic customs in their repertoire. This has become popular in conversation: *Do you know the Masai, or is it the Kikuyu, one or the other, have no conception of an afterlife? The Hopi Indians believe the buffalo is God's spirit released, or anyway God's other nature.* Some people talk about the Yanomami Indians. They have special value because they come straight from the Stone Age to see bulldozers destroying their forest.

Still, his father's poem touches him. As he grew older, his father placed a lot of faith in beauty. He loved gardens and vistas and old buildings, as though there was some eternal truth to be found in their contemplation. It didn't work. He became more confused and embittered. His mother is trying to flesh out the fading spectre by sending him these scraps of paper. She is trying to revive them, like those Japanese paper flowers to which you add water.

– *You look thoughtful.*

– *Thelma, why are you popping in and out to comment on my mental state? My face is mobile. I cannot help it.*

– *Your meeting is starting in five minutes.*

– *Oh good.*

– *Don't forget the report.*

The report is lying where she put it, untouched.

– *Don't worry, Thel, I've read it without opening it. It's a trick I learned in the SAS.*

I am you. And you are me. Made more portentous by the spareness, like those works of art with nothing much in the frame but with a sonorous title, such as *Solitude Remembered*. But he is unsettled. He feels this draught whenever he is reminded of childhood. His parents, despite the romantic revisionism now going on, argued violently. At times he wished they would divorce. It seemed more interesting to be the son of divorced parents. Like being Jewish. Jews are like other people only more so. Fairy stories are on the right track: a large part of childhood is the allaying of fears.

Nelson ascribes much of his strength to herding cattle and goats as a boy, all alone in an endless landscape. We can't judge any more if we are overprotecting our children. Geraldine believes in anticipating all possible anxieties. She thinks many people have had to suppress their memories of childhood, to their detriment. In Rochdale they are dressing up in old curtains and sodomising their children. If it's true. We can't tell if our country is a haven of decent values and good sense or a sink of paedophilia. Nobody knows. This is the effect of the wantonness of information. Somebody, a clap doctor, told him that you can't get AIDS.

Impossible, unless your immune system has been weakened. Yet they keep telling us we're all going to get it. Gays want to believe that. Anthony is sympathetic. Gays are like us, only more so. They don't want to be singled out for it, but the truth is they are gripped by an obsession. There's a public toilet on the little green near the office. At all times of day they gather there. There's something around the eyes, stretched, burning, which he can recognise. To be so obsessed with sex must be disturbing. Yet Anthony believes he understands it. It's just a question of degree.

He thinks of Francine, whose lips drained and whose eyes became almost epileptic during sex. It was a mystery what she was thinking. She probably didn't know herself. Whatever it was, it wasn't him, Anthony. Afterwards in that tropical closeness, as he became impatient, keen to get up and do something, anything, she would cling to him so that he could feel her skin gripping his and her breath, now cooler, breathing her passion on him. He thought that she would do this with any man she slept with, he knew. That's the way it is. You're nothing special. He believes that women are more physical about sex than men, the opposite of the popular wisdom. He wonders if Thelma has ever had sex.

– *Your meeting's starting.*

– *Thanks, Thel.*

– *Don't forget the report.*

– *I wasn't going to, I don't think. But now I'll never know.*

– *I've copied the management committee paper for you. Do you want it for the meeting?*

She is holding a bundle of neatly packaged documents, each one suggesting some weightiness. She has a variety of stuff in her cupboard for turning out documents and folders and spiral-bound booklets. She has many other gadgets, staplers and hole-punchers and page-trimmers. He thinks, sometimes, that what she does is more skilful than what he does. Yet nobody asks her to conferences on skills. He rises wearily. It's already eleven. He's done nothing. And from now until lunchtime when he is seeing Mike, he will be stuck in a meeting about nothing. In his lower gut, on the right side, he feels a rumbling pain. He walks to the lift. The conference room is two floors up, but the hallway outside the lift is a gathering point where you can exchange a few pre-meeting pleasantries. He remembers school, queueing for chapel talking dirty, talking about girls' boobs (but never about masturbation) before going in to commune not with God but with God's wood polish, hand-stitched kneelers, harsh organ music and hymns about the crystal palaces of heaven. God's choice of Anglicanism, which the chaplain implied was the most refined faith, seems now to have been somewhat eccentric, like his choice of Emanuel Swedenborg to explain the cryptic clues to the meaning of infinity.

At the lift he meets the company secretary, Basil Rosewater. Rosewater is detached from the the day-to-day activities of the firm. He's a cheery man, stooped as if his life poring over documents has shaped him. There is a large wart just below his hairline on the right side. It's a puzzle why he has not had it removed. It is more pink than its host flesh, a flat disk like a throat lozenge that has been sucked for a while. Basil is in sight of retirement, which, he suggests, is a great prize. Anthony wonders, but he does not say it, if it isn't just a preparation for death. Nobody talks about death in the firm. Nobody dies. Retirement is a decompression chamber into which the older members of staff go cheerfully, apparently reassured by the valedictions of those left behind.

– *Hello young Anthony, how's tricks?*

– *Fine, Basil. And how's business?*

– *Terrible. But I've still got to push the paper. What's this meeting about?*

– *Skills. Do you need a skills update?*

– *Can't teach an old dog new tricks. I retire in a few months. The only skill I'll be needing is putting. Do you play golf?*

– *Not very well.*

– *Rugby's your game.*

– *Was. I haven't played for seven years.*

– *You were famous. I used to read about you in the* Telegraph *on Mondays.*

The lift comes. Although the building is pastel and contemporary, the lift is erratic, leaping and jolting to a halt. Just as the doors are about to close, Edward Jenkins arrives. He is a busy person. Phone calls delay him at awkward moments. His hair is strangely wavy, like a forties film star's. He is younger than Anthony, and he has been a director for two years. He was headhunted from Margolis, Cadell and Powell. Anthony was not headhunted: he applied for the job. Being headhunted carries a certain prestige.

— *Morning, Basil. Morning, Anthony.*

He is busy with his papers as the lift tangoes upwards.

— *Just read a marvellous book by a man called Lee Shapiro.* Management: Activity versus Process.

— *Oh yes.*

— *You read anything about golf lately?* asks Basil.

Edward Jenkins smiles tolerantly. Basil has passed safely into the twilight zone. But Edward Jenkins causes Anthony's gut to throb. *Activity versus Process.* Which side are you supposed to come down on? Activity may mean headless chicken stuff, process suggests dull routine. He has no idea.

— *Sounds interesting, he says. Who's the publisher?*

— *It's not available in this country yet.*

The carpet on the lift floor extends up the walls to waist height. It's an Otis Elevator. Anthony always thinks of Otis Redding's 'Sitting on the Dock of the Bay' when he takes the lift. He inspects the certificate of inspection (it is certified every two years) as they shimmy upwards in silence. The inspector stamps the paper and then signs his name. The rich families in the world were all in something basic, like Otis or Carnegie or Ford. Now they're in computers and retailing. There has been a shift away from hardware to flim-flam. Each era produces its favoured occupations. In medieval times it was a good number to be a bishop. Now it's investment banking, although even they are feeling the draught in their marble halls.

The lift stops abruptly, like the end of the Latin American section on *Come Dancing*. They exit, wordless, first Basil Rosewater, then Edward Jenkins and finally Anthony. Outside the meeting room others are gathering. He sees Alison Foley, who is head of research. She favours red blazers with full, flowery skirts, symbolising in her dress her dual role as mother and executive. Alison's husband is in hospital. He was snorkelling at a Club Med in Turkey when he was struck on the head by a Jet-Ski. Although Alison never complains, it seems her husband is not going to be able to work again. Nor is he going to be able to claim successfully against a sixteen-year-old Turk. Since the accident,

Alison's face has become smoother and more coloured, like an apple ripening, but it is in her nature to look on the up-side, as she says. There is a growing tendency in the firm for people to speak publicly about their virtues, or strengths. They talk of their benchmark values or organisational skills or game-plans, without embarrassment. Tony Frith is there. He is a bachelor, probably gay, but non-practising, Alistair says. People confide in Alistair. Alistair is skiing in Meribel where his wife's family have an apartment. Alistair says it is a rabbit hutch. Although he is not taken very seriously, Alistar has a talent for making meetings enjoyable and Anthony wishes he was here.

They troop in. There is usually a certain amount of eddying around the available seats. The managing director will sit at the head of the table. For the rest, it depends who is there. Like Solly Zuckerman's baboons, everybody has an idea of their importance which does not necessarily correspond with the true situation. Edward Jenkins always sits two seats from the head of the table, facing the windows. The glass of the windows is tinted a tobacco colour, so that those facing the window look malarial on a sunny day. Anthony takes a seat opposite Edward Jenkins, but moves down when another direcor, Richard Streeter, appears. Richard Streeter has very little hair. He hasn't finally decided how to deal with what remains. He used to brush it across the top of his head, but now he favours a shorter, franker cut. He looks tough with the short hair, coarser and more fleshy. Despite his gangster look, he is a born-again Christian and plays the clarinet. Edward Jenkins is going through his papers, which are held together by eye-catching red plastic clips, so that he looks as though he has important information which has been vouchsafed only to him.

Anthony finds himself next to Alison. He feels shielded from the top of the table. It reminds him of school, where children tried to shelter behind either the thickies like Kevin Harrison or the over-eager like Robin Oldfield, whose hand shot up uncontrollably to answer questions even when he did not know the answer. Alison is often the only woman in planning meetings and there is around her a force-field of femininity. Anthony settles himself into the lee. Coffee is provided in white plastic vacuum flasks with fluted sides. They are all seated. Alison turns to him.

– Hello Anthony. I like sitting next to you.
– Why?
– I don't know really.
– Is it because I am sexually attractive?
She looks at him carefully for a moment.
– I haven't thought of it that way. It's probably your forward planning I find attractive.
– There isn't any.
– Exactly.
She smells of soap. Lavender soap. He would like to ask her about her husband, Ross, whom he met once before he was scalped. It was at the Christmas party and she introduced him proudly to her colleagues. He was a good-looking, squarely cut man from New Zealand. Alison has developed little broken blood vessels around her nose. It is a wintry look. Her hair is sensibly short. *Don't cut it any shorter, Alison. Don't look any more businesslike, even if Ross is a vegetable. It doesn't suit you,* he wants to tell her.

Instead he says, *Here comes the big cheese.*

The air stiffens. The planning committee knows that the managing director is having problems with the chairman, who wants his contract fulfilled strictly if he has to go. The contract was drawn up in better times, when Mrs Thatcher was leading the country to some new mountaintop. They are back in the foothills now, without the map. Mrs Thatcher with her curiously unseeing eyes. Successful politicians are monomaniacs. Successful people generally are monomaniacs. But monomaniacs end their careers disappointed. The managing director was once a big fan of Mrs T, as he called her. He had dinner at Downing Street, with the Prime Minister of Lesotho. – *The B list,* he said. He has a nice line in self-deprecation. The confusions of politicians, the certainties, the promises, the hopefulness, skitter in Anthony's mind as he watches the MD settle down. Nobody believes politicians. The deference has gone, yet politicans carry on with their strangled language and their superlatives. Maybe, like the chairman, like all of us, things have moved out of their grasp. Things are on the slide. But maybe, he thinks, maybe it's just me sliding. All the others seem to have a complete picture of themselves, focusing, benchmarking, proacting. Even Alison, with her damaged husband, and even Richard Streeter, who has separated from his wife and is experimenting with a more rugged hairstyle. They all see the point of things, as if there is some enduring value.

The managing director opens his folder and glances at it, taking in the agenda quickly.

– *Planning committee. Edward?*

Edward Jenkins gives a confident half-smile. He's ready for the pass. (Anthony sometimes thinks in terms of rugby: passes, scrums, sidesteps, tackles. Edward Jenkins is like a fullback, like Hodgkinson, a good catcher of the ball, precise, smug.)

– *Chairman, you may remember that at our last meeting I was asked to look at ways of empowering our staff, to give them ownership of their own projects and allow implementation of management skills. That – as you said – requires a disaggregation. I have followed up the committee's suggestion that we break down the traditional hierarchies and aggregations and re-form into teams. This is obviously going to be a learning loop for all of us. We must be proactive not reactive. That goes without saying, of course, but it is one of those things we claim to believe in without really analysing its meaning. The fact is that we tend to ring-fence our own categories out of a protective instinct. This is our business culture in the UK. So the feedback loop doesn't always function. What I am preparing is a number of seminars for everyone at manager level and over on activity versus process. Before I explain this, let me say right away that this is not something I dreamed up. It comes from a series of papers, now published in the States in book form, given by Professors Shapiro and O'Connell at MIT. They start from the proposition that quality management is not enough without understanding that all organisations are based on a balance between activity and process. Let me explain. Both are necessary. Both have their dangers.*

Anthony is relieved. Whatever they are, they are not in competition for his loyalty. He is not going to have to make up his mind. Edward Jenkins moves smoothly onwards. Anthony doubts if he has changed his hairstyle since he was at school.

The managing director excuses himself; he'll be back in a moment. Alison is making notes. The meeting is settling into torpor. Nelson will be out of jail soon. Anthony hopes that in some way he will make a difference. *Freee-eee-ee-ee Nelson Mandela.* He cannot hear Edward Jenkins any longer. The words have become indecipherable. They have melted, the way the chocolate used to when they lived in Africa. A chocolate bar would quickly lose its whole *raison d'être*, the squares, each one neatly stencilled Nestlé, merging, the crisp bitiness dissolving.

Words. In this place words are used like those roller paints in the Dulux ads with the sheepdog: spread about indiscriminately to cover the cracks with an elastic emulsion. Anthony tries for a moment to imagine how he could be more proactive. But proactive simply means diligent. Or gullible. It's hard to see how you can be more proactive when there is so little to do.

He wonders how Nelson has survived twenty-seven years. The early years were spent breaking stones. The papers say that Mrs Thatcher put pressure on the government there to release Mandela. For more than a third of Nelson's imprisonment, she has been Prime Minister. What took her so long? If Reagan appealed to a slumbering America, Mrs Thatcher appeals to a lost Britain. A country as vaguely perceived as Atlantis. He wonders what people expect from these leaders. Mrs Thatcher gets up at four in the morning and runs around all day tirelessly, while Reagan was hard to rouse from his slumbers, yet the net result is much the same. Brezhnev was a living corpse – he certainly looked like the product of embalming – but he was wheeled out to enthusiastic applause. Still, Anthony expects a lot of Nelson.

Richard Streeter chews his pencils. Anthony has seen him chew pencils down to a stub. As a boy he thought that the lead in pencils was poisonous, like the lead on roofs. If is was true, Streeter would be dead. Occasionally he has to remove the bits from his mouth, which he does with a handkerchief. The managing director returns. Edward Jenkins pauses for a moment. The managing director urges him on. Jenkins is saying something about teams which will have ownership of their own budgets. But Anthony cannot keep up. The words, the torrents of words, are burying him. At home, Geraldine has taken delivery of these thin dry words too. They are words without substance, like crispbread. Now the managing director is thanking Edward Jenkins for his presentation. For the moment Jenkins is making the running. He smiles modestly as all the members of the committee praise him.

– *Brilliant. Very interesting shift of perceptual emphasis*, says Anthony.

Now Alison is talking about a new approach to research. Because they have no work, they are instituting their own research in the hopes of interesting clients. This is very proactive. Alison has begun a programme of questionnaires and documents to be sent to companies in the drug and pharmaceutical fields. She has uncovered some interesting opportunites. Many drug companies lack a long-term strategic direction. Geraldine has discovered alternative drugs, based on the properties of the plants from which they come. She has become interested in the harmful aspects of modern living and the noxious chemicals contained in everyday foods, which seem to affect some of her children with learning difficulties. Plant extracts like evening primrose oil, because of their bucolic origins, are clearly better for you than the things manufactured in laboratories. When Anthony said, *Sympathetic magic,* she did not react as he had expected. She said, *People like you underestimate the magical.* But it's not true. If anything, he places too much reliance on it.

Although Anthony finds it difficult to take in what Alison is saying, he makes notes to lend her support and he smiles encouragement. Sitting to one side of her, feigning interest, he can see that she has a small but evident moustache on her upper lip, which she probably dyes because the hairs are downy and pale. He wonders what colour her pubic hairs are. He wonders if they are glossy and matted, or lightly spread.

Alison believes that they must plan ahead and outline scenarios, as she calls them, because things will inevitably turn the corner. Anthony is not so sure. Something serious has happened to the country. But Alison goes on cheerfully. She shifts from one buttock to the other as she speaks. The spotted dress catches her thighs and pulls down over her pussy, so that he can see its generous bulge for a moment. He wonders if Ross, the New Zealander, will still be able to make love when he comes out of hospital. He knows how important the physical release of sex is to women. Sometimes he feels it dammed up and threatening. It carries also the promise of failure, the failure to be sufficiently aroused. This is probably why in other societies men take more than one wife. It's a reassurance. Sometimes when he makes love to Geraldine he thinks about Francine with her pale lips. It makes him uneasy, but he knows from his conversations with men, particularly when he was still playing rugby, that this is not unusual. He remembers Francine saying, *Our sex life, one failure on top of another*, and smiles. In the bath after rugby matches when they sang obscene songs, he knew that you could live on different levels. You could sing 'the hairs on her dickey-di-doo hung down to her knees' on a Saturday and also love Mozart or one woman or poetry on a Sunday. Human behaviour is infinitely varied. This is what gays want the world to know. There was a girl called Marlene who followed the team for two seasons. She started out as the girlfriend of a flanker who left the club when he was transferred to Northampton. She stayed on and was called 'Blow-Job' by the end of the season, because that's what she loved and that's what she did after a few pints for almost anyone in the team. Nobody despised her or belittled her. She was only about twenty-three. If he tried to explain that to Geraldine now, she would say that Marlene should have had counselling. She would also say that the team was exploiting her. True, once Marlene had extended the service to a visiting team's fly-half and there had been a frostiness in the air. But she redoubled her efforts the next week and was quickly rehabilitated. After three seasons she drifted away, and married a farmer in Essex.

It was eleven years ago now. Jesus. He smiles at Alison and makes some more notes. He writes: *Contact Emanuel Swedenborg asap.* He fiddles with his calculator. Alison is pushing a stone uphill. Her proposals are somewhat desperate. He decides to help her.

— *Could I ask, could I interrupt for a second, if there is a way of including in the light of Edward's presentation on, what was it, activity versus process, his proposals with Alison's proposed client presentation. I am thinking of a synthesis so that Edward's document may have wider circulation. Potential clients would have a short document included in the mailing shot, perhaps entitled 'The drug industry, disaggregation, blah blah, and research with particular emphasis on the concept of activity versus process.' I can see a chairman of an underperforming company finding that irresistible.*

Edward Jenkins looks pleased. Alison smiles warmly at him, her furred upper lip parting over her slightly wonky teeth.

— *I think that is an excellent idea. So what we suggest in all our presentations is that we have some specialised knowledge. Is that what you mean, Anthony?*

— *Yes, that's it exactly.*

– Okay. At the end of the meeting let us set up a team to draft the combined document.

Anthony sinks back. Alison is winding up. She lists the drug companies to which she is proposing to send documents. Do they have any contacts in these companies? Anthony imagines himself in a white coat with a small pipette squeezing coloured liquid on to sugar cubes. They used to take sugar cubes against polio. Do they still do this? On his arm is a small mark like a map of Tasmania, the reminder of the vaccination done on the same day as the polio immunisation. He can remember the doctor in Manzini scratching his arm and applying the vaccine. Followed by the sugar lump, a pleasant surprise. Later he compared marks with his older brother, Clive, who died that same year, before they went back, painfully reduced in number, to England. His mother says that Clive's death did not drive them back. The bank was worried about Africa after Sharpeville and closed its branch in Swaziland. They were sent back to Ewell.

Alison is finished. She is grateful. She squeezes his thigh lightly.

– Thanks. It was getting a bit sticky.

– You did brilliantly. Very focused.

They are pausing for coffee. In these lulls some of the directors leave to take phone calls and messages. Their secretaries push notes in front of them. Thelma is not allowed to appear, except in a case of emergency.

Clive. Who just vanished. The Swazi kings were buried standing up in the mountains near Manzini and for years Anthony imagined that Clive had gone up there too, standing up in his tomb. Like those chillies and pears and so on they put in bottles in France. Although the big, airy house, surrounded by a wide stoep, had been very sombre after that, Anthony had not missed Clive at all. Clive gave him Chinese burns and stole his Marie biscuits. His disappearance was soon forgotten. Anthony thought that Clive had gone on purpose. The idea of death as something terrible passed him by. Anthony wonders how he could have been so untroubled. Later he realised that his mother and father never recovered. The encounter with death, in all its arbitrariness, unhinged them. But he, little Anthony, although suitably pious, was not unhappy. Even now he feels a flush of shame for his insensitivity.

It's more than thirty years later, and he feels his cheeks warming. — *Anthony has got over it quite well*, his mother said on the phone to her sister, *but Freddie is still in a terrible state.*

I got over it well because I thought Clive had gone off and was standing upright in a cave, quite happy, next to King Mswati. That's my only excuse.

— *Alison, I hope you don't mind me asking, but how is Ross?* Anthony asks.

— *He's much better. He can talk a little and he's regaining the motor function in his limbs.*

— *That's good.*

— *The physio spends five hours a day with him. He was the outdoors type.*

— *Will he ever get completely better?*

— *No. He's lost quite a large portion of his brain.*

There are tears in her eyes now.

— *I'm sorry I brought the subject up.*

— *No, really, it's all right. I need to talk about it. It's a release.*

— *Shall we have lunch one day?*

— *That would be nice. You're a sweetie.*

— *I admire you. I honestly don't know how you keep going.*

But he has said too much. She looks desperate for a moment, her face, still girlish despite the executive hair, trembling on the verge of . . . of disaggregation.

The meeting lurches into life again. Anthony has drunk too much coffee. He feels light-headed, slightly crazy. The managing director is talking. He is discussing management options like down-sizing and slim-staffing. He's talking as though this is important news for their remaining clients, but really it's for home consumption: no new directorships, no bonuses, no hiring, some redundancies. Anthony is probably in danger, but his mind is off in the Lemombo Mountains.

When King Sobhuza died, five, six years ago, he too was buried standing up in the mountains. Anthony was once introduced to the king at a garden party to mark the Queen's birthday. The king was nearly seventy then; he was wearing a leopard-skin apron and carrying a sort of axe, which his father said was the royal adze. It was a cold day, yet the old man was naked from the waist up. He spoke to Anthony: *How old are you, young man? Very good. Do you want to be in my regiments when you grow up?* The regiments surrounded the king on ceremonial occasions. They were two horns of the ox's head with the king in the middle. The king's face, close up, was kindly. In his hair there were two red feathers. He seemed to be smiling, without his lips breaking.

– *Yes, Your Majesty.*

Anthony did want to join the regiments, but it was soon after that Clive died and they left Swaziland. Leaving Swaziland was much sadder for Anthony than Clive's death.

Anthony wonders what Nelson will look like when he comes out. Probably like Sobhuza. The only pictures he has seen of Nelson, apart from the famous ghost image on the hospital security video, are of a round-faced man, with a pronounced parting in his hair. He looks less like a lawyer and resistance leader than a jazz man from the fifties. Nelson will have used his time on the island – *the views are sometimes breathtaking, Zinzi* – to good effect, whereas Winnie has been learning blind hatred.

Anthony looks towards the window. He sees a rain-doused blank wall opposite. No mountains. No vistas. He remembers the termites, oblivious of the royal visitor, pouring industriously out of their holes and carrying off the blades of grass from the high commissioner's lawn. (A lot of his life was spent at ground level in those days.) And he remembers seeing some of the king's wives sweeping canapés into plastic bags to take home. At the time it seemed to him a very good policy. You could never eat enough of the sausage rolls and prunes wrapped in bacon. The British guests were, he now imagines, a dismal collection of engineers, soil experts and failed career diplomats. His father, the bank manager, got drunk, what he called 'a little tight', and their car left the road on the way home. Nothing dramatic, just a graceful, prolonged slide on some red mud. Passing Swazis helped them get the car out of the ditch, laughing. Great joke: white man a bit pissed, car covered in mud, the madam tight-lipped. Childhood is a confusion of these memories: the taste of Marie biscuits soaked in milk to make them expand; the termites busy under the feet of the colonials; the mountain pool, full of frogs, where they used to swim and dive through rubber inner tubes; the huge lazy tadpoles; the restless loerie birds (restless, he thought, because their red tails were destined for royal heads); the ochre, clinging earth after rain. Although their usefulness is not evident, he hoards these memories still against the greyness of winter. Nelson is his hope of redemption, his avatar. He knows Mike thinks it's absurd.

– *The nettle has to be grasped. That is the message of the nineties. There's a cultural shift. What impacted on corporate development in the eighties no longer applies. Information, speed of information . . .*

Why does he feel compelled to turn 'impact' into a verb? Does he think it is more proactive in that form? Anthony glances at his watch while pretending to turn over the page of his notes. It's a Patek which he found in a junk shop. It's the only bargain he has ever acquired, although he once won a bantam hen in a raffle and was cheered for a while by the idea that he might be lucky. Many people like to believe they are lucky. The watch has a white face and simple Roman numerals and it has to be wound every day. It's not yet twelve o'clock. He slides it back under the cuff of his shirt. He wears cufflinks which his father gave him on his eighteenth birthday. His father had some odd notions about gentlemanly behaviour, picked up here and there: simple gold cufflinks with a little chain, was one. Anthony has noticed a vogue for coils of gold thread like small cowpats and also for enamel cufflinks, but in his father's memory he persists with the discreet, almost invisible platelets. *Speed of information.* It's speeding all over the place, buzzing and pinging like a fly trying to get out of a window. Nelson will bring some new information with him from his prison and it will not be the sort the managing director is talking about. It'll be more like Swedenborg's claim to supply the language to link the infinite to . . . he doesn't know to what; he hasn't finished the pamphlet although he has established that Swedenborg conversed with angels in 1743.

He thinks of Will Carling flying through the air. In that moment there is something sublime. Probably for the rest of his life, Carling will treasure the milliseconds when he flew horizontal above the turf at the Parc des Princes. Those airborne moments will swell into an eternity. They will become fixed for ever, like the picture of Marilyn Monroe in her pleated dress above the subway air vent. The boulevard of broken dreams. Perhaps in his dry fashion that is what the managing director is saying about the decade which has just dipped below the horizon.

Anthony sees that Basil is almost asleep, perhaps dreaming of golf. His face looks incurably tired. All the feigned alertness has gone. He looks like Sid James from the *Carry On* films. He saw one of them on TV recently, *Carry on Camping*, and it was very unfunny. Out in Swaziland at the Regal in Mbabane they used to split their sides. He heard his father talking about Barbara Windsor's 'charlies' to a colleague from the bank: – *What a pair of charlies, Malcolm.* – *Not half.*

Basil's wart is not appropriate for the nineties. Nor is his hard, melon belly. He has a Jewish tailor's posture. Although Anthony is not sure he has ever met a Jewish tailor.

Alun Phillips suggests that they organise a seminar for their clients on information and communications. Anthony finds his accent soothing as he says, *One of the most important lessons is that hierarchical political power distorts communications.* He and Alun sometimes talk rugby. Alun is disappointed by the Welsh decline. Anthony is gracious. But Alun, although he is Welsh, and therefore obliged to know about rugby, is not really a rugby fan. Caravanning is his passion. He used to have a four-berth Beachcomber, but now he is planning to buy a Bailey Senator so that he can go and camp somwhere in the Basque country. Alun's wife is a librarian in Cheam, who complains about having to stock videos and talking books. Alun looks like a student. He's the last person in the office to brush his hair forwards, like the rugby commentator, Nigel Starmer-Smith. (Hair is going backwards after twenty-five years of advance.) Anthony is impressed by Alun's enthusiasms. Also by his ability to speak as though he is reading in chapel. *And the Lord said that thou shalt not have hierarchical political power. And it was so.* Lunch will be called soon.

But Alison is still lively. Her thighs have become caught up in her dress. They are round and quite fat. He is drawn to her plucky, damp, unruly womanliness, which she is trying to contain underneath her short hair and red blazer. She has had to hire a nurse-housekeeper. Money, she says, is tight. No wonder she is hanging on the managing director's words. They are all thinking about money. Money is the key, the Rosetta Stone, to their language. Even when they are not talking directly about money – endowments, mortgages, school fees – they are under its spell. Everything they have said in the meeting – everything he has heard, anyway – is in the new lingo of money. It's important to speed communications so that the snouts will get to the trough earlier. It's important to have slim-staffing so that the bonuses are bigger. And so on. Every phrase, every 'concept' is about money. Money glowers at them. The lack of it reproaches them. They have retreated into families and forgotten about society. The trouble is, you can't think about society consciously. You can only do it when your mind is free. His father used to say, *I don't like money but it soothes the nerves.* What has happened – perhaps it's been happening for decades and he has only just noticed – is that money has become the only currency. This money talk makes them all strangers, all devotees at their own shrine. Perhaps it was always the same, only dressed up in different language. Now people talk about the cost of the royal family. The cost of the Channel Tunnel. The cost of a mortgage. Everybody knows that since Mrs Thatcher took charge money has become the subject of conversation, but what Anthony sees now is that money has become the grammar of conversation too. Money and language have fused.

Our hieroglyphics give us away. The British Museum, which he visits often, has become for him a chronicle of disillusionment. He sees art, antiquity and beauty but also blind human striving. When he looks at the Sumerian lion hunts, he wants to know why they were recorded in such magnificent detail. What qualities were they celebrating? Did they think there would be chariots and lion hunts and archers and men with spears forever? Did they understand the finite nature of things? In the rest of the museum – he is far from having seen it all – he finds more evidence of this desire to be fixed in the void. He sees invocations being despatched (usually upwards) in many different receptacles: amulets, prayers, chants, tablets, sacrifices and burnt offerings. Now money has become woven into the fabric of meaning, like the thread of a rabbi's tallis.

He feels heavy. Geraldine has theories about blood sugar levels. He is inclined to believe them because he usually feels tired in the middle of the day. He can picture his blood thinning out, the sugar all used up, orange squash with too much water in it. *Lunch. Lunch. Lunch.* To get away from this nonsense. To leave this pastel, creepy meeting room. To be running with the ball under his arm leaving Legisquet, the Bayonne Express, clutching at the air made turbulent by his passing. To be flying over the turf. To be on the launch from Robben Island with Nelson Mandela. To be conversing with the angels in Stockholm. He screams at the managing director: *Time ref, time. Blow the fucking whistle.*

– *I think that will do for today. Very constructive morning. I'm sure we're all grateful to Edward and Alison and Alun for their papers. I know I've got plenty to think about. Anthony, could we have a quick word before lunch?*

Anthony nods. – *Of course.*

He stands up weakly. The others avoid his eyes. They file out fast. He's standing, facing the managing director who is grim-faced. Now he's getting what's been coming to him. All those acts of inner disloyalty are now going to be paid off.

– *Anthony, as you know, things are very tight. There's no point in disguising it. We have had a policy for nearly two years now of not making new directors and allowing natural wastage to take place. But the board has decided, at my recommendation, to make an exception. Congratulations, Anthony. Your appointment takes effect from March first.*

The managing director offers his hand. His hand is moist, although his appearance – his skin, his hair, his eyes – is unnaturally dry.

– *Thank you,* says Anthony.

He feels like a child. When he woke in the night with his hair sticky.

– *Thank you.*

– *Have a good lunch. Enjoy.*

He says 'enjoy' with attempted brio, but brio is not in his range. He gathers up his files and strides out. He's like an emu, dry and preoccupied. Anthony stumbles back to where Thelma's array of pens and files and pads is lying. He must ring Geraldine. Rain is now striking the windows sharply, contrasting with the cheerful mood of the beach umbrellas, deck chairs and ice-cream cones of the prints. Each print is signed with a number certifying its uniqueness.

Thelma is waiting, smiling. He kisses her.

– *Congratulations*, she says. *I am so pleased.* And she is.

– *Thanks, Thel. You must have put in a good word for me.*

– *Will I be coming upstairs with you?*

– *I hope so. I am under no illusions. Without you I'd be the post boy. I'll ask if you can come with me, okay?*

His treacherous heart is telling him what a great opportunity this is to dump her. Her enterprises are doomed. But he knows that the extra salary will help her get a flat of her own, where she can entertain.

– *I'll do it, Thel,* he says, ashamed of his half promise. *You and I up in the stratosphere. Did anybody ring?*

– *No, only Mike to ask if lunch is still on What sort of car are you going to get?* It takes him a moment to understand: he is entitled to a new car.

– *A Rolls-Royce. I don't know. Find out what I can get without looking too eager. I'm off.* He hands her his files.

– *Take your umbrella,* she says.

Only Mike. Even Thelma discounts him. He walks down the stairs. In the reception he sees Alison, hurrying out. She waits just outside the swing doors, seizes his hand and kisses him. Her face is damp.

– *I'm so pleased. Well done.*

– *Alison. I was watching you closely during the meeting. You have wonderful thighs.*

– *You're mad. What does Geraldine say?*

– *She's over the moon.*

– *Are you off to celebrate?*

– *Or shoot myself.*

They stand mute in the rain.

– *Bye, Anthony. You're either very profound or a complete idiot. I can't make up my mind.*

– *Nor can I.*

She covers her hair with a scarf and raises a small umbrella which explodes upwards when she releases the catch. He heads for the Underground. He always tries to get a few tube stops away at lunchtime. Usually he goes to Soho and reads French newspapers in the Bar Italia or Valerie's. He can't understand them entirely, but he can usually piece the sense together. He has the feeling that they contain information which he could use in some way, although he can't ever put his finger on it.

A taxi stops to let someone out. He takes it because it is difficult to find a taxi when it is raining, and because he is a director now. The driver is a young man. He is wearing a woolly jacket which reads, 'Bahamas Yachting Club. Tall Ships.'

– *Where to, guv?* He has just been skiing for the first time. – *Fucking magic.*

Anthony wonders if the taxi driver thinks he's young enough and hip enough to appreciate this relaxed language. Anthony finds it strange that since Mrs Thatcher's arrival the restraints on public behaviour have gone. When you look at Mrs Thatcher, you see a simulacrum of respectability, yet out here they are effing and blinding and drinking cans of lager as though the fall of Rome was imminent

– *Fucking magic. Dynamite. By the end of the week I was paralleling. You ski, guv? I thought so. I can't wait to go again. I'm working nights now, although the business has gone down the fucking plughole. I don't know. Whatcher think? Can't go on for ever. It's the worst I've know it and I've been a cabbie for eight years now. These new cabs cost twenty-four grand. That means you gotta take ninety-two pounds fifty a week just to pay the interest. That's before you eat.*

– *Or ski.*

– *Or ski. Too true. What did you say, Frith? No, Greek. I'll cut up Chancery Lane.*

Anthony seldom takes cabs. They are not allowable any more. They seem to come, like Mrs Thatcher, from the not-too-distant past, with their creaking carriagework, upright seats and many little admonitions. The city outside is framed by the rain-spotted window. It's a large, square, no-nonsense view like the newsreels they used to get out in Africa. Now a shop window of barristers' wigs is sliding by in the comfortably settled landscape. And a shop selling nothing but telescopes, all pointing hopefully up at the impenetrable sky.

– *Moguls. Just when you hit one another one comes along. If you miss one you're fucking dead. Wallop. Skis in the air. I'm lucky I didn't break nothing, to be honest. You going this year, guv?*

– *Maybe at Easter.*

– *Lovely. Lovely.*

It would be good for Fergus. He is pale and formless at this time of year, like the bean sprouts they eat. Anthony finds them tasteless, despite their reputation for budding goodness. People are keen to believe in this purer version of things: bean sprouts; born-again Christianity; mineral water from deep below the earth's crust; dolphin music; herb shampoo. As a director, he will be able to ski and to paint Fergus's room, which is still stencilled with what looks to him like an orgy of eager blue bunnies. He wonders if the managing director had noticed his restlessness. He wonders if he is expected to be more attentive now, more proactive.

– I'm thinking of going to Austria next time. What you reckon? Austria or France. Mind you, I liked Italy, don't get me wrong, but the crumpet was little bit standoffish if you know what I mean. Fuck me, look at this, would you believe it, on a rainy Monday and all.

– I'm early . . . I'll walk from here.

He leaves the skiing taxi driver marooned in the traffic and walks down towards the theatre where *Les Misérables* has been playing since time began. He has never been to see it, but believes he has: *citoyens* manning the barricades, moving songs by the large ragged chorus, headbands of red, costumes of floppy cheesecloth, spectacular scene changes, large helpings of emotion. On the right is a pub where he and Francine once met and which a few days later the IRA tried to blow up, scorching the banquettes. And there's the patisserie where they use real butter to make the croissants. It's decorated like a grotto in Capri, with blue plastic seashells. Real butter as opposed to what? They no longer eat butter at home, but he likes the sound of real butter. He stops at a telephone box to ring Geraldine, but the phone is switched to the answering machine. It's his voice, strangely strangled: *We can't come to the phone right now, but leave a message after the beep and we'll get back to you as soon as possible.* He doesn't leave a message. He wants to give Geraldine the news at a moment when it will have psychological impact; he wants to gain a temporary advantage in the skirmishing of married life. (Perhaps it's not warfare so much as establishing where the front line is.)

This cut-through to Soho he sees as a gateway. It reminds him of the gateway at the end of the garden in Swaziland which led to the ruined farm buildings, the tin roofs largely stripped, the stone and mud walls crumbling, the cattle troughs filled with oily, menthol-scented water from the abundance of gum leaves. Soho is hardly the Barri Gotic, but it is the beating heart of the city. Or perhaps it is another organ, another item of offal, less noble but still vital. They used to call the market in Paris the belly. Sometimes he drops into the Bar Italia to drink cappuccino and look at Rocky Marciano's gloves which hang there. Marciano knocked out his first fifteen opponents in less than five rounds, so his record, which is inscribed there, says. He doesn't believe they are Rocky Marciano's own gloves, but he appreciates the sentiment. There is no irony in their veneration of the Rock. Sometimes he thinks that the country is drowning in irony. The newspapers are full of this cut-price sneering. Marciano's gloves have hung there for ten years or more. Maybe longer, since the Rock fought his last fight. Marciano and Tyson were supposed to be cut from the same chunk of stone, but Tyson went down, stunned. In Swaziland Anthony once saw an abattoir. There was a buzz from the stun gun and the cattle fell over, fatally bemused. It gave him nightmares. Nobody would show children round an abattoir in this country. There it was a regular school outing. He passes a massage parlour down an iron stairway. Idly he wonders what it's like to go down there and be confronted by a provincial drug addict offering to relieve you for an extra twenty-five pounds. *Relief.* As if sex is a sort of boil that needs lancing.

The streets are full of film people and art students. They don't look as though they need relief. They look ecstatic, as though they can't believe their luck to be taking part in this pageant. Mike will be late. He will be bursting to discuss the match. As Anthony turns past the paper shop, which sells a profusion of foreign papers, a strange thing happens: he sees Will Carling hurrying out of a taxi and towards some revolving doors. He is quite small, but very square. His face is bruised, shining as though he has had too many showers, and he is smiling.

Anthony says, *Brilliant, Will, fantastic,* and Will Carling nods modestly as he passes through the doors.

It's stopped raining. He pauses by the Algerian coffee shop and contemplates buying a kettle which has a train whistle. *Will Carling.* The way he tackled Sella and Berbizier was terrifying.

He's just the right height. Anthony can see himself playing alongside him, knowing that Carling would never miss a tackle or hesitate fatally or fail to be there at the exact moment when you've drawn two of them, releasing the ball with your fingertips and wrists just as they crash down on you. Sturdy Will would snap it up. He would be there to grab it if it went loose. He would pull it out of the air if you kicked it. Anthony was always a little hesitant. It stopped him being a really good player. Mike was a good tackler, but he had no overall idea of the game. He couldn't see beyond the moment in which he was involved, so he often made the wrong decisions. But these days he has strong opinions. The two of them are having lunch to commune. At home they were watching separately and now they want to discuss their feelings. They want to uncover the inner meaning of the game. It's the sort of thing which drives Geraldine crazy. She does not see that sport provides them with enjoyment unencumbered by responsibility. He suspects that Fergus has the same relationship to video games, a floating above the surface of the clutching world. Drug addicts probably have it too, the means to remove themselves to somewhere more tranquil. Perhaps Nelson achieved it on Robben Island.

A beggar approaches him, in a sideways, crustacean movement. His face is red, the colour of a crab as it happens, and his hair is wild, so that he looks like Michael Palin in the closing titles of *Monty Python. And now for something completely different.* Anthony gives him money. – *God bless you sorr.* The old Kerry civilities linger on. Once in Aix he saw a gypsy woman begging. She was having a violent coughing fit, coughing up bits of bronchial matter into a square of cloth. Moments after her coughing subsided, a Swedish boy, crisp in crocodile shirt and long linen shorts, gave her a franc. She seized the child's hand and kissed it. Anthony almost ran after the child's parents to warn them to give his porcelain fingers a wipe. It was a strange encounter: a member of the gnarled, prehistoric classes, making obeisance to a hygienic Scandinavian. Geraldine was buying some tourist pottery, which she called 'faience', and he was waiting for her, sipping a *citron pressé* at Les Deux Garçons. Towns are variable. In some you feel all the people joining in a conspiracy of bonhomie. In others, the citizens seem ill at ease, displaced in their own city. Soho, despite the porn shops and strip clubs and rumours of gangster activities, always seems to him friendly. At home in High Woods he has lost that sense. The woods and the lanes and the pubs have become estranged. He sometimes cannot remember the names of roads he has driven down a thousand times.

Yet here in Soho where nobody knows him, apart from a few waiters and the Portuguese girl at the Patisserie Valerie, he feels at home. The Egyptian man who won the Nobel Prize for literature – he cannot remember his name – spends every morning of his life in a coffee-house in Cairo where he plays drafts with his friends. Anthony understands the boulevard life. When people sneer at suburbia, it is not from an aversion to lawns and potting sheds and trees, but an objection to cutting themselves off from human life in its diversity. These are the things which haunt us, what we might have been. He pauses outside the restaurant. It's not yet busy. (As a matter of fact, it is becoming less busy each week, caught in the shallows of restaurant tidal shifts.) Mike's loyalty to the Trat is unshaken, but Anthony would be happy to go somewhere else where they were more playful with the ingredients. But Mike believes that the rump steak with pizzaiola sauce is the best in London. Not that he goes anywhere to verify his theory. Also, he makes no apologies for eating steak. Anthony goes into the lobby where they hang up the coats and make friendly enquiries. A new waitress, tall and shy, tries to identify his name with her scant English. Ludovico wears grey shoes. He comes to her aid. It was only recently that he gave up the open neck and medallion, so derided that the antipathy must finally have got through to his world of Roger Moore glamour. Indeed, there is a picture of Roger Moore on the wall facing, signed with a pleasant note, and pictures of other stars whose dress and hair confirm that the Trat has had its day. The expressions on the faces of these actors and celebrities is perky. They hang there, caught at some moment in their careers, coats draped over their shoulders, cigarettes held jauntily, eyes unnaturally bright. Their clothes are predominantly white, to match their sofas and Rolls-Royces. Bonnie Langford is in a jerkin and hose: Bobby Moore, the cultured footballer, in a suede jacket. Bruce Forsyth, in an elaborate tuxedo, is pictured with his current wife who has a showbiz smile; and Laurence

Harvey, who died at least ten years ago, is stabbing the air with a long cigarette-holder.

Anthony wants to explain to Ludovico something about demographics. Alison could help him. Soon he's going to be stuck with these stiffs and the fossilised menu but no customers. The young waitress brings him the menu and some bread rolls in a basket. He gazes up at her. Her breasts jut out above him against her white silk blouse. As she turns, and the blouse catches, he can see a flower pattern on her bra. Ludovico has relatives in a village near Bergamo who send him their children. They never last long.

– *Mineral water, please. Min-e-ral-e*. He mimes bubbles. *Con gaz*.

Although he can't really speak any languages, he believes he has an ear for them. She goes off eagerly. Her lower legs are stout, nearly as thick at the ankles as at the calves. He wonders if she is a virgin. In his heart, he believes that women should dispose of their sexual hoard carefully. He would hate her to have come to London from a little village only to donate her big friendly body to somebody with herpes or worse. But he can see that already she is weighing the sexual freedoms. Soon her country freshness will fade and she will shave her hair and put rings in a line up her ears. And Ludovico will let her go. Nobody survives London at that age. It has a message for them which they read clearly, a message from its fungal heart, that life here demands some accommodation with decay. Sitting alone in a restaurant waiting to talk to Mike about Will Carling and about being made a director, Anthony feels that this moment will remain with him forever. There are quite trivial things which he remembers, like his father standing poised to dive into the brown, vegetable waters of the stream, the teeming home of mosquito larvae and tadpoles. These moments seem to have become lodged securely in his mind like the insects in amber which his mother wore as a necklace. He also remembers her stole with two foxes' heads, still modish in Swaziland. To Anthony they looked as though they had been found at the side of the road.

The waitress returns. He tries to see the pattern on her bra as she places the green, stumpy bottle of Fontanelle on the table. There is a correlation between the thickness of legs and the size of breasts, athough it has many variants. Mike enters the lobby.

His arrival creates a certain turbulence. He is tall and broad in the shoulder, taking up a lot of space. He is unable to arrive or leave without agitating the air. Ludovico is greeting him. He shrugs apologetically from a distance. They are not yet within human range. His raincoat is wet. Ludovico hands it to the new girl. Mike speaks to her: she smiles broadly. Anthony watches from across seven tables, six of which are peopled only by pink napkins, speaking, like the terracotta army, of promise. Mike comes over. He is holding an imaginary rugby ball in his hands. He dummies past Lagisquet and goes over in the corner.

– *Nice tits. Shame about the legs.*

– *Fresh from the family farm.*

– *All I can say is, fucking brilliant.*

Anthony understands that he is talking about the rugby now. *Mike*, he thinks. *Mike, Mike. Mike Frame.*

– *We should have been there.*

– *We should have been on the field. Signorina bella, un grande Kir royal pour moi. We're celebrating il rugby, comprende? Due, in fact.*

The tall Italian girl has no idea what he is saying, but Ludovico is hovering and smiles his tired smile of understanding. He's seen a lot. He's even seen Anthony and Francine together, sharing a *tagliatelle ai funghi*, but no doubt that's all composted down into the pit of memory. Hotel chambermaids and restaurateurs see many things that speak of the strange, restless nature of human relations.

Friendship. He feels it like the breath from a sun-warmed rock. Their friendship has been beaten airy thin at times, but always it has covered their shapes and frames, like gold leaf. They never discuss friendship. Who can? But they acknowledge it in many ways. Mike once left town to run a yacht charter business in France. It didn't work. He bought a small house near the autoroute, because it was cheap, but one night a party of Dutch Hell's Angels was involved in a multiple pile-up with a truck carrying melons from Cavaillon. The bodies were laid out by the police on Mike's front terrace, all scented with melon. That month one of his boats sank in the harbour and the insurance would not pay up because they believed it had been scuppered. When he told Anthony about the Dutch Hell's Angels, with their fair skin and tattoos and melon pips and blood, he wept.

– Magic! Did you see the picture of Will?
– I've just seen him.
– Who?
– Will Carling. The man himself.
– Where?
– Right outside. Going into a restaurant.
– God has come down to earth.

Anthony tells him about Will Carling's shiny, bruised face and his surprisingly small size. As they talk rugby, they are ghosting through their friendship. They won't get to the subject of Babette until later. Mike prefers to live his life without introspection. He's been dragged reluctantly to discuss the division of their shrunken assets with lawyers. Babette once told Anthony that she couldn't get through to Mike any more. What Anthony understood was that Mike didn't want his inner life disturbed by Babette's sharpened understanding of the world. Also, there was the matter of sex. – *I fuck her. But I'm thinking about other women.*

– Everybody does that.
– Probably, but it's sad.

Forty and beginning to see the score at last. Now Babette has moved to a flat in Greenwich. The Italian girl arrives with the kir, which shades dangerously pink and gold up from the bottom of the glass, like the markings on a venomous snake. Anthony knows that lunch is going to be unjustifiably expensive. But there is no holding back with Mike. Mike's face has lately become slightly lopsided, as though his lack of tranquillity is affecting his facial muscles. He has strong, blond hair, now smudging. His facial re-arrangement is a small thing; nobody would notice who hadn't studied him closely. But his mouth is certainly pulling down on one side.

– Did you touch the hem of his garment?
– I was thinking about him. And I saw him. Spooky.
– Weird. Really, really weird. Were you perhaps dreaming?
– No. Cheers.

They drink.

– To England, says Mike. *Twenty-six seven. Best win since Agincourt.*

Anthony knows that in a way he means it. They're beginning to see themselves and their country in the harsher light which seems to be aimed in their direction. For the moment Will and his boys have made restitution for this painful understanding.

Anthony is about to tell Mike that he has been made a director, but Mike says, *Ant, there's just one thing, before we eat. I've been fired. At least, I've been made a consultant. Same fucking difference.*

– *Oh shit. When?*

– *They told me on Friday. The company's on the skids anyway. Don't worry, I've got a few months' salary.*

– *Oh Jesus. Do you need anything?*

– *Don't worry about me.*

Anthony looks at his friend. His mouth is pulling awkwardly, like a car with faulty brakes.

– *Are you sure you want to have lunch?*

– *Of course I do. I've been looking forward to it every minute since Will went over in the corner. Fuck it. Bella signorina, ancora due.*

The comforting, meaningless language of sport. *Going over in the corner. Building a platform.* Anthony is saddened. What upsets him is the confirmation that the bloom has gone off their lives. When Mike set out blithely to charter yachts, to live in the sun, Anthony knew it would never work. He hoped and prayed it would, but Mike was back after eighteen months, bronzed, thin and broke. Behind him, memories of French and German girls and wild nights in the scent of oleander and thyme. But also the shriek of the autoroute and the smell of diesel and the shrinking of money to haunt him. Now he sits here chatting to the waitress with his mouth tugging nervously, a dinghy chafing at a mooring, his blue eyes filmed over once more by a slick of disappointment. And dulled by the knowledge that he has unmistakably joined the army of the unreliable, the flaky.

Anthony is saddened because Mike's small failures – they're nothing much – confirm his observations over many years, that Mike has failed to read the instructions on the box. They are friends. He read the other day about something called homosociality, which is male bonding, especially intense in institutions and teams. It's thought to be a prop for the inadequacies of men. Men are seen to be lacking in some vital human components. Poor Mike. Poor friend Mike. It seems absurd to discuss rugby, but Mike wants to know what Will Carling looked like: – *Happy, chuffed to buggery, pig in shit, cocky or what?* He feels happier on this ground, this familiar turf. This hallowed turf, as the sportswriters say.

– I only just saw him for a moment. Sort of man's man from an advert. Face was shining as if he had just showered.

– They say he's a bit moody.

– Who isn't? Did you see the way Jerry Guscott was just cruising along beside him as he scored, with Lagisquet nowhere?

Their England. Which hasn't been good to Mike.

– Great kick and chase by Rory.

– Brilliant. He's faster over thirty metres than Linford Christie, I read.

Mike has many facts of this nature. Anthony knows that many of them are inexact. Babette once complained to Anthony about Mike's lack of judgement. She was infuriated by Mike's carelessness with simple facts. But Anthony knows that Mike's perceptions are a kind of cladding for his inner self. Mike says things just to float them in the steam. *– He runs them up the flagpole to see if anybody will salute,* he said that day to Babette, but she sucked in her breath, which raised her solid breasts, a sigh going in the wrong direction, a sigh directed at the conspiracy between men. *Omertà.* Never snitch on a mate. Women like to believe it. Geraldine likes to think there is some suppressed homosexuality in rugby. Men are under suspicion on many counts, but the most illogical is that they are both too masculine and secretly homosexual.

The tall Italian girl is waiting now with her notepad. Her face is thin, despite her generous legs, and her eyes are a worn blue, like painted pottery, like faience. Mike orders what he always has, melon and ham and a rump steak. She writes slowly and carefully, having made the translation. *Prosciutto. Bistecca.* Her lips move.

– For me, I'll have the mozzarella and tomato and some liver, veneziana.

There is some confusion before he remembers the word *fegato. Fegato veneziana.* She writes as if she is going to have to show her calligraphy to the village schoolmistress.

– Very good liver today. Calf, says Ludovico, glancing over her shoulder. *– Very thin. Very nice.*

He glides away on his grey shoes.

— The players said that there was a wall of sound.

— The Supremes. The wall of sound. What's that guy's name who invented it?

— Phil Spector.

— Crazy name, crazy guy.

There have been articles denigrating Spector in the papers.

They know the rituals of friendship. Sometimes they talk about things which happened to them many years ago, like the time they were found asleep naked the morning after a party in the potting shed at Julie Stapleton's parents' house. Anthony woke up with his head on a bag of potting compost. They had no idea of how they had arrived there, nor where their clothes were. They have told the story many times. It reminds them of their integral selves before bits were chipped off.

The drinks have relaxed Mike's face, so that the warring muscles are observing a truce and his mouth has resumed a more natural position. They've had two kirs and they have only been here ten minutes. Anthony drinks deep in solidarity. And to ward off the rainy unease which he now sees in the day. Days have characters. Some days seem to spew helplessness like an overflowing rain pipe. Anthony knows he is easily affected in this way. He would like to have a steadier, more fixed disposition.

The Italian girl has a slightly moist look to her face now as she brings their starters. Although the restaurant is far from full, she is rushing about. Anthony sees her prosciutto legs in their agitation, and he wants to protect her, because he feels that things are not going to turn out well for her.

— Do you think Ludovico is giving her one? asks Mike.

— Probably. That's why they never last.

— Too big for me. Her pussy would be enormous. You would be yodelling in the canyon.

Geraldine would be horrified at the kind of confidences they bandy casually. He could never explain to her.

— Great news about Nelson, says Anthony after they have discussed Ackford's line-out work, which was the platform for success, as the commentators said. Anthony feels the urge to get on to more spiritual matters.

— Did you see his letters? he asks.

– Yeah. I thought the one about how he has been putting on a mask was very touching.

Anthony remembers: *I have been fairly successful at putting on a mask behind which I have pined for the family.* Something like that. His disastrous family.

Mike is eating with an unnatural fastidiousness, as Anthony's mother did when she got false teeth. Suddenly he stops eating. His eyes are strangely insubstantial, lightly cooked egg whites. Behind them Anthony expects to see the workings, like one of those Swatches with no back.

– Ant, do you really think Nelson can do anything when he comes out? Do you?

– I hope so. Don't you?

– I can't see it. Sorry.

Mike knows that Anthony expects a lot from Nelson.

– I can't see it. He's old and there's so much shit he's going to have to wade through.

Mike is reluctant to get off the subject of rugby. He probably feels short-changed. They haven't even finished their starters. Anthony finds the language of eating stilted. *Starters. Entrées. Dessert. I'll go with the steak with the pizzaiola, followed by . . .*

It's an awkward language, sticking in the mouth. Perhaps they are not yet ready to eat in restaurants like French people; there is still a suspicion that it is unnecessary and expensive. His mother ruins their rare visits to restaurants by commenting on the prices: *Seven pounds fifty for lamb chops without vegetables. It's probably best end of neck anyway. Ridiculous.* Or she whispers: *We'll have coffee at home. I've got some nice after-dinner mints. Who is going to pay two pounds for coffee? Ridiculous.* And a craven part of Anthony agrees with her. There is something ridiculous about restaurant pretensions. *It was a bold man who first ate an oyster.* It was a bold man who first charged for meals. And yet restaurants have become a fixed point in his days. In restaurants he slips out of the office raiment, which rests increasingly heavily on his spirit.

He finds it hard to discuss Ackford's and Dooley's line-out superiority – the platform – with Mike, knowing that his friend will be going to the brutal flat in Stoke Newington, above a kebab house, which is all he can afford after paying Babette. Now he probably can't even afford that. One evening they went back there and ate doner kebabs with retsina. Mike said that the only way to come to terms with the kebab house was to assimilate. In the morning, when Anthony awoke on the brown velveteen sofa, the flat was a Somme of retsina bottles, greasy paper and bits of badly bruised tomato. Below, the authentic smells of Turkey and the gourd music had started. There is a sympathy between ethnic junk food and recently single men, a repudiation of the years of clean tablecloths and roast chicken and regular mealtimes. The night on the sofa, the ticker tape of lettuce, the old newspapers, the unwashed aluminium pan, the cheap chipped mugs, the cigarettes in the hallway carpet, the heavy wallpaper parting regretfully from the plaster underneath, the thin, capricious stream from the hot tap, the damp sleeping bag, the smeared windows, the nicotine-coloured lavatory and soused pine smell of retsina, all this made Anthony deeply uneasy. It was the same feeling he had for months after knocking a small girl from her bicycle. (The child was unhurt, but the sudden looming up in front of him kept recurring.) It was a feeling of cosmic unease, like the slippage which he now senses. Yet Mike appears to like this life, emerging each morning from the chaos unscathed, his inner self, like the black box in an airline crash, intact.

Even now, with his mouth settled, the old insouciance is returning: he has established that if the waitress were at home in Bergamo rather than waiting on tables, she would be drinking Pinot Grigio. So he orders some. She smiles, flattered enough to show her teeth which are so young that they look like milk teeth. Teeth are the giveaway, as they begin their long march. – *Pinot Grigio. Nice and cold. Bubbles winking at the brim.* Although Mike seldom reads a book, he can remember poetry from their schooldays. He can recite the whole of 'Kubla Khan' and large passages of *La Morte d'Arthur. The olde order changeth . . .* How true.

Anthony knows it is not an occasion for restraint, even though he will be drunk if he shares a bottle of wine. Thelma will cover for him. Now that he is relaxing, Mike is giving off his familiar briny smell. On holiday he read a book about a man with an exaggerated sense of smell. He believes that there may be a forgotten language of smell. Geraldine is sweet-smelling at all times, even in the morning. Strangely, it is one of the things which bind her to him. But Mike's smell, which he has known for years in rugby teams and on occasions of sexual shenanigans and marriage and fatherhood, is now suddenly strong, as though his turbulent life is disturbing his chemistry. It's like that first, distant whiff of the sea you get as you approach the coast.

– *French forwards do not like running back. Every time they lost the lineout they became more demoralised. I drink to all our forwards in Pinot Grigio: Skinner, Winterbottom, Teague, Ackford, Dooley and the engineroom, Rendall, Moore and Probyn.* Mike values forward play.
– *This is a religious ceremony,* Mike says to the waitress. He crosses himself. *–A religious ceremony, Teresa.*

Anthony sees that the moistness on her face has become a sheen like the skin of a mushroom.

– *I don't think Lagisquet is as fast as Guscott,* says Anthony.
– *I think he's the fastest man in either team over fifty to a hundred yards.*
– *Except for Probyn.*
– *Of course.*

They laugh in sympathy with the legendarily earthbound fraternity of the front row. But as he watches him apparently carefree, the Pinot Grigio winking in his arteries, colouring his face, he cannot bear the idea of Mike going home to his flat alone, jobless.

– *What are you going to do?*
– *I know you will find this hard to believe, but I don't really care.*

He seems to have regained his boyish, maritime jauntiness as proof.

– *I don't care. I feel as if I am floating. Fuck knows where. But floating.*
– *Have you told Babette?*
– *Not yet. I've got to see her later.*

And he hasn't told Geraldine.

– *That reminds me, I must make a call.*

He makes his way to the phone, which is in a small pine-clad nook at the back on the way down to the lavatories.

– *Hello.* Her voice is a little distracted.
– *It's me.*
– *Hello darling. Anything the matter?*

– *No, I just wanted to tell you that I'll be home quite late. Mike's been fired.*
– *Oh God. Not again. Do you want something to eat?*
– *No, I'm having lunch.*
– *Is he all right?*
– *He seems to be taking it well. Can I ask him to stay?*
– *Of course. I'll do something simple. Bye now.*
– *Gerry . . .*

But she's already put the phone down. *Gerry.* She doesn't like being called Gerry any more. At the moment that he should have told her about his appointment, he delayed. He stands reading a card which says 'West End Mini Cabs, Weddings, Special Occasions, Airports a speciality. All destinations. 24 hours'. He starts to dial again, but stops after the first two digits. He pictures Geraldine at home, perhaps with her parents' support group, or patiently reading her textbooks, so full of hopeful jargon, and he can't explain to himself why he held back when the information would have made her so happy. Perhaps he should ring the minicabs, all destinations, and get moving to some far-off destination with his old buddy, whom he can see beyond a large copper jam pot. Sitting alone, his face now looks tired, as if it has softened and become cartilaginous, collapsing into melancholy. His eyes are like a noctural animal's in a documentary, peering timidly from the bole of a tree to verify the arrival of darkness. And at the end of the telephone wire which leaves from here (if there are still wires – he is not sure) Geraldine is reading the agenda, or handing out coffee, or making careful notes, or conducting her tests, unaware of their change of fortune, deliberately if inexplicably kept in the dark.

He returns to the table, executing a careful sidestep around Ludovico, as people do who are nearly drunk. Ludovico is showing some well-dressed Italian tourists, holding Burberry and Liberty bags, to a table. Anthony wonders what they think of their compatriot in his grey shoes and poorly barbered hair, of his restaurant festooned with so much memorabilia that it looks like a grotto to the saint of bric-à-brac? He would love to know if Ludovico speaks Italian with some giveaway, emigrant touches. Perhaps in his thirty years in England he has lost all sense of Italian realities. But then Mrs Thatcher seems to have skipped over the last thirty years as though nothing had happened of any importance. She is lodged in the world of *Picture Post* and Churchill, even if her spirit belongs with the Roundheads. But who can make historical judgements like this with any certainty? Politicians are always plucking them out of the history books. Nelson, he believes, will have picked up some more basic wisdom while he was breaking stones in the lonely beauty of Robben Island. We need it. Mike needs it.

– *Nelson is our man*, he says to Mike.

– *What position does he play?*

– *Utility player.*

– *You're pissed, Antonio. Who were you ringing?*

– *Geraldine. I was supposed to pick up Fergie from karate*, he lies.

– *How is she?*

– *Busy.*

– *They get busier.*

– *They get busier because they were bored at home when we were busy.*

Anthony regrets using the past tense: – *I mean, when we were busy trying to make a living.*

And now Mike may never make a living again. But Mike is making his own accommodation with life. Perhaps, Anthony thinks, he invited dismissal so that he could continue the process. Stranger things have happened. People in marriages are sometimes perversely drawn to throw a stone into the still, dull pond. Geraldine. Once they all called her Gerry. That was in a more perky era. They have a picture of themselves beside the bed, with Gerry in her woollen cap, a sort of medieval burgher's headgear, with flared trousers and a long knitted waistcoat. She is standing on one leg with her arms outstretched, like a pose for a record cover for some forgotten pop group. Gerry, who used to smoke a little dope and whom he loved for her sexy dancing. At parties, she danced with a quietly crazed fervour. She and Babette never really got on. Babette entered their lives too late, after the yacht charter episode. She had been round the track. Geraldine probably envied her her more exotic history. In the Deco-silver-framed picture, Anthony is standing in a swallowtailed admiral's coat, on the sides of his face little hedges of sideburns (which were quickly pruned for the first job interview). He can't put his finger on the moment when their paths divided. The truth is, as Mike is demonstrating, there is in us all an inaccessible kernel.

Anthony sees out of the side of his eye the Italian girl's breasts. With the increased body heat, they are snagging slightly on her blouse. He is reminded of Steffi Graf, going into a third set. She places in front of them, in the wrong order, the liver and steak, but Ludovico is on hand to switch the plates quickly. Teresa and *il patrone* exchange glances which perhaps contain portents of future problems.

– *Nelson's our man.*

– *To Nelson.*

But their conversation has stuttered during the little tension. Like television announcers, they are horribly aware of the silence. Anthony forks up some liver.

– *Not bad. Not too shabby.*

He drinks. He hates getting drunk, but he cannot bear this silence to spread like a stain over to his friend's side of the table.

– *I'm going to Cape Town,* he says suddenly as he puts down the glass, *to see Nelson come out.*

– *I'll come too. I know a few people down there.*

The brief shadow lifts.

– *Perhaps we can go to Swaziland where I was born.*

– *And raised until you were an ankle-biter.*

– *I met King Sobhuza, the lion of Swaziland, when I was small.*

The vortex of the dimly drawn but warmly remembered past draws Anthony down. And at the bottom of the vortex he will meet Nelson. Nelson Mandela. *Nelson Ma-aa-an-de-el-aa.*

– *How's the steak?*

– *Fucking brilliant. And the liver?*

– *Livery. Liverish.*

The liver contains white veins. They remind you of the function of organs.

2

Chanelle Smith's name was Carole, which was her mother's second name. Later she changed it to Chanelle. Sometimes she gives the police other names, like Patti and Laverne. These are the sorts of names she likes. In the children's home they had MTV and she got some of the names from watching that. She still likes MTV. Her boyfriend Jason has it at his other place. The world of MTV looks like fun. Sometimes she wonders if there are people who live all the time, twenty-four hours a day, in that way or if they just put it on for the videos. It's the weather, the big cars and the looning about that she likes. When she was in the children's home they used to mooch about in Clissold Park. It was so big she thought it was the country at first. There were rabbits and things. Now she has to work every day. The crack costs her eighty pounds a day. Jason buys it. He sticks it up his arse in a small plastic bag when he's out on the streets. He comes and he goes. He's a busy boy.

She looks at the clock beside the bed. It's cute, made of pink and green wood, like building blocks, with wobbly hands. It's already eleven. She's got to get to the court to pay her fines or they'll arrest her and Jason will kick the shit out of her if she doesn't. His last words were to get her butt over there. He's left the money for the fines by the bed. She can see it, a hundred quid, not a very big pile. She may get away with less. And she hasn't been to the clinic for two weeks.

She lies back. The pillows and sheets feel damp. Outside it's raining. If it rains in rock videos it rains in a warm, exciting way, crashing out of the sky, wetting the girls' boobs, making the blokes look mean and moody. Here it just dribbles and spits down. It's such a pain to go out and get over to the court. She can't get out of bed. It's funny, some days you just can't imagine how to get out of bed. No matter what, it's impossible to move your legs in the right direction. She turns on her front, but her pussy is sore, and she rolls on to her back again. It's no good telling Jason. He says, *Be more focused, make hay while the sun is shining.* Jason's a funny one. The other day he said, *A bad workman blames other people's tools.* He's ambitious. He is trying to buy a BMW but he can't get credit. There's a three-year-old seven-something which he likes in the A-1 Mart and he's trying to do a deal. He'll get it sorted.

Eventually she has to get up to go to the bathroom. This flat, Jason got it somehow, is in a big block just off the High Road and it's got a huge bathroom. She saw where it said plants like bathrooms and she bought one and put it by the window where there is a lot of light but it died. It had a nice name: busy lizzie. She has a pee, and it stings, which is a bad sign. She runs the tap to see if there is enough hot water for a bath. It's cooling down fast but it will probably be all right if she bathes quickly. One of the worst things on a day like this is to get into the bath and get out colder than when you got in. When they got the flat, this old lady come up to her and said, *It's so nice to see a young couple moving back in here. I hope you are going to have children soon. We miss the sound of little voices.* She is a funny old duck, who dresses up to go to the shops.

As soon as the police started calling, none of the residents would talk to her no more. Sad really. In a way that's how her life has been: people are friendly because she's young and quite pretty, but then they sort of go the other way when they get to know her. They want her to be somebody else. At school they were always on about it. Until they gave up completely. They gave up, and then they blamed her, but if they hadn't started in the first place and just accepted her as she was, they wouldn't of been disappointed, that's how stupid they are.

She gets into the bath. She always slides down the back, which her mother's boyfriend, Alec, taught her when she was little. Now she does it because it's lucky. It reminds her of being happy, which she was when he was there. He was a chef on a boat. When he was away her mother had other boyfriends. Alec lives in Asia or China or somewhere like that now. He must be fifty at least. The water is tepid. She sinks herself up to her neck. She finds a litle bit of red soap, reduced to the size of a cough sweet, and washes herself. It stings; she's going to ask the clinic for some new pills or some cream. The roof is peeling, the paint coming off in bumps like a rash, taking some plaster with it. Jason put green fur around the toilet all over the cistern, which looked good, although it never looked like he said, like Sade's drummer's lounge in LA. Sade used to live in Highbury once. Now the green fur is beginning to look a bit ratty. She tried to pull it off but it's stuck to the toilet so that the underneath part, sort of brown carpet underlay, shows through in patches.

The water, which seemed quite warm a few moments ago, now feels cool. She can feel a chilly patch around her neck and where her tits poke out. The phone rings. It's back on again. Jason bunged someone. Jason has a pocket phone which he uses a lot. She knows it will be him, checking if she's gone to pay her fines. She sinks deeper into the bath so that the water comes over her mouth and into her ears like she did when she was a kid. She's nineteen now and sometimes she feels a lot older. But she can still hear the phone ringing. Maybe he's outside and knows she hasn't gone out. She gets out of the water; her skin is mottled. The towel is wet, no help, but she rubs herself as she walks to the phone.

   – *Carole, where was yer?*
   – *Hello mum. I was in the bath. I fought it was Jason.*
   – *The ponce.*
   – *Give over. What's up?*
   – *It's Brad.*
   – *What's up with him?*
   – *He's not well. He's been crying all the time.*
She feels her heart squeeze, the old ache coming back.
   – *Have you taken him down the doctor's?*
   – *I just haven't had the time. But I'll take him down the hospital tomorrow if he don't get no better.*
   – *Has he got a temperature or nothing?*
   – *I don't know. The thermometer you brung's gone missing.*
   – *Jesus, Mum, take him down the doctor. Or ring the emergency doctor.*

– He's gone a bit floppy. He's sort of tired. Probably from crying all the time.

– You want to take him down the doctor.

– Can't you come up tonight and take him? He wants to see yer.

– I can't, Mum, you know I can't.

– It's that little fucking ponce making you work.

– It's not that, it's the flat and everything and buying some clothes for Brad and all. I gotta go to court before they close. And I'm not even dressed. I was in the bath.

– You're not still shooting up, are yer?

– No, Mum. Don't be stupid. Will you take him to the doctor now and ring me again? Whose phone are you using?

– Nan's. She's out with the OAPs.

– Who's looking after Brad?

– I'm going back in a minute. Don't get yourself in a twist, gel.

– Listen, Mum, I'm freezing. Get 'im to the doctor and I'll come up there tomorrow as soon as I wake up. I'll be there dinnertime latest. And go home now, please.

– Okay. Don't worry, darling.

But she can hear the television in the background. Her mother's television was repossessed a few months ago. She's only thirty-nine but she's become old in the last year or so since Wesley gave her the push. Still, most people think Brad is her kid, she's that young. Ponce. Wesley was a real ponce. Before she went into care, after Alec left, Wesley appeared. Wesley with his big, shiny black muscles and his gold tooth. It was Wesley who drove her out aged twelve. Now he's gone and her mother has deflated, all the air has escaped like from a party balloon, and she has to pay her for looking after Bradley while she's working. And now her mother's warning her about Jason. She doesn't like Jason, because black people are not reliable. Coming from her. Poor little Bradley. He's been sick nonstop since he was born and he's nearly twenty months. And he's black or sort of golden with little twists of hair popping up on his head. It's so cute with his little earrings. He never even noticed when his ears was pierced.

She feels sick. It's the same feeling she had in the children's home and at school when they tried to get her to confront her problems. That was the word they used, 'confront'. What she wants is to be in California or some country like that in a big car with the top down or rolling around in the waves with her clothes on like Madonna, but instead she's got to go to court and then get out on Mount Royal and earn some money and then tomorrow take Brad to the doctor's and also explain that to Jason. Jason is not really hard but he has got a temper.

She towels herself with the bit of orange towel. The colour looked nice and bright when she bought the towels at a stall, but she realises now it was a big mistake. You get what you pay for. The towel hangs limp in her hand. Somehow it never gets dry. Maybe they should get a heated towel rail. She looks in the mirror, which is misty. Her skin is bumpy and rough. It's the crack. She wants a hit, but it's much too early. Every day she wants it earlier and earlier. Sometimes she can't think about anything else, not even Bradley. He's not well, that's for sure. He should have some tests. The number of times she's been down the doctor's with him.

Although the towel is wet and she's getting goose bumps she lights up some weed, the remains of Jason's joint, and draws deeply. There's just enough for one good drag, which she feels not like smoke but like liquid in her lungs. It spreads outwards from there. She remembers that much from school. Before Wesley arrived, she liked school. After he arrived it all went bad. Wesley just cut the floor away from underneath her, so that her mother lived in a new way and nobody spoke about Alec any more. She wasn't allowed to mention his name.

– *Just don't mention that bastard, you hear. I don't want to hear his name no more.*

Alec had found another woman. She was a Vietnam boat person in Hong Kong or China or someplace, and he came home less and less and then not at all and her mother met Wesley who had an import-export business with Jamaica and spent a lot of time in the gym. In the home they asked her if Wesley had ever touched her. Funny thing was, he never, but Alec used to hug her and stroke her legs, even her pussy, and she liked it. With Alec you felt everything was just so. He was the only person she ever knew who seemed to be in tune. He liked being a chef on the boat. He liked travelling. He liked reading her stories. He liked going down the pub with her mum. He liked

■ Justin Cartwright

watching TV. His pleasure in everything he did made everybody else happy. He had a thing he said, which was African, *Hakuna matata*, which he said meant 'no worries'. Only the other day he wrote her a postcard from Thailand saying he had just seen the wild elephant training. – *You must come out east and see the ellies with me and eat flying fish. No worries.*

If she could save anything she would, but there's never any money. There's nothing left after although she sometimes earns two hundred quid in a night. Jason's working on it. He's got a theory that the problem with tomming is that it is too 'labour-intensive'. He's always picking up sayings like that. The other day he told her he was working on his business plan: – *You gotta have good communications.* His plan is to go upmarket. The only trouble is that it's not that easy. You need a luxurious place and the rents are high because they've got you over a barrel.

She's got to get dressed. For court, even though she only has to see the fines clerk, she wears jeans and a big jumper. Not that they would notice, but she wants them to know she's a normal person really.

She swallows a pill and drinks some tea with loads of sugar for energy. Jason says she's too thin. But the crack makes you thin. You hardly ever want to eat. Crack also lets you down further, or maybe she's getting hardened. Your body is very adaptable. Jesus, if anybody had told her that she could take four or five men a day with all the poking and ramming and their hard cocks and their hands all over her tits, she wouldn't have believed it. Although just recently she has been very tender so she tries to get them to take hand or oral if possible. Men are always looking for something more. They don't know what they want. She likes the ones who just get on with it.

She can't go on much longer. Somehow she's got to get some money for Bradley and get a job, maybe out in China or somewhere with Alec. Most of the girls end up dead before they're thirty. Upside-down in a dustbin, like that girl from Glasgow. Jason wants to get a job too, but he's too deep in. It's all talk. The only way he can make more money is with drugs and then he'll be put away for sure or killed. When you get a gun, like Jason, you have to use it one day to show you

■ 76

mean business. Jason hasn't used it yet. She's not sure if he's got the bottle, but he says he is building up his respect. The gun helps. It makes people know you're serious. Jason's big on respect and disrespect. He also likes rap, but she thinks it's too samey. You can be sure the first thing he's going to do when he's got his BM, if he can get the money together, is to put in a system. All black boys have their sounds. Of all the black men she has known, only Wesley was silent and not musical. He never sang a note. It was creepy. What he liked was the grunting and clanking of the gym. She used to wonder what he did with the muscles except look at them. There they were, like pets, doing nothing useful. Her mum loved them. Wesley wanted her mum's undivided attention. And her mum gave it. Now Chanelle can see what happened. It all makes sense. Wesley had these businessmen from Arabia and Africa and countries like that and her mum provided the entertainment. Wesley didn't want some little kid hanging about. He got the lady next door to tell the social services that her mum was on the game and leaving her for days at a time indoors and she was taken away.

Now her mum says you can't trust black men. What a joke. The truth, more like it, is you can't trust your own mum. In a way she's going down the same road as her mum; she would do anything for Jason, even though she knows he has other women and will dump her one day, if she doesn't go first. But at least Jason is good fun, most of the time. He's like a child himself; he's always got a bright idea. Having a gun is really not his game, but all the guys are getting them now and he doesn't want to be left out. Jason was treated diabolically as a kid by his dad, who used to lock him in a cupboard and beat him with wire coathangers until he left home for good. Jason comes from Birmingham and speaks in that funny way they have, as though they are complaining about something all the time. Sometimes people in London don't take him seriously, which makes him mad. Now he's trying to talk more South London, but he finds it easier to speak Jamaican like his mum. And like the Yardies. The police think he's from Kingston, not Hanley.

Jason took her up there once to meet his mum, who is one of those nice old black ladies with a big smile, always knitting. But she spent a long time in hospital when he was a kid. Her liver or kidneys or something weren't working right and Jason never went to school for years. That's when he took up glue and from glue he went on to the weed and then the other stuff. Now he only does weed himself because he's into the Rasta philosophy in some ways. He was one of the first to have a Nelson Mandela leather medallion thing in green, black and gold.

His mum lives in a nice flat which she got when she came out of hospital. She still has to go down the hospital twice a week. She is a trained nurse herself, although she can't work now. His father died a few years ago. According to Jason, he should have been in a mental hospital. – *Total nutter he was.* Jason sometimes makes strange remarks like when he said the Berlin Wall must be made of blocks of ganja the way they were all chopping it down and taking it home. He thinks about all sorts of things.

About half the punters ask her why she is doing this. They seem to find that interesting. Though it's them who are having their cocks sucked and stroked and it's them that want to put their hands on her tits and them whose eyes go round when they come, before they hurry away; still they have the idea that she is doing something crazy. It's no good telling them that they are the ones doing something crazy. She's using them, not the other way round as they think. She's using her knowledge of their real selves. Their wives and girlfriends don't know what they are like, but she does. It's like the wives or girlfriends haven't really found out. Or maybe they don't want to know.

But Chanelle was never given the chance not to know. From the beginning men made no pretences with her. The children's home was the worst. Two of the staff were all over her from day one. At the same time they were always dishing out the criticism, and telling her to confront herself. It was all right for them to feel up some fourteen-year-old, but it was not right to stay out with some boys for the night. Even though the sex which the boys liked was quick and a laugh and not all heavy and sweaty. When she stayed out they locked her up for a few days. They gave up after two months, but they were always trying to get her to talk about herself and her true feelings. If she ever tried to tell them her true feelings their faces went funny, serious and old, their mouths sort of folded inwards. What they didn't understand and what the punters don't understand is that sex is no big deal.

Once she asked Jason what men really want and he said, *They want soomthin wunderful, soomthin they can't have.* (Jason's voice, which some people find monotonous, sounds to her like bees humming.) *The only problem is they have no fooking idea what it is. It's sud. Reely sud. It's a tragedy as a matter of fact.* She makes him laugh. But when he's angry he is frightening. Once he kicked her in the face and she didn't want to work with a split lip, but he sent her out. He warned her not to do oral because of the fluids.

She must get dressed. The court closes at three. If Jason finds out she's still lazing around she'll be in trouble. She looks in the wardrobe, one of those white ones which you are supposed to assemble yourself and last about ten days. Jason wants a BM because it's well made, he says. She would like a place where everything was brilliant like in the videos: warm and light and beautiful with big flowers in bowls. The other hinge comes off the wardrobe. She finds a sweater and some jeans, not the tie-dyed jeans with a zip up the leg which most of the girls from up north like, but proper Levis. The funny thing is, though, from the age of twelve men have always seen her real self too. There's no hiding it. It doesn't matter what she wears, they know her. Just like her mum, really. One look at her mum and it's obvious. It's in her face and her angry stupid eyes. And Chanelle knows she's getting it too, that look. She sees her own eyes sometimes, that they look sort of bruised from the inside. Before Alec left, she had bright eyes; you can see them in photos, bright eyes which show how happy she was. Now she's only happy when she's had the first rock, and that doesn't last too long.

Bradley, Bradley, little Brad. Now she's got her skates on. She must get everything done, all those things, so she can go and see Bradley tomorrow, her golden syrup boy. Brad is the first and only thing which is all hers and she has to leave him with her mum. Even though sometimes when he's staying here she gets really edgy because he's always whimpering. Jason goes out. If he stayed in he would probably hit Bradley. He shook him once and banged him on the floor. Jason's always got something to do, people to see, weed to pick up or drop off. She scoops up the money Jason has left for her. When she was in the home, this sort of money would have been a fortune. Now she knows that money is not easy to hold on to. Not only that, it seems to lose its shine. You think you want money, and then when you get it you never have enough and you can get quite pissed off with it, blaming it for your problems. It's almost like money has a life of its own, as if it's looking at you to see how you're getting on. She tried to explain this to Jason one day but he didn't want to know: – *Shut yer gob.* He was thinking about something at the time. When he thinks, he gets a crease between his eyes and his nose. But it's true about money, it's not what she thought it was and yet she needs it more than ever.

Some of the other girls have pimps who started them off on drugs on purpose so that they would have to go on the streets. With Jason it was more just doing a few drugs together when they were lonely and then needing some money. She feels sorry for the girls with pimps. Most of them call the pimps boyfriends, but everyone knows the score. The police say, *How's your boyfriend?* to her too, in that way. The sergeant says, *Need I ask what he's doing now?* He always says *need I ask?* For example, *Good evening, young lady, need I ask why you are standing here?* But he's quite a nice old geezer really. Unfortunately there will be a new lot on next week. They change them round every few months.

It's time to go. Just as she's patting and pushing her hair, she hears keys in the door. That noise gives her the creeps, that scraping and jangling of keys, locks turning, doors opening.

– *Jason, I'm on me way,* she shouts, hoping to rush past him and out of the door. There he stands. In his hands he's holding something. He's smiling.

– *Not so fast. No rush.*

– *What's up, Jace?*

– *This is a great day. In my hand I have the signed agreement for the BM.*

– *Brilliant. Have you got it?*

– *Not yet. There's a few details to be sorted.*

He's bought himself a new LA Raiders jacket and cap, and new sunglasses to go with the car. He looks great, in fact he looks ready to be in a video, with one of those rap groups he likes. Big clothes with plenty of pockets. The black boys don't want to look as though they have any financial worries. Jason always has nice new trainers and big jackets or hoodies. When they walk down the High Road together they are telling all the little white people that they are big and loose and free. They want respect. You have to respect them and their world, not try to make them into whities. That's what they are saying. Chanelle wonders if they can win this one, but she never tells Jason that. Jason has started calling his mates his homies, or homeboys. He likes these American words. Recently he said to her, *Don't put my business on the streets. It means don't gossip*, he explained. Now he's standing there, all in black, with his face, the little she can see, smiling. She's happy too, now.

– *Wheels. The deal's going down tomorrow. Seven series, bad, bad, bad.*

– *Brilliant. I got to go down the court, Jace.*

– *No rush.*

He's hopping about now, as if he's playing basketball. He sidesteps, feinting to swish or dunk or skyhook or something, even though he's too short for basketball really. She hasn't learned the lingo yet, but Jason knows it.

– *And guess what. Listen to this. Nelson is coming out. Our man he's coming out to lead us home.*

– *You what?*

– *He's coming out of captivity. He's the Lion of Judah. He is the Emperor of Africa.*

– *What's up with you, Jace? You been on the ganja already?*

– *Let me explain to you one more time. They going to let Nelson Mandela out of jail this week. He's my Haile Selassie. Nelson's coming out. Free Nelson Mande-e-la.*

Jason is very excited. He gives her some crack right there which she puts in a stem without delay and looks for some matches. Two rocks. And there's more for later, he says.

– *I got a plan. I been working on it.* He explains to her that he needs a couple of grand by the morning and how she's going to get it. Then she can go and see Bradley. In fact he'll collect the new car and take her there, although he hasn't got time to take them to the doctor's as well.

– *Brilliant*, she says, *what I got to do?*

He explains. He's got it sorted.

3 ∫

There is nobody left in the restaurant but them. From somewhere down the narrow stairs to the kitchen beyond the basement comes the noise of washing up, clanking and banging. It's a melancholy sound now that the customers have gone. In documentaries about restaurants and great chefs you always see them frantic and shouting at each other in pidgin French. You never see the washing up. Here, where all was bustle a few hours ago, a heaviness has fallen. The light outside is already weakening. Winter days suddenly give up the fight. The trees threw in the towel a long time ago. The only trees in Soho are in the square and outside the bombed church, which they are now rebuilding from the back as offices. Outside, Soho is turning up its own light, as though a gas mantle is glowing gently. This light doesn't extend out into the suburbs or even beyond Piccadilly.

Anthony thinks about being dead. It's the light of a stained-glass window, filtered by mortality. It may be the sugar problem causing these thoughts, although he has had plenty of sugars, both natural and refined, including a tiramisu, an Italian trifle which Ludovico says is the best in London. Like ciabatta, tiramisu has suddenly appeared from nowhere. Down in its rich, soaked depths there was plenty of sugar and cream and dark almond liqueur. But as he prodded it, he felt for a moment as if he were looking into a coffin lined with silk. The oddity of the thought upsets him. It's the way things are moving, inexorably, that has got to him. He decides never to come here again. Even as Ludovico is pouring them a second complimentary sambuca from a bottle which looks as though it is made of an ice sculpture, his treacherous heart is telling him that this place is dying, but dying in ignorance of the reasons, like some old dear with cancer who believes that taking a few pills will keep her going. The trouble with death is that the closer to it we get the less able we are to discern its true shape.

Down below they are clanking away. It sounds like gongs.

His uncle Ken tried to manage his own funeral. As he remembers Uncle Ken's funeral oration, delivered by Uncle Ken himself from a ghetto blaster placed beside the coffin, his dark thoughts fly.

– *You are listening to me not from beyond the grave, but before my death. It's probably a spooky feeling, but I wanted to do it this way because I didn't want my funeral to be a solemn, sad occasion. I've had a good life, thanks to Debbie and the family, and some success in my business affairs, and so I thought, once I knew I was ill, I would record this message. Please treat this not as a gloomy affair but a celebration of life. God bless you all and goodbye.*

It was surreal, shocking in its unexpectedness. It made the local paper in Cobham and got into *Private Eye*. It was alongside a story of a man who had ignited a gerbil which ran up his rectum. His uncle's voice, a little shaky in his last days, still retained plenty of the assurance which had given him, as he said, some success. Unlike Anthony's father, Uncle Ken was obsessively well organised. There was something irritating about his narrow focus; he never left the street where he was born and leapfrogged from the purchase of one truck to another for many years in a game of draughts, until his trucks were a common sight all over the South-East. In the meanwhile Anthony's father was encountering termites and tribal customs out in Africa. By the time Uncle Ken died last year, his company was insolvent, though that only became apparent after the funeral. Uncle Ken's voice coming from the ghetto blaster was a moment of madness, made more enjoyable when the vicar pressed the reverse button instead of stop and they had the whole speech at high speed backwards. Anthony had buried his head in his hands as some other mourners were doing, their shoulders shaking. Aunt Debbie was sitting bolt upright, her face composed bravely, but the mistake by the vicar upset her and her eyes suddenly dried as they turned on the technophobe in his dog collar. Priests seemed to be recruited from the dysfunctional, to use one of

Geraldine's words. You treat them the same as you would a Jehovah's Witness at the front door, with sympathy, knowing they are in the grip of a delusion. It's becoming increasingly difficult to be good without looking like an idiot. Goodness is not in demand, in fact it's regarded as a deliberate appeal for attention, like having six earrings in one ear or wearing a velvet hat. It's out of tune with the times. There was that film *Wall Street* a year or two ago where Michael Douglas played a financier, he can't remember the name, who said greed is good. Nobody knows for sure, but Anthony thinks the policy of encouraging everybody to look out for number one may have been a mistake. At the Spice Mall they subscribed a little late to Gordon Gekko's – that's his name – credo.

Aunt Debbie had laid on a large tea, but the vicar made himself scarce. He had a parish management meeting. Debbie muttered, *Farce, what a farce*, but she didn't mean it. She meant tragedy. They are always talking about farce in Parliament. But politics can never be a farce. A farce is something like the tape-recorder running backwards. Or the science and sex teacher causing an explosion in a test tube which singed his eyebrows. Pure joy. Tears of pleasure. It's funny, because it will never happen again in the same way, even if the universe is infinite, which Anthony does not believe. (What is interesting is not that the universe may be infinite, but that we are able to think about it.)

Sitting with Mike, he thinks that the accumulating years, the disappointments, the sense that things are sliding, may come from a related sense that the things which made them so happy were irreplaceable. It will never happen again. (There's a song he remembers with that line in the cracked, junkie voice of Tim Hardin: *It will never happen again*.) Maybe this is why Geraldine is rooting around in the past, trying to recover memories. So much springs from the knowledge of death and the quiet frenzy of trying to subdue it. If you can capture your memories, perhaps you can restore your lost self. Geraldine says that the idea is to recover your lost innocence, which is the same thing. By recovering your lost innocence you recover your lost esteem. Self-esteem is a new issue. It's very important to have self-esteem.

Mike is talking to Ludovico, who never sits but hovers, his

eyes always on the move. He's like a captain on a sailing ship checking the rigging and the tide. The Italian girl, now in her coat and carrying a cheap black leather bag, is leaving. They halt their conversation. She smiles shyly. She is wrapped against what she may find out there on the streets.

– *Bye bye Teresa, ciao*, says Mike. His voice is not slurred so much as elided. It's rich with lunch and Pinot Grigio. Even when he's drunk, he is never insensitive. Ludovico smiles his wan smile. Down in the basement the clanging is loud.

– *We should go*, says Anthony.

– *We're going to Cape Town.*

– *Now?* asks Ludovico.

– *Not now, Friday.*

– *We're going to see Nelson Mandela.*

– *I never been there, but my cousin got a restaurant in Cape Town. He say it got very nice fish.*

People see the world from their professional standpoint: good fish. No Nelson Mandela for Ludovico. Just fish: grilled, fried, baked or poached.

I can imagine that someone who has lived in different circumstances from mine has contrary ideas. He can't remember who said that, but he thinks that it is true, and if so it confirms his fears that everything is on the slide. There are no fixed ideas. It's a terrible thought. It's what plagued Swedenborg. His mind is full of fragments. He can't arrange them in any order. Geraldine has her facts marshalled. They are ready for use, like the spices she has in the swing door above the stove in bottles like a myopic schoolboy's glasses. Some of them are used more often than others, but they are ready to go at a moment's notice. His facts, like Swedenborg's angels, have no obvious use. But he remembers all sorts of things about rugby which he doesn't need. He can remember which year Serge Obolensky scored his famous try. He can remember all the tries Gerald Davies scored for Wales. And he'll remember for ever Will Carling's try on Saturday. Why? Why, when he can hardly remember from one day to the next the files and the projects they are working on?

– *We're going to see Nelson Mandela come out of jail. Let's go. Let's get the tickets.*

Mike has no sense of urgency, just as he had none on the

rugby field, although he tackled with wild enjoyment. He and Ludovico are talking about soccer in Italy, which is now shown on Channel Four.

Only free men can negotiate. Prisoners cannot enter into negotiation. Will Nelson be nervous? After twenty-seven years in prison he may be afraid of the hubbub of the world. Maybe he was freer there, out on the island looking across the sea at the strange, flat-topped mountain like a side of beef. There are different kinds of freedom, that's for sure. Nelson has been most in the company of one man, a warder called Gregory, for twenty-two years. What have they said to each other? Are they friends, in the way he and Mike are friends, friends whose ties are beyond the reach of facts? Did Mandela miss Gregory when the launch took him to the mainland on leave? Gregory and Mandela, a prison officer and a prince of the Tembu tribe, together on a wind-scoured island. Islands are introspective. They are defiant. They have self-esteem. Who knows what Nelson has decided out there? Anthony is drunk, at the very least tight, as his father would have said, and the light outside is dying and so perhaps his thoughts are unreliable, but he is sure that Nelson will be bringing back from there, like Moses from the mountain, essential knowledge which will put a stop to this drifting and sliding. Nelson has been set free of all the humiliation and reverses that ordinary people suffer.

Ludovico tries to pour some more sambuca. Anthony refuses. He can feel the stuff already in his system, rolling around like mercury. Anthony produces his Barclaycard. Some people at the office delight in having an array of credit cards. It seems to Anthony evidence of gullibility. Credit cards have less merit than the badges Fergus wins at Cubs and karate. Ludovico heads for the cash register holding the card respectfully, as though it is a ducat.

– *What are you going to do?* Anthony asks Mike.

– *Now, or with the rest of my life?*

This is the English way of conversing. English people are ironic. It's almost a speech disorder.

– *You know what I mean.*

– *Let's go and see Nelson. Let's see what comes along.*

Anthony doesn't persist. He doesn't want to put his fingers

in a wound. He remembers his own, undeserved promotion. He thinks of the randomness of the arrangements, like Alison's husband having his head pared by a motorboat.

– *How much do you think the tickets are?* Mike asks.

– *I'll pay.*

– *No, I'm not completely skint. Although I will be if Babette gets what she wants.*

– *You can pay me back when you've got that sorted.*

Ludovico arrives with the bill. He walks in a strange way, like a man who has mastered an old-fashioned dance step, a foxtrot or a quickstep, and is practising at home. He glides around the empty tables, which are already set with melon-coloured cloths for dinner. Anthony signs. He waves away Mike's attempt to pay. He feels the weight of his promotion; it brings increased social responsibilities. The bill seems enough for two or three meals, but Anthony smiles at Ludovico as he accepts the pen, which is a promotional item from Panificio Italiano. Seventy-two pounds. VAT, £10.30. Service, optional, £8.20. Total, ninety pounds. Jesus. He thinks of Geraldine and her collections and sponsored lunches. They are lunches where people fast and give the money they would have spent to Children in Need or Great Ormond Street Hospital for Sick Children. It must be the richest hospital in the world. (Maybe there's a reproach for him in her choice of charity, considering his failure to father more children.) She and Leonora and Jacqui collected about fifty pounds a few weeks ago by denying themselves, and here he is handing over nearly a hundred in some sort of gesture for his wounded friend.

Now they are out on the streets, surprised to find another, nighttime world has descended on Soho. Ludovico shuts the door perhaps a little too quickly behind them, maybe fearing they will change their minds and take him up on another free drink. Sometimes in books you read that the cold air sobers people up. It's not that. It's the realisation that while you have been eating offal and drinking wine and digging into rich desserts, the world has been busy. That sobers you up. It's startling, like waking in the middle of the night to a phone call. A heart-stopping phone call like when his father died or when Francine rang at four one morning and pretended to be the international operator: – *Will you take a call from Mr Spring Roll. – We don't have a Mr Roll, there must be some mistake.*

Geraldine sat on the bed, her face uncomprehending, but perhaps even in her tiredness and confusion suspecting something. Francine was very apologetic the next day, but Anthony found it difficult to forgive her. He wouldn't have but for the attraction of the sexual vortex.

We couldn't fulfil our wishes, as we had planned, to have a baby boy. Nelson's words. He feels tied to Nelson. There is something stunted about his family, just Fergus growing up in a goofy, over-analytical world. His every action and thought is likely to be examined. He is constantly shepherded and coached and counselled. He is never allowed to discover the consequences of his actions for himself. Consequences can be banished altogether.

Anthony decides to get Thelma to order some ski brochures. Skiing is uncomplicated. He'll take Fergus and they'll get an unhealthy suntan and grapple with the elemental. In Swaziland nobody bothered about his state of mind. He played endlessly in the old farm, or walked up to the edge of the mountains until the baboons barked at him, or fed ants into ant-lion traps, or drank warm milk from the milking buckets and enjoyed the undemanding companionship of a dog with ticks. Looking back, he can see that after Clive died, his parents were puzzled about how to keep him entertained; but he can remember no unhappiness, simply endless days of activity near ground level involving insects and frogs and walking with Willie, the dog. The dog was supposed to provide advance warning of snakes. In Swaziland he used to save his pocket money to buy aniseed-flavoured sweets called niggerballs. It seems hard to believe. *Four niggerballs for threepence.*

They are standing outside a gay sex shop which sells poppers and manacles. In the window is a picture of a beefy boy in black briefs. The look on his face is hard to fathom, knowing but stupid, someone who hasn't quite got the whole picture.

– *Do you want to come and get the tickets with me?* Anthony asks.

– *No. I've got to sort something out with Babette. I'll catch up with you later.*

Mike walks off towards Shaftesbury Avenue, placing his feet carefully. He has to go and conduct this painful business. Maybe he doesn't want to suffer any expressions of concern for his future.

Two men with very short hair approach the sex shop. They appraise Anthony frankly. To him they look parched and hungry. He avoids their gaze. Their faces are eloquent. They may be in the true image of the last decade of the century. This restlessness, this displacement, is not the result of poverty or individual misery, but of uncertainty, a deep uncertainty about the explanations. Gays have tried to put their own sexual uncertainties into a wider context, to suggest that they are part of a cosmic uncertainty. The lean, foxy faces and the tough clothes say, look, we're living on the margins, we've seen the way things are going. It's your problem too. Putting our cocks up other men's arses is not what you straights think it is; no, it's all a part of the same thing, the fragmentation of certainties. Anthony is not sure they are wrong. But he finds the eloquent faces a little too literal and the sexual remedy a little too basic, the part of the equation he can't quite follow although he can well imagine how it came into being. He wonders what they are doing in there, what they are buying to ease the cosmic worries.

Next door is a Vietnamese restaurant, probably run by boat people. Thelma would appreciate the aromas wafting out into the indifferent Soho air. Ginger and garlic and something sweet, possibly lemongrass. He turns the corner past a shop full of waiters' and chefs' clothes, a shop as dead as a case of armour in a museum. And then a shop selling American clothes, as if everybody in America went around like Marlon Brando in *On the Waterfront*. And a pub with its fruity beer smell. It's a place where Dylan Thomas used to drink. Dylan Thomas was the poet he liked most at school. *It was my thirtieth year to heave, woke to my hearing from harbour and neighbour wood* . . . You didn't think then you could reach thirty. And over there the Free French used to meet in York Minster, *A tous les Français*. Out in High Woods there is no history, except the history of skies and trees which means nothing to him, although Geraldine is excited by the knowledge that the surviving wood, from which the housing estate gets its name, is a patch of the original forest which swathed England. England was a leafy place, and in the glades frightened people huddled. Now their troubled descendants go into sex shops to buy poppers to dilate their anuses. He's not condemning them. Why should he? We are past the age of condemnation; we have entered the age of no consequences. Except for AIDS. AIDS presents a tricky problem of explanation.

The Italian grocer, its windows packed with basil and spaghetti and wheels of Parmesan, is crowded. There is so much food in there, the customers seem like an afterthought. And here's a place where they sell cut-price air tickets to Milan and another sex shop where they sell underwear in red and black PVC and, if you look in, rows of dildos, some of them puckered like tripe, and here's a Chinese restaurant with the bodies of ducks hanging in the window and bowls of noodles and rice, made of plastic or something, to give you an idea of what's available inside, and over there they sell nothing but boots, which everybody in Soho wears and now he is walking past the window of a film company which advertises a film with Tom Selleck, *Three Men and a Little Lady*. He saw the earlier one, *Three Men and a Baby*. It was funny. And here's a tapas bar, selling Spanish and Mexican beer which everybody drinks. The richness of it all, just in these few yards. In the darkening streets – it's night but still afternoon – this is evidence of the range of human restlessness. There is some pink in the sky. It's not easy to see the sky. His eyes are drawn downwards. He often looks at paving stones as he walks. The art of the paving stone is dying. When they dig them up they replace them with something synthetic, but these new stones are compounds which lack the staying power of the slabs of York stone and granite. And now he is passing a preview theatre where film people look at commercials and movies. And here's a place that sells the T-shirts and caps that belong to this world of movies, and joke clapperboards. People like to identify with the movies, as if there is some distinction in wearing a T-shirt which says, 'I'll be back'. And now he's passing an alleyway, heavy with urine, almost steaming like a pissoir, where red lights above the bells say 'model' or 'new model' or 'busty new model'. And here's a place which sells and repairs violins. Violins apparently need a restful setting: they are posed on winding sheets of velvet. The streets are busy with people rushing home and people reluctant to go home and some with no home at all, who wander with beer cans in their hands and amused expressions on their soiled faces. This category is multiplying. As a drunk stumbles past him, Anthony sees that the familial sentiment can drag on your soul and force you into radical new lifestyles and yet your soul (if you have one, which he can't quite decide despite the help of Swedenborg) is nothing without it. And then he swings past the market, a vegetable world, with a touch of the fairground: the traders are shouting and the stalls are hung with strings of naked light bulbs. They have a rawness he likes; let's not take this too seriously, let's not get tied down. And now Anthony feels a tap on his shoulder. He turns around a little too quickly. A small, sturdy woman, perhaps thirty or thirty-five, is standing there, bundled up in a cheap coat. He recognises her with a flood, as though his blood has lurched.

– *Francine.*

– *Hello Anthony.*

– *I'm drunk. I must be.*

He kisses her, but their faces scrape and bump.

– *Don't worry. I've got fat. Nobody recognises me.*

– *When did you come back?*

– *I slipped back, almost two years ago.*

He feels his blood keenly. It's agitated, like mineral water. Why hasn't she contacted him?

– *Don't take it personally, Anthony. I've found my level. It's not too high. I needed to go to Australia to find out. I don't want much. You wanted a lot.*

She still talks in this disjointed way, now with the trace of an Australian accent.

– *I needed some space and some time. I am more comfortable with who I am now.*

Everybody over a certain age talks like this. They have flow charts and goals for their personal development.

– *Terrible about shooting Ceausescu like that, on Christmas Day,* she says.

And he laughs as he remembers her strange mind, so unpredictable in its sparrow-hops.

– *Are you married?*

– *For the second time,* she says, with an apologetic shrug.

– *What's he do?*

– *Why?*

– *I don't know. I just want to know.*

But of course he wants to know where in the herd she has found herself.

– *He's in central heating.*

– *He's a plumber?*

– *No, he is not a plumber, he's a central heating engineer.*

She laughs, her puffed-out face, which has forced her eyes into retreat, very merry. Her laugh is the same – staccato, slightly insane.

– *What are you doing in Soho?* he asks.

– *Oho, Soho. I work up the road at Marks. Checkouts. I'm part time. And you? Still with the firm?*

– *I am. I know it's surprising. They made me a director this morning and I've been celebrating with my friend Mike. That's why I'm drunk.*

– *Sounds reasonable to me. Is that the same Mike?*

– *Yes.*

– *The one with the nice flat we used?*

– *He's fallen on hard times.*

– *Do you still cry sometimes when you come?*

– *Jesus, Francine. Francine, why did you go to Australia?*

Behind him they are marking down the Chilean grapes, loudly. They shout: – *Owny fitty two pee a pand. Chilean gra-a-pes. Juicy gra-a-pes. Fitty two pee a pand. Luvverly gra-a-apes.*

– *It wasn't to get away from you. Not really. What are you doing here apart from getting pissed?*

He's upset. Some careful reordering of the past eight years is going to be required.

– *I'm buying some air tickets.*

– *You and old Geraldine going off to do a spot of skiing? Yodel-lo-di do hi ho?*

– *No, I'm going to Cape Town.*

– *Brilliant. What for?*

– *To see Nelson Mandela. It's going to be historic. A lifetime experience.*

– *Fuck, that is incredible. Can I come in your luggage?*

She has been married twice. He tries to imagine how this could have happened. He looks for some clues in her face, but all he sees is Francine, fattened up and cocooned. He feels demeaned, although he is not sure what right he has. His memories of Francine, particularly Francine in bed, have sustained him. Yet she has married twice and grown fat while he's been contemplating.

– *How many kids have you got?* she asks.

– *Just the one. Just Fergus. He's nearly nine.*

– *I've got three. One's stayed in Australia with my ex.*

The pigeons are not yet roosting. Maybe they are confused by the lights on the barrows. They hardly ever get airborne.

Francine. What a tumult in a few years! Three children, two marriages. He can't imagine how you would find the time for so much upheaval. These facts of her biography are more shocking than the way she's aged. But then he's aged too. His hair is thinning and his features have begun to settle in unwelcome ways. Perhaps she's as uneasy meeting him as he is meeting her. If she is, she shows no sign of it. She seems to be quite relaxed, married to a heating engineer. She obviously experiences no guilt about not getting in touch. She should have been truer to their . . . but he can't think of a word for it. It wasn't love. She can probably hardly remember the moments that he has hoarded. He is like one of those glossy-headed termites which used to run around the ambassador's lawn when he was living at ankle level, storing up blades of grass somewhere underground. He was laying up stores of eroticism and abandonment against the winter which was coming. But why should she place any weight on their affair? (He hates the word.)

– *The child you have left in Australia can't be very old.*

– *Nearly six. Ross got custody. I hadn't behaved myself very well. I went off with someone else.*

He doesn't dig any deeper now. He doesn't want to.

– *God, you've lived,* he says sadly.

– *I've lived, and now I'm fat and reasonably happy.*

– *I sort of assumed, I sort of assumed that . . .*

– *You sort of assumed that I was holding a little candle for you or that I had gone into a fucking nunnery?*

– *You didn't use to swear before you went to Australia.*

– *I learned it when I came back.*

– *From the plumber.*

– *Anthony, we live in a world of specialisation. My husband is a specialist.*

– *What are you talking about?*

– *You don't want to face the facts.*

– *Like?*

– *Like we're all getting older and our hopes are never really going to be fulfilled. That sort of thing.*

– *This is not the greatest moment for a discussion of my personal philosophy. But I can assure you that it's a bit more complicated than that.*

– *That's probably why you're going to Cape Town. I think it's beautiful. And I'll be in St Albans doing the weekly shop. We've got an estate car. How's Geraldine?*

– *She's fine. She's doing a diploma and teaching disturbed children. You were an antidote against Geraldine. That's what I thought, and then I realised you were an antidote against myself.*

– *My first husband was bitten by a snake in Victoria. A bushmaster. His foot went brown.*

– *Francine, can I ask you now if you loved me?*

She looks at him for a moment. Her eyes, now recessed, are the same hazel brown. He is rapidly becoming used to the new Francine, with her padded features, but he is trying to keep a fix on the old, the one whose pubic hairs found their way into his teeth. That is the sort of intimacy he is trying to preserve. He remembers the way her eyes rolled backwards and her limbs shook. He remembers her begging him to come on her face. Why are these things – really so banal, practised by millions daily – so precious to him? It's not for the reason Francine gives, although she's not too far off the mark. Behind them the fruit-sellers are having a competition as he waits – how long? – for the answer to his question. One shouts and another takes up the cry. Edward Jenkins should come down here to see activity versus process at work.

Francine's mouth has become smaller, crowded by the flesh.

– *Yes. I loved you. But the truth is that I forgot you in Australia. Not in the sense that I couldn't remember you, obviously, but you went on to the back burner. I had a hectic time. At that stage you're desperate to get into something permanent, whether or not you realise it. It's female survival.*

– Did you sleep with a lot of people?

– Quite a lot. It's not the big deal you think, fucking. Not always, anyway.

He wonders if he comes into the 'not always' category. She used to say she liked sex too much. He wonders if the specialist plumber has had his problems with her. Maybe she's lost her sense of being doomed. Or maybe she's on tranquillisers. He's read a lot about the new generation of tranquillisers which can make everybody happy, even if they are not loopy. It's not a bad idea. The dosage would depend on how dark your thoughts were. You could bring everybody up to a sort of plimsoll line of happiness. Or possibly the sun and the outdoor life changed her.

– Will you ring me at the office?

– I will. I'm on from nine until three thirty. It's all new technology. We can meet for coffee.

– Or a drink.

– Or a drink.

– Francine, what's your husband's name?

– Chris.

– His second name, your name, dumbo.

– I know I'm fat, but that's not nice.

But she's laughing.

– His name, our name, is Batt. Chris and Francine Batt. And their children Shane and Sara.

And the one abandoned in Australia.

– Where are you going now? he asks.

– I'm going to the post office, right here, and then I've got to go home. I've missed one train already.

– Okay. Will you ring me?

– Of course. There's no need to get all intense.

They kiss briefly, their cheeks together and the corners of their mouths just making contact. He holds her arm, which feels full, above the elbow.

– We can do it if you like, she whispers in his ear. *Mr Director.*

He watches her go stoutly into the post office before he moves.

They are digging up the pavement here. He passes a building where policemen live and beyond that a building site. Something is rising above the hoarding, but it is still too early to tell what it's going to be. The concrete pillars and supports could be anything when they are finished. They all start in anonymity. The house at High Woods is one of six on the estate. Each one is different in some superficial way, but when they were being built you could see the essential sameness. Maybe now that he's a director they can afford a proper house, built by someone. The developer of High Woods planted two Japanese cherries outside every house to make an artful chain. Anthony is alone in wanting to cut them down. Everybody else thinks the burgeoning cherry forest is quite a feature but Anthony rebels, inwardly anyway, against this imposition which comes garishly to life each spring. He refuses to admire the over-abundant pink blossoms.

Francine, whose element was the bed. How could he have imagined she would have stayed the same? While he was nursing his false memories, she had put him on the back burner. He thinks he should take her up on her offer to renew his acquaintance with her body. If she means it. He feels weak at the thought.

Here's a pub, with very high ceilings. Inside, another group of convivial strangers is meeting. Next door is a doctor, Dr Pelz. Good name for a doctor, suggesting skin disease. Francine says he tries to avoid the facts. What he wants from Nelson Mandela is to find some new facts. The ones we have don't seem to be doing the job. Just as the voyage of the *Beagle* showed Darwin the shadowy outline of natural selection and evolution which became public knowledge, so Nelson has discovered something about the nature of being human on Robben Island. He remembers the smiling face of King Sobhuza looking down on him. Sobhuza was a convinced pagan. He wanted to return to the Swazis the easiness they once had with their world. It was a hopeless task. But this is what Nelson Mandela will bring from prison, a simple but previously undiscovered truth about humanness. He will stop the drift.

Anthony is passing a store which sells ghetto fashion. Black boys in huge sports clothes hang out there. They need Nelson's testament too. The music from in there is rap, which sounds like a threatening harangue to Anthony, but then he remembers what his father said about the Rolling Stones. Now you hear rap all over the place, especially when black kids appear next to you in traffic. It's harsh music. Anthony wonders why these kids are so entranced by looking cool. They walk or stand about as if they have a lot of time. They are readying themselves for something, a record contract, a party, a new car. But they seem to have missed the steps on the way to success. They are waiting, but they are not doing. The connection has been broken. And here's a place which sells nothing but left-handed goods, scissors, mugs, pens, paintbrushes, toys, toothbrushes. And a sports shop, specialising in boxing equipment. On cue a small man with a broken nose comes out smoking a cigar. Anthony has the feeling that the city goes on forever. It's a feeling like being caught in heavy fog on a mountainside. It's a feeling of helplessness, but pleasing at the same time. He remembers skiing once in dense fog. He had no idea of where he was going until he skied up a bank and fell on his back with his skis way above him. All these streets, all these shops and cafés, all these people, and you can't see the end. No, it's not the facts he can't face. Far from it. He's as keen as mustard to face the facts, it's just that he wants Nelson to tell him what they are. He wants Nelson to answer Swedenborg's questions in plain English. At the office he hears them busily talking up teamwork and quality management, but he knows they are just whistling in the dark. They hope to get something out of the use of 'teamwork' and 'teams'. He resents it. Sport is the isle of joy in a troubled sea. Sport is fact. It may not signify much, but you can't get away from it, every match has a result. It's finite, it's concluded.

And here's a shop selling candles. Wonderful things, with the promise of light and scent and religious experience. And next door is British Airways.

– *How may I help you, sir?*
– *Two tickets to Cape Town, please.*

4 ∫

Chanelle goes to pay the fines. Jason's good mood, the thought of going up to see Bradley with Jason at the wheel of his new car, the wad of notes in her bag, the cold but dry afternoon, the crack in her blood, everything seems to be clean and orderly. What she misses, it's like a buzzing you can't locate, a fly trapped behind glass, is the idea of where she's going next. Sometimes when she's in a car with a punter she's envious. They're always going somewhere. They have houses and families and jobs and holidays. She doesn't mind when they tell her. Some of them tell her to feel better about what they're doing. They may be stopping off for a quick fuck but it's just a sideshow in their lives. They want her to know that for some reason. Now she feels happy, but she knows that when she's coming down this buzzing can become loud. When they drive off in their Escorts and Astras and Renegades and dinky BMWs and she's left by the side of the road, she wishes she was going with them. They all have plans for next week, next month even.

She's tried to discuss this with Jason.

— *Do you mean getting off the game, like?*

— *Yeah, sorta, but I mean, I mean what are we doing like, in general?* She can't explain it to him properly.

— *I told you, I'm getting it sorted. We've got to get a plan.*

But his plan, she knows really, is just a day-by-day arrangement to get more money. As soon as he's got some in his pocket he thinks everything's fine. His new plan, to pay for the BM quickly, is not a plan for security. It can't last. In magazines the girls want security. Girls are always asking the fellers to marry them or get a job or a house. But all she can do is to earn enough money to pay her mum and pay for the crack which gives her some good times when she doesn't think about security. Like now, except that she is thinking about it. It never goes away completely; that's because she was in care. All children in care dream about a warm, safe bedroom with proper parents downstairs, like on television. The staff talked about security as though it was just regular meals and clean sheets and so on. It wasn't for her friends. They all had a huge hole in them through which the wind blew. They were all doomed and they knew it. One boy is already dead, murdered. Patrick O'Shaughnessy. He was a rent boy at fifteen.

Still, she's looking forward to driving with Jason in the new car to see Bradley. You take it where you find it. Jason seems to think it will all turn out all right. It's just a question of getting the plan right. Sometimes, particularly if she's stoned, she believes him. But she doesn't want to see him get heavily involved in drugs, which is his only hope really. They're all crazy. He'll end up dead. The funny thing is, with all those black boys, winding up dead is part of the game. It wouldn't have any point if that was not a real possibility.

There's a street near the court which looks like those streets in *Mary Poppins*. The front doors are all gleaming and there are neat trees and bushes in pots and boxes. Each house seems to be occupied by one family. She always walks up this street, even though it takes longer. Down in the basements she can see bright, tidy kitchens. The floors are tiles or wooden planks. In one kitchen she can see children sitting down at a long table. It must be a birthday party: there are streamers and balloons and cakes in blue and red, and a small Asian lady in an apron is handing out jelly. The mothers are drinking wine and admiring their children who are creating a right old mess with the cakes and party poppers. Chanelle is standing there smiling, watching this as if it's on television. She's out of her head really. One of the mothers looks up at her and she walks on, avoiding the joins in the pavement. She still does it, aged nineteen. She says, this is where I am going to live with Bradley. But she doesn't believe it. She knows she's going to wind up like her mother. Or dead.

They know her at the court. Just like they know her at the clinic and at the police station. They treat her all right, but with a little bit of distaste. The are able to suggest by the way they speak to her that she is to blame having to wait and sign a form or hand over her money, or sit while they talk about her as though she's not there and ask personal questions as if it's for her own good. Once you get taken into care, you become public property. That's what Patrick used to say. He wasn't far wrong. They also think they can just ignore her if they're busy. Sometimes when the police take her in she has to wait three hours in the van and in the charge office. Three hours wasted. They all know she will just have to get out there again or Jason will get angry, or hold back the crack. Jason and some of the others make sure that nobody around here will sell the girls crack. Sometimes if she is desperate and she has a bit of money she can go up to King's Cross or score off one of the other girls. These fines are a joke. The trouble is, if she doesn't pay them she can be locked up for weeks or even a few months. Her mum's quite good with Bradley, but she doesn't trust her. God knows what would happen to him if she had to spend two months inside for non-payment.

Some of the police are okay. There was one boy, a Welshman, who used to talk to her in that funny voice.

– *What you doing standing out in the cold, lovely? Why don't you go and work in a massage parlour? Or a get a flat, love-ly?*

– *Rowlands, don't piss in the wind. Need I ask what you're doing here, Carole?* asked the sergeant.

– *I'm waiting for Constable Rowlands to come off duty, sarge. I think I'm in love with him, sarge.*

– *If I see you again I'll nick you. I'm just being lenient because I don't want to break Constable Rowlands' heart. Go on, hop it, Carole.*

– *Chanelle.*

– *It says here Carole, sometimes known as Patti or Laverne. Or Madonna.*

– *That was a joke.*

– *All right, Chanelle. Off you go back to the material world.*

And then she would have to hang about at the café or Nero's until they went off at one. Like everybody else, the vice squad has homes and girlfriends and plans.

Mrs Baxstead is just closing the office.

– You've had six and a half weeks to pay the fines and you arrive at one minute to four on the last day, Carole.
– At least I come.

Mrs Baxstead has worked here for many years. She has a light down on her face and dresses very smartly, as though she, at least, still takes the court seriously. The truth is it's a tired place with bored magistrates and exhausted ushers who couldn't care less.

– At least you came. I suppose we should be grateful. Have you got the summons?
– Oh shit, no. I had it. It was seventy-eight quid something. Something like that.

With a shake of her head, a sorrowing, barely audible mutter, Mrs Baxstead opens a box file and finds the papers.

– Nearly right. Eighty-seven pounds and seventy-three pence.
– As much as that?

Chanelle hands over the money. Mrs Baxstead gives her a receipt and the change, which she takes from a small safe.

– I suppose we'll be seeing you again in the not-too-distant future?
– Probably.
– Look after yourself. You're only young once.
– And you look after yourself.

But Mrs Baxstead doesn't want her good wishes. Chanelle's good wishes are not worth anything.

The court has a big, echoing hall which is plastered with signs and information that nobody reads. The floor is a mosaic, showing St George and a dragon, but so worn out by feet that St George's white horse has almost been erased and the dragon could be anything, because its fiery nostrils and its tail have been wiped out. It was Jason who told her it was St George and the dragon. At his school in Birmingham they used to have a badge like that, although only the nerds wore the school uniform, he said. Now Jason is wearing his green and gold and black necklace thing to show that he's a Nelson Mandela supporter. That's a badge really.

It's dark. At least it's dry. She hates going out when it's raining, because it doesn't matter how hard you try, you can't keep the rain from getting down your neck and into your shoes. And less punters come out. There's a shop here which sells toys and games. She goes in and buys a cute green cat, or perhaps it's a dog, it's hard to tell, it's so furry, for Brad. It has pink eyes and a red tongue. It's only £2.50.

As she goes by the big houses again, the children are leaving. Volvos and other cars like that – she knows a lot about cars – are picking up the children. A woman wearing a quilted green jacket says, *Say thank you for the leaving present, Lucinda. And you, Charlotte. Really super, super party, Luce*. She kisses another woman. The children who are leaving are holding presents. At this party everybody gets a present. The children are bundled into cars and safety-belted in. Down in the basement the Asian woman is washing up. It's going to be quite a job.

Chanelle would like to live like this, in a bright, busy way. As the little boys and girls whizz off in the solid cars, she thinks of Bradley alone while her mother goes out for a drink or to watch television at her nan's. Poor Bradley. Poor little bastard. She feels tears rising up. They seem to start under your eyes. Sometimes the blow makes it harder to control your feelings. You're up and down. She holds the green toy tight as she waits for a bus.

5

The plane tickets are in his pocket. They are glowing in there. It's a miracle, once you make up your mind. On Friday they will launch themselves up on a gentle parabola ending in Cape Town. Nonstop. He has no picture of Cape Town, beyond the obvious one of the famous mountain which doesn't look to him like a table, but like a topside of beef which has been sliced through. (By his father, after much knife-sharpening.) As he walks down past a shop for rent, abandoned after Christmas with the decorations winking hopefully and blearily, like a drunken reveller who has missed the last bus, and as he passes a boy with his lower half in a sleeping bag, sitting in the doorway of another vacant shop, he thinks not of going to Cape Town but to the house in Swaziland.

The huge quiet rooms kept shuttered against the summer heat and the pulsing, vivid, throbbing garden, where monkeys descended in lightning raids on the walnut trees and the vegetable enclosure. That house was probably not so big. Everybody knows that your childhood home shrinks over the years. But it had twelve rooms and they all opened on to the garden. Sometimes in books Anthony has read, gardens seem to take the form of art, as though gardening is the same sort of thing as painting or writing a poem, only with bushes and shrubs as materials. But this garden had nothing artistic about it. It was a trucial area between the house and the wildness of the mountains behind, where the kings were buried. It was exciting. He traces his route through the gate to the old farm, under the flame trees, past the water-trough, past the old ploughs into the stand of gum trees, which appeared to be suffering and dying but which were, his father said, as tough as old army boots. This short journey was full of anticipation. There might be monkeys or even a baboon, or snakes, or huge beetles ahead. There were always birds, including the loerie with its highly desirable red feathers.

Now Anthony thinks of these rooms opening on to that garden as his true destination. The house was brown, of local stone, with a thatched roof and a wide verandah, looking down to the floor of the valley where the Swazi huts clustered in small hamlets. Next door, in a similar house, lived the Watsons. (It was to Mr Watson that his father had said, *Look at those charlies, Malcolm.*) Anthony sees himself going back there to recapture the enchantment.

Maybe our lives are more governed by the rooms we were brought up in than we realise. At this moment Anthony thinks that he would like nothing better than to go and live in those spacious rooms again, with the loud garden outside. Now he's passing a man in mittens selling chestnuts from a brazier, apparently unaware of the changes which have gone on in the world. For a moment he can feel its heat. He remembers entering the coolness of those rooms from the insistent noisy heat of the garden where his khaki shirt sticks to his back.

Rooms. Francine's room. The progress from the big, still, spare rooms in Swaziland to Francine's little room, where the night shift at the postal sorting office opposite could almost certainly see them on the bed. A cramped, enchanted room with one small window. And the move to the new bedroom at High Woods, with quality finishes gifted by the developer. This is his whole life, really. God, a life is a quick sprint. Three houses which tell his whole story. But what is his story? He seems to have become infected with the idea, so prevalent, that he should have a personal history. People say *Get a life* nowadays. They are not entirely joking. Everyone believes they are entitled to a life. And who could argue? Mike's life, too, does not seem to be conforming to any narrative.

From the lithe, demented Francine in that small room to the new, chunky, philosophical Francine duck-walking through the vegetable-trimming streets of Soho is only a progress of a few years, yet she has lived a whole life, two lives, while he has been taking comfort from his recollections. His recollections and his musings have provided him with rich sustenance, like one of those concentrated drinks they sell at the squash club. You sip them and replenishing minerals course through your veins.

In his pocket he feels the ticket. He feels the queasy moment when the engines take a grip on the 747 and heave it into the air. A miracle, but still something like a bus which is flying by mistake. And in the morning they touch down in Cape Town, which is, of course, hundreds, probably thousands, of miles from Swaziland, but he sees himself easy in those big, restful rooms. With his old pal Mike, eager to be shown the garden, then the waterfall which tumbles over smooth rocks (lethally slippery) into a turbulent pool, where he had to wait until his father and mother were finished with the plunging and gambolling. Sometimes they dived from a rock into the brown water and he would wonder what life would be like without them if they never came up. There was a nervous wait before their heads broke the surface. His father's was something like the ambassador's lawn, a large denuded ring revealed by the action of the water and sunlight.

He wonders what Mike and Babette have to talk about. Babette has a long memory. She latches on to failings or omissions reasonable people might have forgotten. Mike's life has been a series of exits. He has brief enthusiasms. Babette complains of his attention span and will not accept Anthony's pleas in mitigation. Anthony's argument is that at least Mike has enthusiasms, but it cuts no ice with Babette.

– *That's so typical of you. Do you mean that boat-charter business that you encouraged him in?*

Why does she resent something that happened before they met? Perhaps she is reproaching herself for not heeding what must have been a clear sign. In her heart she knew Mike was unreliable, yet she married him still redolent of lavender and seawater and blood. Of course Babette is shrewd; she sees that the boat-charter business was the end of innocence for Mike, where youthful adventure became flakiness, which has been cruelly confirmed today. But Babette does not understand that Mike is fearful of losing – actually he may have lost it already – his careless, attractive self. Babette, like everyone else, wants to nurture her own self too. But it demands a pound or two of flesh from Mike, which he can't spare.

Anthony passes a Burger King exhaling those American meaty smells which have become part of the sensory landscape and he thinks that he, Geraldine, Babette and Mike are all suffering from this same unease: how to make good their expectation. There's uncertainty in the air. Mrs Thatcher seems to have run up against the buffers: if she doesn't know where we're going, who does? At least old Reagan never really asked the question; he knew enough to understand that politicians can't give answers, only assurance. But the cruel thing for someone entering a political career is that we don't give our trust to just anybody. We give it to people who don't deserve it as freely as to those who do. What we want to believe is that they know something we don't. Mrs Thatcher had that, but it's gone.

Griddled hamburgers, roasting chestnuts, kebabs, pizzas all mingle on this corner of Piccadilly Circus. He wonders what London smelled like a hundred years ago. Above him starlings are nesting in the warmth of the neons: FUJI. COCA COLA. KODAK. FOSTERS. Suddenly the starlings rise into the air in a huge, squeaking flock of disquiet, looking like vampire bats against the darkened and bruised sky, before they settle again. There are plans to get rid of them. They are a menace. He can't remember what the problem is. Droppings or lice.

He's walking aimlessly now as though all the time until he leaves is dead time, like being in the departure lounge. He cuts back up a side street, past a hotel and a theatre running a sex comedy: 'Pure bloody farce – *Express*.' His blood has been disturbed by seeing Francine again. Francine has children, a husband in the plumbing business, an ex-husband in Australia. It seems a reckless way to dispose of what she had, a talent for sex. Of course you couldn't put that on your CV, but it was her only talent. Once Francine had said to him – which he remembers but she has almost certainly forgotten – that the moment she introduced him to some of her sexual repertoire he began to discount her. That's men, she said. It wasn't true. He valued her more. But sex has led her to dumpiness. Because sex is by its nature a wasting asset. It's not built to last. When you fall in with an expert like Francine you wonder how she can keep this to herself, and then you ask yourself where this could be leading. Like the roller-coaster in Disneyland which he and Fergus enjoyed so much, it's going nowhere. That's the nature of sex, he thinks: it has no destination. And it's also an illusion. Fat little Francine has popped the illusion as deftly as the kids pop balloons at Fergus's birthday parties. Geraldine makes a cluster of them around the Georgian knocker on the front door and over the party table and sooner or later they are all popped, except for the few that escape over the fence to puzzle the cows on the smallholding.

His mind is wandering. It's skittering nervously, expectantly. Nelson must have spent all those twenty-seven years without sex. Is this more of a hardship for a black man? King Sobhuza had – they said at the club with a little added emphasis – one hundred wives. It was understood that black men were very nearly insatiable, which was reflected in their 'physical development'. As a boy, Anthony was unable to see the point of having a hundred wives, but now he thinks that the opportunity to renew the sexual frenzy every night could have been a big perk for an African king. Anyway, powerful men are accorded sexual privileges. Even ugly men like Onassis. They are given honorary youth.

Mike is trying to hold on to his youth. But does Mike really know what he is doing? Anthony doubts it. He is hunkering down in response to elemental forces. He still has women above the kebab house, although he doesn't talk about them, but in truth he is on the defensive. Fergus has a book, richly illustrated, which explains Norman castles, the outer ramparts, the curtain walls and so on. And right in the middle, the last resort, is the keep. That's where Mike is. In the keep. The enemy have got the rest.

Geraldine is aware of Mike's shortcomings, but she also knows the affection Anthony has for him. She had a three-month fling with Mike, not too long before they were married, when she was dancing and wearing her wacky hat. Once you've slept with someone, no matter how long ago, there is a certain understanding. It's probably transmitted in the fluids.

He's walking aimlessly, even though he's a big cheese back at the office and there would be pleasant things to discuss with

Thel: the new car, the arrangement of pictures, a choice of desk. He's already on his way to Africa. He's showing Mike the caves of the kings. Old men guard them and keep you at a distance. Yes, he should go back to the office and he should ring Geraldine, but there is something unsettling about his promotion. He's disappointed he hasn't been fired, like Mike, so that they could make a new start out there. Mike won't come back to England, which has turned its back on him in its casual, indifferent fashion. If Anthony had been fired he would see it differently. That's how we are. He walks back up past the sex shops and peep shows and vegetable stalls to the Bar Italia and orders a cappuccino. There are mirrors on the wall but he avoids them and keeps his eyes fixed on Marciano's record – the first fifteen fights all inside three rounds – while Ornella scoops up the coffee for the giant Gaggia.

What a performance to make a single cup of coffee! The coffee is placed in the circular holder, like an ice-cream scoop, the jug of milk is injected with steam, then swirled around, the great lever comes down, a trickle of coffee descends into the cup, and the milky froth and the dark coffee settle into a pleasant alliance. He drinks. The drawing of Rocky Marciano which decorates the bar looks like an illustration from a children's magazine of thirty years ago. Anthony wonders how long the Rock would last against Mike Tyson. Rugby players are getting bigger too. Everyone is changing physically. He read the other day that the average age of menstruation among girls was seventeen in the nineteenth century; it's now thirteen.

His father was quite a small man, though he took pride in his height which was five foot ten. He took Anthony to see the great Ncwala, the ceremony of renewal of the king. The whites, the women wearing gloves, sat awkwardly on a platform with a canvas roof while around them a torrent of the king's warriors seethed. Actually, some of them were gardeners and herdsmen and the postman's assistant, all dressed in their impala and leopard skins and brilliant loerie feathers. Every single man was carrying a stick, a knobkerie, and every pair of ankles, circled by porcupine quills, was whirring and clicking like mah-jongg counters and rattlesnakes in movies. When the warriors hit the ground in rhythm, the ground shook. The faces –

even the face of Cephas, the garden boy who waved at Anthony
– were ecstatic in the sight of their king. And as the sun sank
behind the mountains, they released a bull into the huge kraal
and young warriors, completely naked, ran forward and tried to
seize it. Terrified, it galloped around the kraal until they caught
it and overpowered it, and beat it to death with their fists.

– *Should he be seeing this, Freddie?* his mother asked. *It's a bit
gruesome.*

– *It's part of life, dear.*

The king appeared again and danced with his regiments. Some
of the whites became restless.

– *Letting the side down*, said his father.

The king was in his late sixties, yet he danced for hours,
holding a sort of axe and wearing only necklaces and amulets
above his skirt of leopard-skin.

– *He is the lion, and his mother is the she-elephant*, said his father,
who prided hiself on his local knowledge.

His father said that the bull was cut open after being smoth-
ered. It inflicted some injuries. One young boy had his cheek
gouged, but still fought on frenzied. His cheek flapped as he
ran by them. The blood underneath was darker than the blood
Anthony had seen at the abattoir which all the children visited.
He imagines the outcry if the head teacher at Fergus's school
announced a school outing to an abattoir. The bull ran two
laps of the sibaya (his father said that was the correct word:
Very important to know these things, increases their respect) before it
was subdued, even though there were at least a hundred naked
boys after it. How big their penises were, mostly. This must be
the physical development his father had mentioned.

When the sun was nearly down, the whites were shown the
way out to where their cars were parked, guarded by the police
still on duty in their neat uniforms. For some reason, his father
took their appearance as a personal compliment. They drove
away, saluted by the policemen, into the bleeding night. As a
matter of fact he didn't think of it then as bleeding, but more
like the milk shake of mixed flavours which you could get at the
Indian café, where he also purchased his niggerballs.

The king with his saintly smile, the thousands of warriors, the
singing which soared up above the kraal and must have reached

the kings – and Clive – in their upright tombs, and the thudding of the earth as the regiment danced had thrilled and frightened him. Particularly when his father said, *And now they get down to business*, when they were safely on the National Road, which had just been tarred for a mile.

– *Freddie, really, what do you mean?*

– *Oh, there are things they won't show to Europeans. Believe me.*

– *What sort of things?*

– *Little pigs have big ears. Enough said.*

And anyway Anthony was soon asleep on the leather seat so that he had to be carried into the house and put to bed in his khaki shorts. And now, aged forty-one, he knows that Nelson, when he comes out, will be able to express what King Sobhuza was trying to say. Nelson's daughter, Zeni, is married to one of the king's sons, a prince, although princes are two a penny. Nelson will have been thinking about what it all means. He's a prince himself, and also a man familiar with both the brutality and the nobility of the real world. 'The real world' is such a stupid phrase. *Welcome to the real world*. People in busines think that's where they are. But someone keeps flying the scenery, moving the goalposts, shifting the boundaries, changing the rules, tilting the playing field, fixing the game. That's the real world. A lantern show. Its realness depends on your vantage point.

The coffee is strong. Ever since an Italian friend described the location, with a flat-handed gesture against the back of his neck, where coffee strikes, he has been able to feel it there. God, his mind is disordered. They must have been crazy to make him a director. Names tumble through this day like garments in the laundromat: Marciano, Mandela, Sobhuza, Will Carling. And Francine. Little, fat, waddling Francine. She seems happy, like a snitch or a grass who has been given a new identity. In the real world strange things happen. Former lovers marry plumbers. Friends get fired. People come out of jail. They're popping up all over the place. Or they get shot, like Ceausescu, for having been the mirror image of the people who shoot them. But back at the Spice Mall they are still hoping that a new management strategy is going to impose some sense on the unruly world.

– *Another coffee, Ornella.*

Her right arm, the one that pulls down the lever a hundred

times a day, is no bigger than the other as far as he can see. He's never spoken to her by name before, although he's heard it spoken many times. Today he feels the warmth of the tickets in his pocket spreading across his chest and the rumble of the earth as the warriors dance coming right through his childish sandals. He's tuned up. He's wired.

His life, so ordinary, is full of strange things. Thelma is going to Thailand, with the obduracy of a salmon leaping upriver; Francine, who once asked him to fuck her up the arse, is now married to a plumber; Geraldine is learning how to unearth lost memories; Edward Jenkins is dreaming of a balance between activity and process. And he and Mike are off to see Nelson Mandela. Why not see history, the real stuff, being made? Why not follow England, and Will Carling, wherever they go? He feels released. A life without freedom is no life. *Free-ee-ee Nelson Mande-e-e-la.*

He moves down the room to phone the office. The television screen at the end of the bar runs MTV. An old man, his face giving no clues as to how he might have looked when young, holds a cup of espresso, one finger arched, an overcoat of fawn camel hair just holding on to his diminishing shoulders, an émigré's pork pie on his head, watching the screen where Kim Wilde is singing. She's sexy. The old man sips the espresso. Perhaps he has had many girls as lovely as Kim Wilde. Anthony is put on hold, listening to Vivaldi played thinly until Thelma comes on.

– *Hi, Thel.*

– *Where are you?*

– *Just finished lunch.*

– *It's nearly five. Have you been celebrating?*

– *Yes.*

– *When are you coming back?*

– *Any rush?*

– *I think you should come now. Anyway, your briefcase is here. And there are some messages for you.*

– *Shoot.*

– *Mike rang. He's left a number. He'll meet you somewhere. He says he's coming home with you.*

– *Yeah. He's coming to stay.*

– *Everybody's so chuffed. It's brilliant.*

– I'm chuffed too.

Kim Wilde finishes. She crosses her arms in front of her so that her breasts are squeezed upwards. The old man wipes his lips with the back of his hand.

– And Mr Rosewater wants a word in your shell-like. He sends his congrats, by the way. The company secretary. Are you there?

– Viva lemongrass, Thel.

– Are you drunk?

– A little.

– You deserve it.

– Don't overdo it, Thel. Did Geraldine ring?

– No.

– Thel, I haven't had a chance to speak to her yet. Don't tell her if she rings.

– Are you keeping it a lovely surprise?

– Yeah. That's the sort of thing. I'll be over in half an hour.

He puts the phone down. Now there's a rap group in military fatigues and dark glasses on the screen. Rapping was a word for chatting once. Now it seems to be about scaring whitey. Or boasting about gangs and violence. He's all for it. Nobody wants to be ignored any more. In the past whole groups of people just trudged along or ploughed fields or pushed paper or darned socks and then died. No more. You've got to make your mark. You've got to make your move. You've got to advertise your existence. In truth, this group don't look too menacing. They look like extras in a made-for-TV movie, with the fat one, wearing ski glasses and a woolly hat, mouthing the words and the bodyguards in their dark glasses and berets trying to have as much attitude as possible while doing nothing. *Yo, Public Enemy. All right.* The old man in the trim hat is not looking at the screen now. Kim Wilde, that's music. That's sex on a stick. But these overweight black guys in Raiders jackets and impenetrable shades don't appeal to him. He's talking to the tall thin boy who prepares the toasted sandwiches. He has a very prominent Adam's apple. It's a lifeless conversation, like dry leaves barely stirring in a breeze.

6

Jason's gone off somewhere. He will go to great trouble to get things, not just drugs, which he needs, like a Raiders jacket or a CD. He likes 2 Live Crew at the moment. To get some other tapes he goes to special shops miles away. Jason thinks she should do an hour or two before putting his plan into operation. He says it would be good if the vice saw her down there, and anyway there are always a few customers early on. There's one punter who arrives every Monday after work. He looks for her. They never exchange more than a few words and she tosses him as he drives around the Common. It never takes more than one circuit.

She heats up a little crack in the stem and draws in deeply. There's not much left but she gets one deep hit and feels its warmth. It's a kind of numbness which makes things easier. Not that she has much trouble with the punters, usually. They're quite frightened of her. They don't know how to treat her. Some of them are apologetic, some of them are brisk, as though it's a chore they've got to do; some of them want her to provide more than they can say; some want it as basic as possible, up against a tree or in an alley. But very few of them are frightening. Over at King's Cross there were more nutters, vicious and deranged people. Not here. That's why Jason thinks his plan will work here. It's got to work, he said, but she wasn't sure if he meant she's got to make it work

She tidies the place up a bit. It's difficult to get everything exactly right. She should get the fur off the toilet; it doesn't look good any more, but she'd better ask Jason first, even though he spends more time at his other place. She puts the funny green dog or cat on her pillow so she won't forget to take it in the morning. She's got a terrible memory, like her mum. She used to have a lot of animals sitting on the bed until Jason threw them out of the window. One night he put his cock in one and said, *The letter F. F is for . . .* like *Sesame Street*. That was funny. After he threw the animals out, he promised to get some more but he never.

She's wearing a short black skirt which is a little tight on the hips, and long black boots. Jason says she must come back and change into some other clothes for his plan after she's made some money. He's going to meet her at McDonald's at about seven, which means eight.

What the punters don't understand is that Chanelle is doing a job. For them it's something outside their normal life, something exciting or disgusting or maybe something they don't understand. But for Chanelle it's a way of making money, and there are things you learn like on any job. There's ways of making them come quickly. There's a way of getting the condom on fast. There's things like never getting into a car with two men. Or making sure they don't lock the doors on their cars. On some cars they can lock you in. There's ways of speaking to them so they do what you want. But really the main thing is to get them in and out as fast as possible without too much pain or mess. It's as simple as that. If they want to kiss you, you get out of it without upsetting them too much. There's a moment or two when it can turn ugly, when they realise what they're doing. She never looks at their cocks even when she is giving them French or even if she says she is. She's not interested. They like you to comment for some reason. They think of their cocks as funny characters, or tyrants telling them to do things as though it's not their decision. She can get rough if she has to. In a car, in a small space, strength isn't that important, although she is strong enough. Also, they're frightened of trouble or of being scratched. If you say, *My boyfriend's just over there in that car*, it scares the shit out of them. They're also frightened of the police, who sometimes caution them and write down their car registrations and threaten to send letters to their home address and their work. The old sergeant can be very sarcastic with the punters, telling them that kerb-crawling is a crime and so on.

She turns off the television. Without it the flat becomes dead. It doesn't look like those bright basements near the court, which are always clean and pretty, that's for sure. She wonders where they find all that nice stuff. In one of them she saw a chicken sitting on the counter to hide the eggs and big knives in a block of wood. What would you cut up with all those knives? Herbs and dinky bits of cheese like in those ads. She and Jason eat crap: chips and burgers and kebabs. And her mum gives Bradley any old rubbish, if she remembers, even though Chanelle pays her to buy decent food for him.

– *He's got to have some fruit and stuff, Mum.*

– *He don't like it. He won't eat it. Only Hula-Hoops and oven chips.*

– *He can't live on that.*

– *And yoghurt. He likes his yoghurt. The ones with the little Mr Men on them. The whatchamacallit ones.*

It's not surpising he's always sick. She rings her mum, just to make sure he's not got any worse, but there's no answer. Her mum is so lazy, it's unbelievable. She's always making excuses for herself, as though being useless was a full-time job. She can never find anything or remember anything or make anything work. She leaves the taps running and puts the rubbish in the hall and forgets to take it to the bins for hours. A phone ringing unanswered gives Chanelle a very sick feeling, even now when she's had a few good hits. When she was in care she used to ring her mum and she was never there or the phone number had been changed, 'discontinued'. Sometimes she rang people she didn't know just to pretend she had a family. She puts the phone down. God knows what she's done with Bradley. The thought of Bradley alone in that dump with the phone ringing, which he can't answer, makes her feel weak.

She tries to relight the last burned-out rock but there's nothing there, just a black and charred bit of gunk on the foil. She's so angry now she wants to punch her mum and smash her nose. She makes some tea to calm down, and loads it up with sugar. She drops the milk bottle on the floor, but luckily there's not much milk in it.

After a while she feels better. Her mum has probably taken Bradley to the pub. She locks the flat and slips the key into the crack in the wall. The steps down to the hall are wide, made of something which looks like it's got tiny chips of black and grey pebbles in it. You can see that there was once a brass railing all the way up, but now you've got to watch it because it has been replaced most of the way by a timber handrail, nailed not too expertly in place. Some of the old ducks who live in the flats blame 'her kind'. But they're scared of saying it to her face now and certainly not to Jason. Jesus, are they scared of Jason, even though he's not tall.

In the beginning they were saying, *What a nice young couple and lovely to have a baby in here, bring some life to the place, in the old days families lived here, it was all families as a matter of fact, there was a lovely Lyon's Corner House, you could eat your dinner off the pavement, no need to lock your doors, the Queen come down here to open the new hospital, she was Princess Elizabeth then, there wasn't any violence nor loud music, the traffic wasn't so bad, the milkman used to have time for a chat, this was a lovely area, beautiful houses down by the Common, Arding and Hobbs used to deliver, and the butcher – that's right, and the butcher. Remember his big old bike? And those twins were born here, now he's a weatherman and the other one's a commissioner in the Salvation Army . . .*

Once they discovered she was on the game that all changed. The good-looking boy Jason turned out to be a black devil. But they were scared to complain when he played Salt 'n' Pepa and LL Cool J and NWA and his current favourite, 2 Live Crew. Now he's more or less gone, they give her the stare and the intake of breath again.

As she passes the Odeon there are a few people going in to see the six o'clock of *Three Men and a Little Lady*, or *Karate Kid III*. There's a choice. She's seen them both. She crosses the road. They always know: somebody shouts at her from a car, *Slag*.

– *Fuck off, wanker*, she shouts back and makes an up-and-down motion with her fist. Normally she doesn't bother, there's no point, but she's that upset about Bradley. In fact, she's behaving just like her mother, who's the one that set her off in the first place. She's got to have another hit when she meets Jason or she's not going out again. She walks past the Greek restaurant, the Kleftiko, which is always empty apart from the owner's family, and she turns off the High Street just by the Reformed Church. It's a spooky place with a large, cheery sign in green day-glo letters saying 'The Best Present at Christmas is Jesus's presence'. That's clever. Some of the girls take their punters into the churchyard at the back late at night. She walks down Mount Royal Avenue. There are some lovely houses down here, with big front gardens and bow windows and that black wood and white walls, the Tudor look, and some houses that have gone a bit downhill but are still big and roomy. The best place to stand is just down at the corner, near the Common, so you've got three roads covered and you can keep a watch for the vice squad in their van. The other police don't bother you unless they get a complaint. It's cold, but dry. The skirt is too tight even though she's thin. She passes a woman pushing one of those trolleys with a leather bag for the shopping. She has probably come up on the bus from the new Sainsbury's. Most of the people around here have cars. There are some BMWs, the little ones. The woman with the trolley crosses the road to avoid her. It still makes her sad when this happens.

She takes over the corner, keeping just a few yards away from the front gate of a big house that faces the Common. It's called Rosemead, written in gold letters on a slate. The woman who lives there is very quick to get on the phone if she sees you. On the Common, under the bare trees, there are joggers. The fast ones are skinny and serious, but you see more and more slow fat ones, some women plodding along, almost walking. She would like to try jogging to get thinner, but her life is too complicated. It's a mess. To go jogging you would have to get a jogging suit and a Walkman and running shoes and put a ribbon in your hair. She's never going to have the time. It's the life. When you're not working you're thinking about crack. You can't think about anything else. You can't get out of it, although some of the girls talk as if they can.

On the Common a horse goes thundering by. The rider has lights attached to the footholds, the spurs or whatever: *doomba, doomba, doomba.* And the horse snorts with each stride: *ffwy, ffwy, ffwy.* And then it's gone into the dark. She wonders where they keep the horses.

A Passat that has passed once comes back again, slowly. She can see the driver now, a timid-looking bloke with a round face and thinning hair, the streetlights making his glasses yellow. He'll stop. She knows him.

7

When they moved here Fergus was three. These days Geraldine measures time by how old Fergus is. They bought the new curtains when Fergus started playschool. They put in the climbing frame, which she can see out of the kitchen window, when Fergus was five. Fergus is like the sundial in the garden, the shadow moving around and giving meaning to the numbers it strikes. Anthony wanted an old sundial, of course, but they cost hundreds. This one has aged quickly and sits in summer in a thicket of lavender and petunias on some slabs they got at the garden centre. Needless to say, Anthony rejected this at first because they were composite stones, not the real thing, but now he seems to have forgotten.

Sometimes she thinks Anthony hates High Woods, although he doesn't say it directly. He talks instead of buying a vicarage or farmhouse when they can afford it. What he doesn't realise is that to finish off an old house to this standard would be almost impossible. Leonora said that when Jim built the barbecue and games room they nearly split up. And now he's in Saudi anyway. But still, she admires Anthony's dreaminess. That's his mother's word. He was always dreamy, she says. But it's not really dreaminess, it's the hope that there is something finer, more noble to be had. They don't discuss it in this way, but that's the text. She understands why Anthony doesn't like High Woods; for a start there are five other houses, all basically very similar. But it's also the fact that they didn't do it themselves. In some ways they are growing apart. It doesn't worry her. There's so much nonsense talked about growing apart. All that happens is that you lose some of the things you shared when you were young as your own personalities develop. There's nothing to be afraid of.

Geraldine tidies up the games and puzzles. For her pupils she now has a range of remedial and educational aids which she sends away for, mail order. She's become more organised since she took the course, more focused, while Anthony seems to be less and less interested in his job. And of course he resents that, so that she tries to have all the toys and the mothers and the meetings out of the way by the time he comes home. Now she has homework for her course, which she has to do in the morning before her pupils arrive.

Fergus is at karate. Jocelyn is bringing him home. He loves karate and is apparently fearless. Anthony was a rugby player when they first met and he was completely fearless, even frightening. He was famous for his tackling, head on. People say he could have played for England, but things were not so professional in those days and he was ignored for a while. Fergus has inherited his physical directness. She has discovered that the genetic influence is very strong in children. Children have many sorts of abilities. Sometimes she is troubled by the idea that there are different forms of intelligence too. The parents, no matter how badly the children are doing at school, want to be reassured that they are not stupid. In some ways it's true. From the moment she sees them write a sentence or do a wooden puzzle she can tell how they are getting on in class. Much more work needs to be done on these parallel worlds. A person who can memorise a whole symphony after reading it once obviously has a different kind of intelligence. A person who can do numbers and mathematics without any learning at all has another. A person who can draw has another, innately. She sees her job now as reassuring the parents. It's not always completely honest, because some of the children are genuinely stupid. But then, what is stupid? If you take that boy who can draw St Pancras station perfectly after looking at it for five minutes, but who can't really speak, maybe that just points up how restricted our notions of intelligence are.

None the less she's glad Fergus is doing so well at school. Anthony accuses her of shielding him, of anticipating all his problems, but she knows that success is often the product of confidence. That's what she aims to give her pupils, as well as reassurance to the parents. It's surprising how they listen to her, and it's amazing how her ability to help these people has helped her to become a much happier person. Anthony hates any talk of personal growth; he thinks it's all jargon. But the funny thing is, he is looking for it himself although he would never say it. When she tried to talk to him the other day about the importance of repressed memory and recovering repressed memory, the course that she is doing, he said, *Jesus, is there really anything you won't swallow? Next you'll be telling me your father dressed in a bath towel and practised satanic rituals in the garage. And your mother stirred the cauldron.*

She laughed. The garage was a very important place for her father, where he fiddled endlessly with his car, the lawnmower and his power tools. The tools seemed to have a religious significance, like her grandfather's Masonic kit. They had to be sharpened and oiled and charged constantly. Her mother once said that the tools were looking for a vocation.

With Fergus at karate she's got time to make something for supper. Although Mike's life is so disordered, he is a polite and helpful guest. He behaves as though he has to be on his best behaviour in the presence of family life, which for him is something exotic. Anthony says his flat is unbelievable, a tip, but he clearly retains the memory of family life. While he's here he folds up the towels and offers to wash up. It's almost apologetic. Although it was fourteen years ago, she can remember the taste of him. She can remember small details of his body. Of his cock. They were smoking dope then. It wasn't a long phase in her life, just after she dropped out of teacher training and before she started working at Masterton's in personnel, which was a dead end.

It was through Mike that she met Anthony. They had been at school together and played in the same rugby team. The truth is that she loved Mike for a few months more violently than anyone else. But then, like an ice-cream on a summer's day, he just melted away. He vanished to the Atlas Mountains after Marc Bolan's death, on a pilgrimage of some sort. She can't remember the details. But melting away has proved to be his speciality. He was full of schemes then, which involved semi-mystical subjects: clouds, mountains, Tibetan music, ashrams, whale communications. It was probably the dope. Anthony hardly smoked dope. He was playing rugby seriously, getting into the Southeast team and so on, and he was working at that direct mail company. He took the job instead of university, which he regrets. Direct mail was big in those days. It might have just reached this country then, she thinks, and it was going to revolutionise marketing. Marketing seems to exist in a state of revolution. He was taking a course at the poly as well, although he didn't sit the exams. She's at the same poly now, fourteen years later, doing her courses.

Mike came back from his jaunt wearing a fringed djellaba, and he seemed to have forgotten her. It was hurtful. The things they had cherished, small, intimate things, had apparently gone entirely from his memory. He made no reference to them or to their shared memories. Now she can see that he was probably suppressing them because of his chronic lack of security. He avoids any responsibility when it becomes insistent. She gave him her body, every fold and oddity of it and a lot more too, and somehow he came back and behaved as though it had never been. He treated her like a friend, but not too intimate a friend. And yet. She still remembers him naked and erect. She wonders if she'll ever make love to another man except for Anthony. Probably not. Although she did, just after Fergus was born. Twice with the squash coach and then with the group manager at Masterton's, Mike O'Donnell, who was a completely transparent rogue. It was fun. At the time she didn't feel guilty; it was something she deserved, a treat, and it made her feel whole again. Now she knows that it's a common reaction after having a baby. Anthony was off on a rugby tour to France at the time. He broke a cheekbone and came back early, which was almost disastrous.

She chops some parsley in a cup with scissors. She's no cook really, but when she's got time she likes doing simple things. Women who are wonderful cooks probably really want a career but can't bring themselves to admit it. So they cook sophisticated things involving rare ingredients to show that they are still in touch. Mind you, once you start on this line of thinking, what people are repressing and what they are compensating for, you can come up with some ridiculous conclusions, which Anthony loves to exaggerate. She glances at the recipe. She makes a cross on the top of five large tomatoes with the point of a knife before dropping them into boiling water. This will release the skins more easily.

Outside the lawn is gleaming in the light from the house, the grass frosted and the path snaking away, the flagstones like cubes of gleaming coughdrops. The back garden runs away to a field where the farmer, who is more a rural wheeler-dealer than a proper farmer, sometimes keeps bullocks for fattening. He runs a boarding house for cattle and he sells secondhand Land Rovers. Geraldine loves to see the bullocks playing and browsing in the summer, with their fat, naïve faces, like Ferdinand the Bull in Fergus's book. The tomato skins come off easily. The secret, which she learned on a television programme, is to leave them in the water just long enough without cooking the flesh underneath. She slices them and squeezes out the pips. Then she chops them roughly. Fergus likes spaghetti bolognaise and Mike likes meaty, simple food. She browns the mince with a chopped onion and adds a drop of red wine left over from the committee meeting and throws in the tomatoes and some concentrate and puts it on a gentle heat. If Anthony's had lunch he will only nibble.

He says that the office is losing its way. She wonders if it isn't more a question of Anthony losing his, but she would never say it. Although he is not always completely with it, Anthony does come up with some good ideas. The managing director told her so at the Christmas party. She was not a hundred percent sure it was a recommendation, what her mother would have called a 'backhanded compliment'. The annual Christmas party has become an ordeal; there is a lot of false jollity, which cannot quite cover the fact that the wine bar in Farringdon Road is not the same as the private room at the Savoy where it used to be held, in better times. She loved going to the Savoy, all brass and lacquer and chandeliers. It looked to her as though it had been put together over the years by a tasteful eccentric.

Anthony should really leave if they don't make him a director, but everyone says the fringe companies, service companies, are suffering worst. Nobody is leaving. Yet down here Geraldine is leading a full life with the school run and the support committee, the remedial teaching and her courses. She lifts the lid off the pot and adds some dried herbs, oregano and some others called *herbes de Provence*, which sound romantic, but smell a bit like tea leaves. She lays a place for Fergus in the kitchen. He always comes in from karate starving. She longs for his return. For the feel of him, his unfinished carpentry. There are dangers for the single child, but Fergus is well adjusted with plenty of friends. He's going to be big, like Anthony, well over six foot. He has Anthony's very direct gaze and square shoulders already. His hair looks thicker than Anthony's ever was. She loves Fergus's enthusiasm. When he comes in there's a new joke, a new story, often about the teachers, and usually a request:

– *Mum, can I have a lemur for Christmas?*

– *No, I don't think so. Who would look after it?*

– *I would.*

– *For about a week. Like the guinea pig. Anyway, they're an endangered species. You can't just go out and buy one. It's not practical.*

– *You always say that.*

Although she's losing her grip these days, Anthony's mother was always very enthusiastic. Now she's channelling her energies into a running critique of her new neighbours. Poor Anthony. He deals with her very patiently. At least she's not going gentle into that good night. Anthony's favourite lines from Dylan are, *Woke to my hearing from harbour and neighbour wood and the mussel pooled and the heron priested shore.* And now it's her fortieth year to heaven. They never read poetry now, or novels for that matter; she has to read a lot of textbooks and manuals, and Anthony has started reading history books and biographies. But she tries to get Fergus to read to her every evening. It's a struggle. Children have so many more exciting things to do these days. It's difficult to explain to Fergus why reading is more rewarding than video games, particularly as she and Anthony don't really read. Still, she would like to write something. A children's story or a textbook. She'll get round to it. She feels full of energy. She is reluctant to use the word 'empowered' which they do on the course, but that's what it is.

Jocelyn is always in a hurry. She toots the sharp little hooter of her Mitsubishi jeep. By the time Geraldine gets to the door and opens it, she's already turned. They wave and Jocelyn shouts something as the jeep gathers speed. It sounds like, *Speak later*. Fergus, in his karate pyjamas, is halfway up the path, already through the cordon of cherry trees which are bare. No trees are more bored in winter, less deeply asleep, gathering themselves for their spring burst of glory which she loves so much.

– *Fergie, where's your coat?*

– *I left it at school. What's for supper?*

– *Spaghetti bolognaise.*

– *Wicked. Did you hear what happened to Mr Tyzer?*

– *No?*

– *He got locked in the gym by the caretaker. All afternoon. Brilliant.*

Fergus is laughing at the recollection. She laughs too as she hugs him.

– *How was karate?*

– *I smashed them.*

– *Fergus!*

– *Well, I sort of smashed them. Not too hard.*

– *Come in before you get cold.*

– *Is Dad here?*

– *Not yet. He's coming later and Uncle Mike is staying the night. Probably. You know how he is.*

– *Brilliant. Mum, why did they put Nelson Mandela in jail for so long?*

– *Ask Dad when he comes home.*

– *One of the boys says he was a murderer. He blew up people with bombs.*

– *I don't think so. Ask Dad, you know how he loves Nelson Mandela.*

His face is warm and reddish, a little clammy. Below his tunic, which is too short, his thin, thin calves and ankles protrude. His hair is going backwards and forwards at the same time. She feels her heart, her whole being, swell with love for him. She fusses him into the house.

– *Tell me everything that happened today.*

– *Nothing much. I got a good mark for English. Can I watch television while supper is on?*

- *It's nearly ready.*
- *Just a few minutes. Please.*
- *Okay. Come when I call.*
- *Thanks, Mum. You're a doll.*

Mothers and sons. She goes to put the spaghetti into the pot. She wills it to soften and collapse quickly so that she can summon him to her. It takes its time before it subsides gently into the water. She counts the minutes. They are almost unbearably long.

8

Basil's office, although identical in outline to the others on the fourth floor, has retained something of the old world of Dyson Chambers. Basil has framed photographs of his family – stagey, highly-coloured pictures of his daughter's graduation, her first child, his son's barmitzvah, a family holiday in Spain, his wife in an apple-coloured suit and his son making a speech. On the wall behind his desk are five certificates, some dating back to the early 1950s. When you look at him seated, they form an aura of certification. Anthony has plenty of time to study the pictures, the diplomas and the imitation rosewood bookcase while he is waiting for Basil to come back from the kitchen. Basil has insisted on making the coffee. His secretary has gone. Indeed, the whole building is quiet, although Thelma is waiting downstairs for instructions and the surly man from the security company, who has a birthmark like Gorbachev's, although a little lower, will be standing there as if he can't wait to take over the building.

Basil's furniture has survived the move intact. It's a style which reminds Anthony of those early *Saint* series on television, spindly furniture and a glass-fronted bookcase which could double as a cocktail cabinet. Basil's desk is weightier, covered with green morocco leather.

The building is empty. In the old building, not so long ago when times were good, they were often there until eight or nine o'clock, huddled together, in shirt-sleeved knots, churning out documents, celebrating their successes and unreasonable demands – the timescales, timeframes, deadlines – which clients placed upon them. They complained about the pressure, but how they loved it. Now people say they have a meeting at four o'clock and doctor's appointments or prospective clients to visit and slink away from the Spice Mall as though the new building itself is to blame for what's gone wrong. There was a place in Swaziland, a hot spring, which some Swazis avoided. The bubbling water was thought to be malevolent. When they were in Yellowstone on their big adventure with Jet Tours, Anthony had been less entranced by Old Faithful than the others. To him the pressure from down below somewhere hinted at trouble. He understood the Swazis' suspicions. The new building is eloquent: it tells them how flimsy everything they recently believed in was. They start each day with plans and hopes, but by the middle of the afternoon, when the phones are silent and the fax lines produce only circulars, they become demoralised.

Basil, because he is retiring soon, is philosopher-king. He understands cycles in business and he is determined to be meticulous and methodical to the last. He's the old bosun who can stand on the deck in the worst storm. Also, his hands are clean: as company secretary he has never taken part in the hysteria of the recent past, in the false hopes and unwise diversifications.

Anthony can hear him in the little kitchen down the corridor making the sort of old people's noises which his mother does. All her teapots and cups are chipped and she swears as she takes things out of cupboards or the fridge. He hears water running and the lavatory next door flushing. Basil is thought to have a prostate problem. He comes in with a small tray, complete with cloth, and a china pot of coffee. He places the tray carefully on one of the low tables balancing on its thin, tapered legs.

– *Great moment for you, Anthony. Congratulations.*

– *Thanks, Basil.*

– *Overdue, perhaps, but welcome all the same, I am sure. What does Geraldine say?*

How can he tell this old man, with his family pictures, his wife in her bright, flowery suit, and his certificates of chartered competence, that he hasn't told her yet?

– *She's over the moon.*

– *Over the moon. I should think so.*

– *Have I got to sign things? Thelma seems to think so.*

– There are a few things. Nothing that can't wait.

Basil pours the coffee. Anthony knows that he doesn't drink. Perhaps Basil is trying to sober him up. As he pours, his suit jacket catches on his tight, melon paunch so that it is tugged apart, held only by one straining button right in the middle like a wine waiter's. Despite this paunch, he's a slight man.

– Anthony, I wanted to congratulate you, of course. Also, I wanted to explain to you, now that you are about to become a director – technically you already are a director, I may say, after the board meeting – I wanted to explain what that means.

There's something of the *hausfrau* about him. Anthony thinks that Jews are much more attuned to the details of life. The cough drop on his head seems to be pulsing as though it has an independent blood supply. His eyebrows grow strongly, the individual hairs crossing. He has that bland kind of Jewish face, none of the obvious characteristics, but kindly lidded eyes and a neat mouth that are unmistakably Jewish. What is it exactly? It's there in the eyes and in the skin, as a watermark. It's also in his voice, the way he says, *Great moment for you.* There's still something of old Europe about 'great', a little extra tweaking of his mouth.

They are sitting now. Basil is at his desk and Anthony on the uncomfortable Scandinavian chair. Nothing dates like up-to-dateness. Basil puts sweetener in his coffee.

– Anthony, thanks for making the time to see me.

– Don't be silly. Thanks for waiting for me. I appreciate it.

– It's nothing. I'm tidying up. July is approaching fast.

– Are you really going in July?

– Yes. I had the option to stay on for six more months, but the time has come. The golf beckons. And my wife – he gestures towards the twenty- or thirty-year-old picture of her – *says she wants to see more of me. Though it beats me why. We've got a flat in Spain near Fuengirola. Anyway, Anthony, there are certain responsibilities associated with being a director. Under the terms of our incorporation, there are two boards. The inner board, which, as you know, consists of four, and the bigger board, which is all the directors. The inner board is in reality a partnership, and the partners controlled the company. But things have changed. Some of the partners are no longer able to meet their liabilities. So the proposal is for the inner board, the partnership,*

to sell out to the directors. This would be largely a paper transaction but the directors would then be directly responsible for all the company's finances.

– It's a public company, though, isn't it?

– Yes, the operating company is, but its finances were guaranteed and controlled by the partnership. Being a director meant, in the financial sense, very little. But now it's possible – I am only saying possible – that the banks could hold you, the directors, responsible directly.

– So you're saying that I have been made a director to help take the loss if we go down?

– Not exactly. What I am saying is that I would take the papers to an independent lawyer before I signed anything. I am telling you this because I want you to be fully aware what the new arrangements could mean. I am telling you the worst-case scenario, as you whizz kids like to say.

Anthony considers why Basil would have given him this information. He feels the shifting ground, the earth tremors.

– Do we have large debts?

Basil sips his coffee.

– Anthony, the company is technically insolvent. The pension fund is collateral. I'm sorry to say this. It grieves me. The inner board have been given a few months to find new money.

Basil's face has a sheen in the light from the small spots which dot the roof. Anthony always looks closely at Jewish faces. He expects to see something there, a certain wisdom, a certain worldliness: the etchings of history. On Basil's face he sees a greyness, which is accentuated by the light falling on his evening beard, which is coming through strongly. If he allowed it to grow he would have a rabbinical beard of purest white. He sees also a little man, a tailor, a clerk, who has been beaten.

– Is your pension safe, Basil?

– I hope so. There are a few problems, I must say.

– Jesus. You didn't need to warn me, Basil. Why did you?

– I've always liked you. There's something special about you. There's something about you.

Anthony feels his slippery heart lurch as he stands up.

– Thanks, Basil. I won't tell anybody.

Anthony wants Basil to know that he understands that it would have been a lot easier to say nothing. It's possible that his pension depends on a smooth transfer of the company's liabilities to the directors.

– *I appreciate it, Basil.*

– *I would have done it for anybody.*

He doesn't mean it. He means that he would not have done it for just anybody. As Anthony leaves his office, his snug parlour, he feels deeply sorry for Basil. Basil has spent a lifetime in offices, with documents, guarantees, contracts, company registrations and so on. And now he is seeing, just as he should be moving off cheerfully content, that all this form-filling and paper-pushing has been for nothing. Behind him are rows of box files, each one containing some transaction which he has approved, signed, stamped, filed. Out of sight somewhere are disks full of computer information. And each one of these forms and documents is without meaning or importance. Whatever they were intended to solemnise no longer applies. No one cares. Contracts and agreements have lost their original purpose: they are now to protect financial dealings from scrutiny and channel money in unusual directions. Anthony sees Basil as one of those elderly refugees in cities which have been bombed, standing in the rubble of their houses and apartments, hopelessly confused, as they try to understand how their home, their books, their photographs, their china, their furniture, their bundles of letters, their pets – everything that old people cherish – have gone: scorched, bombed, burned, destroyed.

Anthony feels himself lightened by the information that Basil has given him. It explains a lot, and it confirms his own understanding of the way things are. He feels better. He feels better about Mike, and better about not ringing Geraldine.

Thelma is waiting, of course.

– *Thel, has Mike rung?*

– *No.*

– *I'm going home now.*

– *I've got all sorts of things for you to look at.*

– *My father always said you shouldn't eat all your sweets at once. He said you should save some for later. He always left a small amount on his plate. In this way you feel superior to the other kids who have gobbled theirs. See you tomorrow. If Mike calls before you leave, tell*

*him to get me in the car or just to come down to the house. But don't
wait for him. Go home.*

– *What did Mr Rosewater want?* asks Thelma, perhaps alarmed
by his manner.

– *Oh, he wanted to make sure I understood the directors' pension
arrangements.*

– *Are they good?*

– *They're under new management.*

He walks towards the lift, but turns to wave in response to the
barometric pressure from Thelma. He sees her standing, looking
after him, her broad face puzzled, and probably hurt.

The streets are almost deserted. The evening rush convulses
and then dies quickly. He passes the sandwich bar where the
mozzarella took a direct hit. It's a cold night, but dry. It's
been dark for nearly three hours and it's only seven o'clock.
Leonardo's bustles in the morning and then closes completely
in mid-afternoon. Edward Jenkins could explain to them the
better deployment of their assets. The trays of tandoori and egg
mayonnaise and crispy bacon and smoked salmon and cream
cheese and chicken tikka and mozzarella are transferred to a
huge fridge, like a mortuary safe you might see in a cop film,
where some poor relative has to identify the body. Patterned
tea towels are laid out over the shelves. An insect electrocuter
glows like a neon bagel in the back of the shop, near the hanging
garlands of dried onions, peppers and garlic.

Anthony cuts down an alleyway where almost every building is
for sale or to rent, and he emerges just outside Dyson Chambers,
'for disposal on very easy terms', but now unmistakably doomed,
with boarded windows and rubbish and cans accumulating in
the gothic niches. Not so far away are the offices of a charity
for HIV-infected people. Dyson Chambers is terminally ill also,
too late for any vaccine to save it.

The Underground is empty too. It becomes furtive so soon after
the rush is over. The transformation reminds him of Aix after the
summer, when the locals come back and take possession of their
cafés and restaurants again. As soon as the commuters have been
dispersed – all Anthony's communicants – authentic Londoners
come out again. In their almost infinite diversity he detects a
stubborn self-regard. The boy with the matted hair which falls

like a rope that's been picked by convicts from the top of his head, over to the shaven sides of his skull, drinks his strong lager with self-congratulation. His long, thin legs, finished off in heavy boots which they hardly seem capable of moving, are sprawled in Anthony's way.

– *Oh sorry, mate*, he says, tidying them up with a smile, as though he's doing something mysteriously clever.

If anything the air down here at this hour is more exhausted, thinner even, than in the morning. It's as though the millions of people, now mostly gone, have sucked all the goodness out of it. Mike, born in the suburbs like him, has become a Londoner. That's a clue to his intractability. And now Anthony sees, as the mineshaft walls rush by all coated in mineral waste of some sort, that in the face of the capriciousness of this city – which he has just witnessed in Basil's homely office – this pride in one's own weaknesses and follies, so characteristic of Londoners, is quite sensible. The boy with the fraying Mohican opposite catches his eye. He scratches his balls as though there is some complicity between them and indeed there is, a bond of understanding.

He finds the journey unsettling without the presence of his usual companions. It's like visiting a house where you once lived to find everything changed. The train rattles along, the doors open and close, the familiar stations are shadowy and almost deserted. The primitive nature of it is cruelly exposed, like looking underneath a car and seeing the pipes and brackets. The boy opposite burps and winks at him. Anthony returns the smile but in a matey, masculine sort of way as if he too would like to be drinking strong lager if he weren't forced by the military-industrial complex to wear a suit to do their bidding.

He reads the *Standard*. He finds something about the rugby, but already, Monday evening, it's a small story. That's how it is with sport; it has no weight or permanence although it must fill a psychological need. He's begining to think like Geraldine: there are psychological vacuums into which explanations rush. The French are going to fire their manager, according to this report. That's the French way: if something goes wrong there must be a solution. Anthony has come to think that there is seldom a single solution to anything. Or a single explanation. The French believe that their style of play must change. They must become more hard-nosed, the way the English have. Anthony sees that this English team have achieved more than that, more than any English team before: they have entered into the higher realms of sport, which sports fans recognise. He and Mike understand that they have transcended tactics and determination and achieved in this match at least something of the sublime. Geraldine can't understand his love of rugby, but the love of sport, because it's so irrational, cannot be refuted by any rational means. It's no different from what painters want to achieve, some sort of perfection, which is never going to happen, of course.

Poor Basil. His attachment to reason and order – perhaps there is something in his Jewish memory which makes him seek it – has not held up well. Irrationality survives. That's why religious cults are springing up and alternative beliefs, often quite mad, are flourishing. Like suppressed memory and satanic abuse. You don't want to underestimate the pulling power of the irrational. Reading Swedenborg is hard work, but you see that Swedenborg was trying to reconcile the irreconcilable. Irrationality is making a comeback in all sorts of disguises. Perhaps it never went away. When he was a boy his father liked to use the phrase 'the twentieth century' as a term of approval: French plumbing hadn't entered the twentieth century; the Swazis were some decades away from the twentieth century. The twentieth century, despite Hitler and so on, was completely different from other centuries. It was the first century to be free of superstition and ignorance. Now it seems that his father's judgement may have been hasty. What happened was that irrational thinking got dressed up in the clothes of science. Geraldine believes in psychotherapy. Edward Jenkins believes in global management, process versus activity. A lot of people believe that you can acquire the skills for living. Anthony sees that Mike, in his haphazard way, has resisted these blandishments. He doesn't want to acquire any life skills.

The empty stations fly by at high speed. The speed makes him feel disoriented. He fears that he may miss his station and shoot on down into unknown tunnels.

Mrs Thatcher led them to believe that there were simple, scientific mechanisms. Everything could be fixed. And now she looks increasingly confused. She wants to stop the Germans reuniting. It's no coincidence that in this confusion, made worse by the collapse of Communism, they are releasing Nelson Mandela. They too are hoping, as Anthony is, that Nelson is going to tell them what it means to be human. He and Mike are going to be there in person. In Cape Town.

The skinny boy with the rope of hair stands up, burps and winks again.

– *Ta-ra mate*, he says.

He stumbles as the train stops and rushes out of the door unsteadily, as though someone has pushed him in the back.

9

Jason has had his hair done. He says it's the wave. His hair stands straight up in a ridge on his head, with the very top bits flopping on either side in ringlets. He's copied it from a singer in some American band. She's never heard of them. The hair on the sides of his head has been cut very short, with a zigzag pattern shaved in it.

– *Look*, he says.
– *At what?*
– *At my hair.*

He turns slowly. The zigzag reads 'BMW'.

– *Brilliant.*

It is cute.

– *How much do you think it cost me?*
– *I dunno.*
– *Twenty-five quid. Good deal. How much you made so far?*
– *Seventy.*
– *Not bad.*

He unwraps some more coke. He explains that his plan will only work if she's completely focused. He loves words like that. Maybe he means out of her brain.

– *Just one rock now and some more later when we've finished, okay?*
– *Okay, Jace.*
– *I'm going to be there as backup. We want to do this without getting heavy. We don't want anybody running to the police.*

She has the crack heated up and in the stem. She draws and feels herself floating. Some of her is completely calm and the rest is racing, going mad. She tries to kiss Jason, but he steps to one side and whacks her impatiently on the bottom.

– *Keep your eye on the ball, girl.*

– *You're not taking the gun, are you, Jace?*

– *I'm taking it just in case. But I'll only get it out if they're showing some disrespect.*

He thinks he's in a video or something. He's talking very slowly. He's talking as though he's briefing his homies. She's so far gone, maybe it's her that's listening slowly. He's got a new jacket, 2 Live Crew, and his new haircut and he's already driving that car.

– *You haven't forgotten Bradley, have you?*

He hits her on the side of the head, hard.

– *Fucking shut up. Get your head together. I don't want to hear any more of that shit.*

She feels the side of her face. It's swelling.

– *Jason. You promised.*

– *Are you all right? I shouldna hit you. Yeah, I'll take you. Soon as I've got the new car.*

– *You won't forget, will ya?*

– *No way José. A man's word is his bond.*

Now he starts to laugh. He has an amazing laugh, very high and sudden. She loves it when he's happy. Some people don't realise how nice he is really. Sometimes he's more of a child than Bradley. Bradley, with his streaming nose and poor hearing and his screaming. Ever since he burned himself he cries for no reason, almost. Now she's crying.

– *What's the matter now?*

– *Nuffink. I was just thinking about Bradley. It's the blow, it makes me funny.*

– *We'll see him tomorrow in the new wagon. Promise. You better wipe your ear, there's some blood. Not much.*

It doesn't hurt. She wants to laugh just as suddenly as she wanted to cry a moment ago. Jason is rubbing his face with his small hands, rubbing his cheeks and his eyes as though he's rubbing in cream or something, and his wave begins to dance. She starts to laugh, almost screaming.

– *What's so funny?*

– *It's your hair. It's gone all wobbly.*

– You crazy girl.

– Why are you speaking like that, Jace?

– You got to get serious. This ain't chopped liver.

She doesn't know what he's talking about, but she laughs until the tears are running again.

Jason goes through it carefully, but she finds it hard to listen to him speaking in this funny voice, like *Beverly Hills Cop* or something.

– I'll drop you just by the lights at Norwood Road. Then I'll go and wait at Bevan North. You know where I mean, don't you, in the garages? Cool? You sure you know? Okay. I'll be there out of sight, but I'll keep an eye on you until it's time to make a move. Okay? If there's any trouble, hit the horn.

– What do you mean, hit the horn, Jace? Do you mean the hooter?

– Yes. Beep the hooter. Tell them your boyfriend is just over there. Let's go. You look just right. On the money.

She's wearing a spotted skirt and a white blouse with a round collar which he bought at Marks. He says she looks like a student. When she sees herself in the mirror she can see what he means. And that makes her want to cry again, but she stops herself. Students live in a world of complete make-believe, from what she has seen on television, but it looks nice, with everybody discussing things, relationships and books they have read and so on. She's not sure if students can afford leather coats like hers, but she puts it on anyway.

They walk down the stairs. *Coming and going at all hours of the night,* as the old dears say. He's got his car round the corner.

– Last time we'll be in this old banger, he says as he fiddles with the keys of the Escort. He's pulled on his Raiders cap, but it is sitting up a little with his new haircut. The car doesn't always start first time. It lurches a bit before the engine gets going.

– Jason, I got to get Bradley some new trainers tomorrow with some of the money, all right? On the way.

She knows Jason doesn't want to talk about Bradley, but she can't stop herself. What she wants is to have a life which is more certain with more nice things. Maybe if Jason's plan works the way he says it will, she can save some money and go on a proper holiday to Disneyland in Paris which everybody says is going to be great, just like the one in America, only newer.

She knows loads of people who have been to Disneyland in America.

They drive up the High Road past the Greek restaurant, McDonald's, the other cinema, the Italian place, the fire station, the Reformed Church, Nero's, and out on to a stretch of the road where there are not too many houses, only the DIY store and then a big intersection and some trees round a war memorial. It's quite open, with the grass, not that you can see it, running away up the hill to the waterslides. Jason says this is the right place. He pulls into Norwood Road. He puts his hands on her new blouse and rips it open, so that there are no buttons left and the collar is torn.

   — *Rub your eyes. That's it. Get it smeared around a little.*

   — *How's that?*

   — *That's good. Fingerlickin' good. Now remember, undo your coat before you go up to a car. You got it?*

   — *I got it.*

   — *If you don't show within an hour, I'll come back for you and see what went wrong, okay?*

Now that it's time, she feels nervous.

   — *Are you sure it's going to work, Jace?*

   — *Of course. Just don't give them time to think. I'll be there.*

She feels lonely here, away from the lights and the familiar streets where she knows every turning and tree and yard and the nice houses where she usually stands. And where the vice come round from time to time, which is also quite reassuring. Here she feels exposed in her student clothes. She stands by the war memorial. Jason says she should come out from behind the bus shelter at the right moemnt. She can see that it's not going to be that easy. For a start you don't want to come out when there are lots of cars around, just the one, and then you have to pick on the right person, not too young, in a company car. Jason has in his mind a person from one of those television shows where really straight people live in the suburbs and are always having problems with their neighbours and misunderstandings with their wives, which turn out okay in the end.

He hates shows like that, without music or action. Without burners, his new word for guns. She smiles. She can't help it.

10

Geraldine sometimes says that Anthony doesn't give his feelings a chance. She believes that feelings and dreams and desire and grief need an airing. As he unlocks the car, Anthony wonders if he should be feeling angry. The truth is he feels happy to know the facts. He's not so happy that the company is insolvent and that his promotion is phoney, but he is relieved that there is some logic in this chaos, even if it's only the logic of retribution.

God knows where they go from here. He doesn't care. He's off to Cape Town to receive enlightenment. Nobody would take him seriously if he tried to explain what he's expecting from Nelson. And if he did, he's not sure that his feelings, brought out into the open, would stand the scrutiny. Not even Mike believes in Nelson as he does. Like Swedenborg, Anthony believes that there must be a link between what's going on in everyday life and the infinite. (If he understands Swedenborg right, which is far from certain.) And Nelson will provide that link. It won't be in a textbook or a manual or a management course, but a flash or revelation, a restoration of faith. Swedenborg, who dabbled in anatomy, thought the soul was located in the brain somewhere. Anthony is not interested in its geography, but in its existence. If he explained this to Geraldine, if he gave his feelings a chance, she might suggest therapy in order to find his real and hidden agenda.

As he turns out on to the A23 his phone rings. It's in his case so that it is stifled, like the noise of young birds in the eaves of a house. He fumbles with the catch and gets the phone out.

— *Hello. It's Mike.*

— *Hello. I was just thinking about Cape Town. Where are you?*

– I'm at Babette's still. Can you come over? Where are you now?

– I've just picked the car up from the garage. What's the problem?

– There is a problem. I lost my temper. She's locked herself in the bathroom and she says she'll call the police unless you come over.

– Why me?

– Fuck knows. She thinks you understand me. And her.

– Did you tell her about Cape Town?

– Yes. That's what started it. She wanted to know what I was using for money. You know how these things go. I hit her.

His voice is flat.

– Oh shit. Don't do anything silly. I'm just near the Oval, it won't take more than twenty minutes.

– Thanks.

– No probs. Tell her I'm on my way, I'm just doing a U-turn now.

He has changed direction. He usually drives home without thinking about the route, as though he's hooked up to the car, his hands moving the steering wheel and his feet pumping the pedals as required but with no volition on his part. Once you're clear of South London it's not a bad journey. He's hardly aware of it. Now he's heading into less familiar territory. Babette lives near Greenwich in a flat which she took when she and Mike split up. While Mike has been content to live in squalor, making no decorative, or even hygienic, impact on his flat, Babette has fitted her place with stuff that makes a statement. The nature of the statement is that she is an independent woman, with her own books, CDs, pictures (mainly art posters) and her own estimable and ordered life.

As Anthony understands it, and his information comes largely from Mike, at first she enjoyed her independence and the rituals of setting up on her own. She was ready. But nothing much happened. Life without Mike proved to have less downs but also precious few ups. That's Mike's version. Anthony wonders if she was hoping for an exciting new sexual dimension to her life. In his experience this rarely happens as planned. These women find that at forty-odd they are prey to a tribe of men who are not very securely moored to reality. Mike says Babette occasionally has one-night stands. She is a very good-looking woman, with high cheekbones, dark, strong eyes and dry blonde hair. She dresses powerfully. But there is something too assertive about her. She's got it all worked out, with no time for the little lies and flatteries which men, in their delusion, require. Mike once told him that in bed she was too ardent and too detached.

Anthony takes a wrong turning at a roundabout and finds himself heading towards Deptford, which is one of those places – there are many – in London which you know exist but have never visited. He makes a turn by backing into an alley next to a a takeaway which is selling Chinese and Polynesian food and fish and chips. He remembers a documentary in which Polynesians buried whole pigs in pits and covered them with banana leaves and tropical fruits before raking ashes over them to cook for twelve hours; he wonders how Wing-Lo takeaway is duplicating the authentic taste of Polynesia alongside the chip fryer. There are red tassels hanging in the window. The Chinese believe red is a lucky colour. This part of South London is choked and haphazard. Gasworks, bus station, towering council blocks, disordered streets which go nowhere, soiled parks, hole-in-the-corner minicab offices, boarded-up churches, abandoned seamen's misions, flaking houses, mean shops and quantities of metalwork: road barriers and signs and bus shelters and railings. It's a landscape that makes him uneasy. It's overloaded, but it seems to have no purpose.

He can't imagine Babette crouching nervously in the bathroom threatening to call the police. But then he can't imagine Mike hitting her. It pains him – not, he's ashamed to admit to himself, on Babette's account, but on Mike's. There's a certain honour in being hit, a vindication, but there's nothing but shame for a man who hits a woman. It's weakness. It's a sign of desperation or, as Geraldine would say, low self-esteem. But with Mike there is this kernel of Mikeness which will never be disturbed. It infuriates Babette. Perhaps she went too far in trying to disturb it, he thinks.

He's glad to find himself back on the road and then to be approaching the Naval College. The College and the hill with the observatory above it are completely still and empty, frozen like an eighteenth-century landscape painting in this cluttered, Cubist South London. He slows the car to look down at the river, which is gleaming, grey and shining in the clear night beyond the formal, deserted terraces designed by Christopher Wren. Or was it Christopher Wren? He can't remember. There are so many things that he is not sure of. He's not sure, for instance, what all those countries are that have suddenly sprung up in Eastern Europe or Yugoslavia. Where were they all those years? And in personal matters he seems to have lost the plot as well. Why is Geraldine into – he hates the phrase – her psychotherapy? Is it to make up for something he is lacking? Is it a sort of reproach to him for being insensitive to her needs? He longs for the easy intimacy they once had. And he doesn't know why the country has lost its confidence. Greenwich Mean Time was invented up the hill and out in Swaziland they certainly had great faith in the old country. But he doesn't know if this loss of faith, like yuppie flu, is all in the mind. And he doesn't know if they really are drowning in satanism and child abuse and ignorance or whether people are just as decent and law-abiding and civilised as they used to be, or thought they were.

At the very least, their rugby team is doing well. Geraldine would say he was clutching at straws, but he and Mike understand what it means. It's like being able to hear music that others can't.

He turns into a maze of small streets. These must once have been seamen's cottages. Babette has the top half of a small Victorian house in Jellicoe Street. Who was Jellicoe? He can't remember, but guesses that he might have been an admiral. He parks the car. The ground floor, mercifully, seems to be empty. He would not like the other occupants to have heard the thuds and screams, muted but none the less audible. He rings the bell. It is marked 'Lesaux', her maiden name. *Babette Lesaux.* She is of Huguenot descent, which confers on her some distinction, although it is not clear why this is. The absent people underneath are called Pickering. A light comes on in the common hallway. Mike's tall silhouette fills the corridor. He opens the door.

   – *Come in.*

   – *You okay?*

   – *Yeah. As well as you can be when you're under the cosh.*

   – *Did you hurt her?*

   – *No. Just a fat lip.*

   – *Oh dear.*

Mike looks deathly tired. He's not wearing his jacket or shoes. Perhaps they made love before the row.

Anthony follows him up the narrow stairs. They both have to stoop for fear of knocking their heads on something. This little house emphasises how big they are. They could never have gone to sea. Directly above the stairs is a big sitting room and kitchen. Another, narrower stairway leads up to two small bedrooms and the bathroom. Mike's discarded clothes lie on the pale, fleecy carpet.

– *Anthony. Is that you?*

He hears Babette's voice from above.

– *Yes. It's me. Why does she want me?* he whispers.

– *She wants you to witness.*

– *I'll go up. Does she know you're coming to stay?*

– *Yes.*

Anthony makes the short journey up the stairs.

– *Hello Babette, it's Anthony.*

– *Anthony, I hold you responsible. It's your fucking fault.*

– *What is?*

– *You know what I'm talking about. You've known him for years. You know what he's like. You've encouraged him.*

From behind the bathroom door her voice sounds less forceful than usual. He knows that Babette is suggesting that he and Mike are complicit in some plan to defraud her of what she is owed, emotionally and sexually. It's a feeling he often has, that he is emotionally in debt. What he wants to tell Babette is that he has been thinking about this problem. He has concluded that we are neglecting the links with the magicial and he wants to reassure her, by telling her about Nelson Mandela and King Sobhuza. And he would like to tell her that Mike will come back from Cape Town with new knowledge.

– *Babette, I don't mean to state the obvious, but aren't you and Mike legally separated? So what's the point in going over his inadequacies?*

– *Thanks,* Mike whispers from the top of the stairs.

– *If he has any,* Anthony adds.

– *Did he tell you that he attacked me?*

– *He mentioned that there had been some pushing and shoving.*

– *Pushing and shoving, shit. He hit me and split my lip. It's still bleeding.*

– Do you want me to look at it?

– No. I'm going to live. I wanted you here on a more serious matter. Did he tell you why he came this evening?

– Not really. He said you had a few things to sort out.

– He came to tell me that he had been fired, and that he couldn't pay the mortgage on this miserable flat and that he would leave the country if I raised any objection.

Anthony looks at Mike, who is sitting just below him on the stairs.

– Is Mike out there? Anthony?

– No. He's downstairs making coffee, I think.

– In other words, after four and a half years of marriage, nearly six years in all, after giving him my best years, he's saying he has no responsibilities to me.

Giving him my best years. Anthony repeats the phrase to himself.

– Anthony.

– Well, he hasn't got a job at the moment.

– Whose fault is that?

– I don't think it's that simple.

– Look, Anthony. I'm just about to start at Surrey University. He knows that. I'm going to try and make something of my life, even if it's a bit late. But if he pisses off, then what? If he does, it will all be your fault. Anthony, you've got a side to you which in your oh-so-innocent way is really very anarchic. You like a spot of trouble. You're probably enjoying this, me in here bleeding all over the bathmat, your mate Mike stumbling about or earwigging our conversation and you egging him on to go to South Africa.

Anthony thinks that there is some truth in Babette's analysis.

– Babette, let's just assume for the moment that everything you say is correct. What can I do to help? Now? At this moment? It's probably too late to be spreading the blame around.

– You're the only one he will listen to.

– Open the door, Babette. I feel silly talking to you through a bathroom door.

– Anthony, I'm going to call the police and have him charged if I don't get some reasonable assurance.

– Can we talk about it over a cup of coffee?

– Okay, she says wearily.

He gestures to Mike and mimes, 'coffee'.

– *Mike's just getting it.*

– *Tell him to make me a verbena infusion. It's just above the hob in a small jar marked 'tisanes'.*

– *Mike*, he calls, although Mike is still at the top of the stairs, *Babette wants some verbena tea, it's in a jar marked 'Titian'.*

– *Tisanes. It's French.*

– *Tisanes*, he says.

– *Okay*, calls Mike, strangling his voice, *the kettle has just boiled*.

Mike goes down the stairs to the kitchen, smiling. Babette opens the door. She is wearing a dressing gown of a quilted pink material decorated with old roses. She is holding a bloody Kleenex to her lip with one hand and she has a portable phone in the other.

– *Are you all right?*

– *No, I'm not.*

The bathroom releases a charged atmosphere. It is rich with the scents of sachets of herbs and capsules of oils and colourful soaps, which he can see in a bowl, looking like large cod liver oil pills. Anthony feels excited and curious.

Babette walks through to the bedroom regally. He follows her. One wall is lined with cupboards, some of them open, the aftermath of the row, he thinks. He gets a glimpse of her vivid selection of clothes before she shuts the doors. She sits on the bed and he sits beside her. He reaches out for her hand, and holds it between his two hands. He glances at her. Her bottom lip is pushing forward, with a small, glistening split in the middle. In rugby it would be nothing; in marital relations it may be criminal. They sit on the bed where she has, apparently, tried to revive her sex life. There is a tasselled silk scarf over the bulbous lampshade by the bed, lending some uncertain sensuality to the light, and a poster of a naked girl standing by a fireplace, from an exhibition at the Metropolitan Museum. Her hand feels large and oily. It may be cold cream. Her hair is falling forward over her injured face.

– *Babette, we'll sort something out.*

She releases her hand, but not without squeezing his first. It may be a gesture of thanks or a reminder of her emotional reserves. She reaches to the bedside table for a tie for her hair. Anthony has always been fascinated by what women keep by their beds, and in their handbags. She pulls her hair back deftly, tying the band around it as she turns to him.

– *I'm so miserable, Anthony. I can't tell you.*

– *I don't think Mike is much better.*

– *Don't take his side, Ant. Not automatically.*

With her hair back and her strong face with its emotional sheen, she looks like Elaine Page in *Evita*.

– *I'll tell you what. I'll drive him home in a while, we'll talk in the morning – I'll take the morning off – and I'll try to work out something.*

She says nothing, weighing the suggestion. At least the threat of the police with their heavy irony seems to have been lifted, he thinks.

– *Don't let him go to Pretoria.*

– *Why not? It's Cape Town, by the way.*

– *Timbuctu, I don't care. He'll never come back. You know how he is. He's like water, just flowing wherever there's no resistance.*

He is pleased she hasn't said 'downhill'. He decides to leave the question of the expedition open, for the moment.

– *We'll talk about that in the morning. Will you be here?*

But he's pushed on too fast for her.

– *Wait a minute. I want to get something agreed before you leave, taking the boy wonder with you. At least I know you will try to stick to it.*

Babette's voice is harsh. It's strangely aristocratic, swooping, as though she is addressing people at a few paces. She's also from the suburbs, but she spent a few terms at drama school in Bristol or somewhere and this minced delivery of her words is the legacy. When Mike first introduced her five or six years ago, after the yacht charter disaster, Anthony found her jagged, over-precise voice exciting. It seemed to promise knowledge and experience. He has even imagined having sex with her, with her full, firm jaw matched by her assertive breasts. The way women regard their own breasts, the question of display or concealment, is another puzzle which intrigues him.

– *Ant, what's getting to me is that I've wasted six years on him. It's terrible to realise how stupid I've been. I'm paralysed by the thought of how we're never going to get those fucking years back.*

How casually women use the word 'fuck' now. He thinks of Francine swearing from her unfamiliar, padded mouth.

– *We're all finding that. We've reached that kind of age.*

– *Yes, but you haven't made a complete fuck-up of your lives as we have.*

He sees she must be including Geraldine in this. But he resists this, thinking of his own emotional life as distinct and precious.

– *I wouldn't put money on it.*

– *Don't be silly, Anthony; you like to think you live on the edge, but it's only in your mind. In reality you're quite shrewd and well organised. You've got a nice home, although you think it's a little bourgeois, and you've got Geraldine and Fergus.* (Yes, and I've got the big house under the mountains, he thinks.) *You've had the same job, however boring, for years. I don't know. Mike has undermined everything I hoped for. He's like one of those fucking termites in Africa, he just nibbles away until one day everything collapses.*

Mike says, *Tea's up, coffee's up,* as he mounts the stairs noisily, so that they aren't embarrassed by being found talking about him.

– *Herb tea and coffee.* He doesn't look directly at Babette as he places a tray on the bed. She dabs her lip.

– *Are you two finished discussing my inadequacies?*

– *Not quite,* says Anthony. *It's a big job.*

– *I'm sorry about your lip.*

– *No, you're not sorry about my lip. You're sorry that your friend has seen what you're capable of.*

– *That's also true,* says Mike.

– *Let's not go back on what happened now,* says Anthony. *I think we should sleep on it. I've said to Babette that tomorrow we'll work something out.*

– *Mike must sign the guarantee form for the flat and pay this months's mortgage before you go. It's two weeks late already,* says Babette. As the injured party, she is entitled to make demands.

– *I'll sell my car tomorrow. The company let me have it as a farewell gift. You can have all the money, probably about four thousand, and I'll sign the undertaking. Where is it?* says Mike.

And so this is what it has all come down to, a question of money, a few months of security for Babette. Anthony feels drained now, as though his essence, his human soul, has been siphoned off by the meanness of the transaction. It is also clear to him that Babette is only getting a deposit: the full debt is far from being paid. Mike signs the form. He is responsible for the payments. But he is only signing because he hit her.

There is some problem with the pen. Babette stands up to look for another, and her dressing gown opens. Anthony sees her breast, large and brown-tipped. He can easily imagine her having one-night stands, but he can also see that her impatience and directness might work against her. She finds the pen and hands it to Mike, who makes a pretence of reading the document. His blond hair, now slightly muddied by grey, is thinning and his face, his tired face, has acquired the unnatural contours it had at lunch. His mouth is starting to jib again. It's protesting against this surrender. Anthony takes out his chequebook. He wants to join in the fun.

– *Here's a cheque for a thousand pounds. Cash it if you have to or give it back to me if things turn out okay. No, I insist. As you rightly said, I am to blame for seeing anything of value in this person.*

But he is thinking, *There goes Fergus's ski holiday.*

She takes the cheque without reluctance. Anthony doesn't feel aggrieved. Like his conversation with Basil, this negotiation has been another tutorial. Increasingly he imagines that he can see the inner workings, not only on the personal level but going out in concentric rings to business and politics. It's reassuring, like being shown a cardtrick or learning to ride a bicycle. When he watches American football on Channel Four he sees that the experts can detect all sorts of subtleties and stratagems in the clash of the fat people in the front line. He's becoming an expert on the inner workings of things. It's taken him a long time.

Babette is prepared to let them go now, although she lingers over her herb tea and offers to make them another coffee. But Anthony says they should go. He cites Geraldine: she must be wondering where they are.

– *You can call from here.*

– *No, it's okay, I'll ring from the car when we're on our way. It's a hell of a schlepp from here. The traffic's terrible.*

— It's only terrible along the river.

— Do you use the river bus?

— No, it's hopeless, it can't cope with the rubbish on the Thames. You can't rely on it.

— Can I have a pee before we go?

— Of course.

He leaves the combatants together sitting on the bed and goes into the bathroom where Babette was recently holed up. The air in here is close and fragrant, but the fragrances are at war. He pees, looking at his face in a mirror which also shows him his back view in another mirror. He inspects, intrigued, his surprisingly broad back and dark hair which is gathering into untidy tails at his collar. It surprises him to be reminded that he is so solid-looking. He realises that this is what other people see: a big man. A few drops escape on to the fluffy mat which surrounds the lavatory.

Babette is worrying about the years she has wasted on Mike, as though he was a poor mount in life's horse race. But Anthony is concerned with the dead time which is piling up. When he was a child time seemed insatiable, pressing against the outside of his head with the urgency of its demands. Now it seems to be flaking, like paint from old ironwork, or falling like the dead particles of skin which we apparently shed.

This is the way my mind is going, he thinks: *I pee on the floor and think of infinity.*

5

Chanelle is coming down now. That's one of the problems with crack. If things speed up, the highs and the lows coming ever faster, she won't last. Still, it's better than her mother's way, which is slow and steady but headed in the same direction. God knows what will happen to Bradley if she ends up in a dustbin. That is what the desk sergeant said to her the other night:

– *How's Jason? Don't say I didn't warn you if we find you upside-down in a dustbin.*

He's talking about the Irish girl, Jacqui.

People have always been warning her. Even her mother, when she was on the the game herself. There was a girl in the home whose mother used to inject herself fifteen times to find a vein. Sometimes she would inject herself in the tummy, straight in. And she was always hitting this girl, Shelly, for coming in late and so on. Eventually Shelly was taken into care. Chanelle knows that Jason is not going to be around forever, but he's been good to her and he's not too bad with Bradley, except for his temper.

When Bradley was born he was very small, four and a half pounds, and they blamed her, in that caring voice, for smoking and taking drugs and drinking. He looked yellow and red and unready. She thought of tandoori chicken in Costcutters. Jason once asked her a question. He asked her if she ever knew who its father was. But she doesn't think like that, even though it was probably her boyfriend before Jason, John. Because of the colour, people think Jason is the dad and he doesn't mind as long as he doesn't have to be bothered with him. He can't be around Brad for more than a few minutes before he gets on the phone or goes out on his business. Sometimes when Jason is talking on the phone, she has to laugh. Although he wants to be cool he has trouble hiding his feelings, and his free arm begins to go up and down and his accent becomes more Brummie, so he begins to sound frightened instead of cool. That's why he's talking like Axel Foley now, because the Birmingham accent doesn't sound cool at all. His temper comes out when he can't quite get on top of a situation or people disrespect him. The police don't treat him with respect. And the drug dealers don't either. He believes his BMW will get him proper respect. What he calls 'props'.

Jason's plan hasn't worked out so far. The first guy only had fifty pounds, which he handed over, and the second tried to throw her out of the car until Jason arrived. He had twenty-five and a car phone. His cash card was only good for a hundred. But Jason says it will work. *The night is young.* They've made two hundred plus so far. She stands by the war memorial, so that she can keep an eye on the cars as they slow down for the lights. Jason says she's picked them badly, but that's easy for him to say. She's only got a few seconds as they slow down, to decide. She's stopped trying to be focused. It didn't help and she doesn't know what it means.

She sees a Saab approaching. It slows and stops. She looks back up Norwood Road. It's clear. She runs to the car and starts to open the door. The driver is a bald man about fifty in a suit. He doesn't want to hear what she wants. She's just saying, *Please, please help me*, when he accelerates through the red light almost ripping her arm off, shouting, *Piss off, piss off.* As he goes, he reaches across and pulls the door closed. Bastard. She would like to kill him, with his brand new G-reg Saab and his stripy suit. Her fingers are quite sore. It's lucky nothing got caught up. She knows his sort. Once they've come, they can't wait to get you out of the car. Bastard. He didn't even listen to what she was trying to say. What if she really was a person in distress?

The wind is bitter, sweeping down off the grassy hill behind her. She can't stand out here much longer waiting for the right car. It's fine for Jason, sitting eating Kentucky Fried Chicken or smoking some weed, all nice and warm. She wonders how many cars she's looked at in this way: looking at the lone, shadowy figures inside, guessing what they're like, trying to match the cars to the people inside. In her own way she's become an expert on cars.

12 ∫

Mike wants to have a drink. He knows a pub, he's seen it anyway, just past the Naval College where the road takes a sharp turn. Because Mike is saddened, and perhaps embarrassed, by what has gone before, Anthony agrees, saying, *We both need a quick one,* even though he would now like to go home and unravel the day, and make amends for his reluctance to ring Geraldine.

As they swing into the car park beside the Admiral Hood, Mike says, *Ant, I'm sorry you were involved in that. But she wanted to call the police. She would have unless you came.*

– *That's okay.*

– *I know I shouldn't have hit her, but Jesus, she was asking for it.*

– *Are you sure she was asking for it?*

– *Literally. She wanted me to give her one, she was waiting in her nightie, and when I wouldn't she wanted me to hit her. It was terrible. It was like being caught up in a TV play. You know the sort of crap where men are all violent bastards and women are finding themselves and everybody talks meaningful rubbish, that nobody would in real life? That's how she talks these days. She said to me, 'I suppose you want to hit me now, because you are such a failure you can't get it up.' And so I did.*

Anthony begins to laugh. As they enter the car park they are laughing like idiots. They sit in the car, unable to move.

– *Oh Jesus, it's not funny,* says Anthony, but he is laughing so much that he feels weak and ecstatic, just as he used to when his father tickled him. But, like tickling, it goes on too long and becomes unbearable. Mike hit Babette and they are laughing like baboons: it doesn't make sense. He could never defend it, but then, he thinks, why should I have to? They walk into the pub.

Anthony hardly ever goes into pubs, but Mike likes them. He has found that they are tolerant and forgiving. This one is large, with huge, fake beams and a long bar stretching away around a corner. The bar is hung with mugs and plastered with naval memorabilia, navigation charts, signal flags, ships' crests and cap badges. Anthony can imagine that life in the Navy might be very reassuring.

As they approach the middle of the bar, where the beer pumps are, they see that round the corner a stripper is performing on a raised dais. She is down to a camisole and a G-sring.

– *Let's go and take a look*, says Mike.

They carry their pints towards the smaller bar. It's not crowded and the spectators are hardly paying attention. But Anthony pays attention. He sees that this girl has an eczema burn behind her knees, only partially obscured by make-up. Perhaps this sort of work is stressful. He looks closely at her tummy, revealed as she slides the camisole off, one of her reddened knees pushed seductively forward. The poses are all secondhand. She is definitely a mother. There is just a little looseness, not much, about her skin. Her breasts are small, but with an upward curve in them. He has hardly inspected her face, lean and earnest, before another stripper is announced.

– *Give a good welcome to Linda.*

She's a black girl who dances twice as energetically as the previous girl, as if being black demands extra physical exuberance. Although the spectators glance at her, none seems rapt. Even the mystery of women's bodies is not a mystery to anybody except Anthony. He watches her. Her breasts are held tightly in a waspie corset and her hips are muscular, at odds with her legs which are almost impossibly thin below the knee. On her head she has a chestnut blonde wig, or hair extension, which makes her look as though something has landed there and she's trying to shake it off. She takes off her waspie without slowing down. Her breasts are round, completely symmetrical, with deep brown nipples and almost purple aureoles. Her face is blank. It reminds Anthony of Winnie Mandela when she is angry, a kind of steely emptiness. She goes off to light applause. They are told that there is to be an interval before the next act so that they can wet their whistles after that steamy little number.

– Mike, what are you going to do? Babette says you will go abroad.
– I might.
– You know, after you left, I saw Francine today.
– You saw her, or you are seeing her?
– I saw her. She was just about to enter the post office. She works in
Marks and Spencer in Oxford Street.
– How is she?
– She's married, for the second time.
– Jesus.

One of the secrets in the exchange of hostages that makes up
their friendship is that Anthony used Mike's flat to meet Francine
sometimes. Mike, in his less encumbered days, was seldom there.
He never said a word to discourage Anthony. There are many
ways they are tied together, which include Mike's few months
with Geraldine. The giving of secrets with absolute confidence
is, Anthony thinks, one of the signs of friendship. Behind them
and around them the pub is full of noise: the rumble and clank of
fruit machines, the sighs of the beer pumps, the thunk of darts,
the alcohol-steeped laughter and the beer talk.

– How was she, Francine?
– Fat. Like a dumpling. She seems to have had a conversion. She's
married to a plumber and left one of her children behind in Australia.
It was a shock, because for all those years – how long? eight years – I've
had a picture of her. And I thought maybe she was keeping herself for
me. Or at least keeping a little bit of herself. But it seems she forgot me
almost completely.
– She was a funny one. Quirky.
– Do you think we have been more than averagely useless with
women?
– No. About average. The problem I have with women is exactly the
same problem they have with me.
– And that is?
– They turn into something else. You go out with, or marry, one type
of woman and she quickly turns into another.
– Maybe you drive them to it.
– It's possible. But I always feel they want more from me than I
bargained for. I noticed when I was very young that girls, little girls,
are always grading their friends. This one's up this week, then she's
a right cow, and another one's favourite. Perhaps they don't change.

My sister used to spend all her time making her friends cry. It was ruthless.

His sister, Mandy, now lives in British Columbia and is married to a man who sells algae-resistant marine paint. Mandy used to do ballet and hung around Sadler's Wells until she was seventeen. Mandy once let him put his finger in her, but only once. He wondered for a long time what he had done wrong. He was searching for her erogenous zones but he obviously hadn't made contact. She was like Mike, easily switching her attention to something or someone else.

– *Ant, you know when we see Nelson Mandela, I hope you aren't expecting too much.*

– *What are you talking about?*

– *I worry about you. You seem to be getting religion.*

– *The only religious feelings I have are for Will, Jerry and the boys. 'Swing Low' is my anthem. Did you see the Standard? One of the French papers called Parc des Princes, 'Parc de Waterloo'.*

But they can't divert down the road of rugby. Mike is at a watershed and Babette's fat lip is the proof.

– *What are you expecting from Nelson?*

– *I expect Nelson to bring to the world some new information. Nothing more.*

Now that he's said it, now that he's put it out in the open, Anthony feels moved by the idea.

– *What sort of information?*

– *Some information about what it is to be a human being. Don't laugh. I am expecting the same sort of elevation people got from listening to JFK's inauguration speech, or Churchill. Or even from seeing Will flying over the French try-line. That's what I'm expecting. It may sound crazy, but I want to feel that exhilaration. I want to get outside myself. Don't you feel ourselves, our lives, I don't know, our habits and so on are dragging us down?*

– *You should get pissed more often. You get quite interesting.*

– *That is a rugby club kind of remark.*

– *I am a rugby club kind of guy.*

– *Yes and no.*

Another stripper comes on. She is wearing a velvet ballgown which they can see has Velcro tabs that are going to be ripped apart. She has big hair. The ballgown is dusted with dandruff or perhaps stray particles of make-up. Sure enough, the Velcro soon comes into play: she opens her dress at the back with a loud tearing sound.

– *We must go*, says Anthony.

But they don't go immediately. Although they have caught the general indifference, they find it impossible to leave the pub while a girl is taking off her clothes. It's the thought that something new will be revealed. Some new information; some information about women that they lack. They watch idly as she dances, ripping away at the Velcro.

– *It's Thatcherism*, says Mike.

– *Of course. We're here to study market forces. Activity versus process, as we say at the Spice Mall.*

– *Do you want another drink?*

– *No, but I'll watch you.*

As Mike walks to the bar, Anthony wonders if there really are watersheds. In films and books, although he doesn't read much, people seem to arrive at watersheds or turning points. They know when they've got there and they either accept their fate or they overcome it. It's nonsense, really. It doesn't work like that. With Mike there has been an accumulation of things, but they all stem from the way he is. He was attractive because of his elemental, primitive blitheness. He held something back, and people, particularly girls, thought that they could find what it was. One stoned girl told Anthony about the depths of Mike's eyes. But now his eyes are wounded. They are wary of the light and other sensory shocks. His eyes have taken refuge in a face which no longer displays them to best advantage; they seem to be lodging there uneasily, rent unpaid. What was once seen as mysterious about Mike has proved to be a lack of focus.

When he played rugby, he could never read the game as Anthony could. He would make the wrong pass or put in an enormous tackle when it wasn't needed or fail to anticipate where the ball was going to land. Anthony would spend all of Saturday morning and most of Friday night in a state of increasing nervousness, his stomach painfully active. Mike would never give the game a thought in advance; sometimes he would turn up having forgotten who they were playing. Anthony tried to control his nervousness, to be more like Mike, but he couldn't. He always woke early on Saturday morning, after a troubled night, and started to fuss about his boots and his kit, and then he would wonder if he wasn't too tired to play properly. He remembers the dressing room, the stamping feet, the fat thighs, the smell of embrocation, the bandaging, the running on the spot, the nervous jokes, the urgent noise of the other team in their dressing room, the expectant murmur of the crowd outside, the constant tying of the boots and the final quick passing of the ball around the room which numbed the fingers. He can remember exactly how the ball felt, the new leather slippery, the lettering on the side bold, the stitches firm and even, the smell still of the shoe shop. The menacing ball. The ball which is somehow in charge of the players.

And Mike? He was hardly aware. Sometimes he would be reading a newspaper while Anthony was bending and stretching and retying his boots. Once, before a very big match against Quins, Mike had to be sent for from the lavatory, after the kickoff. Not even the cavalcade of studs on the concrete floors and the shouts outside had disturbed him. Nor did Mike share Anthony's deep, almost cosmic, unease if they played badly. It never mattered to him. And now it seems he has neglected to understand more fundamental matters than rugby.

Anthony still puzzles about the ideal that he was seeking in rugby. It must correspond to the ideal in the mind – or the soul – which writers and painters are looking for: the ideal of the perfect poem or the perfect painting. It's unobtainable, but it's unmistakably the goal. What a strange thing, to crave something which can never be obtained.

Anthony watches the girl with the dry cereal hair as she bends forward to pull her G-string away for a moment so that they see her dark and glossy mound, as some sort of reward, before she goes off. As she leaves the stage, she stumbles. One of her heels has broken. She quickly bends forward to pick up her shoe. Anthony sees her buttocks part and her breasts appear between her legs for a moment. He finds this defenceless posture touching and erotic, because it is unforeseen.

To aim for something which you have never experienced and will never experience: there's no such thing as a perfect game. On Saturday they came tantalisingly close, probably as close as any English team ever has. But with Mike there was never a quest for the unobtainable. It was enough for him to play and enjoy himself. Some great players can play the game without rational thought. Intelligence doesn't come into it. Geraldine says there are probably different kinds of intelligence anyway. What Swedenborg was looking for was the link between our ideals and infinity, or God. But perhaps you don't need God to accept that we have a notion of perfection. Our notion of perfection must correspond in some way to the nature of being human.

And now he sees clearly at last: Nelson is going to reveal that human striving – *My life is the struggle* – is the human condition. He sees now that to be human is to be compelled to seek the ideal, without any expectation of achieving it.

Here comes Mike after his negotiations at the bar. Sadly, he looks like a man who is familiar with this journey from bar to table, holding a drink. The drink is slopping over the side because he is not walking steadily.

Anthony wants to tell him about Nelson, but this is not the moment.

13

In China they are allowed to have one child. All those hundreds of millions of people and tens of millions of only children. Geraldine goes in to see her only child. He is sleeping with his nose poking upwards, greedy for air. His neck is strangely angled too. It doesn't look natural, but she doesn't move him. When he sleeps he sometimes talks and grinds his teeth, as though the events of his day have not been fully resolved. Nobody really knows what dreams are or what their purpose is. She used to dream and sleepwalk as a child.

She wonders if the Chinese will change as a people. There must be a huge difference between a culture which was accustomed to five or six young children in the house and one where the norm is a single child. If she had been able, she would have had three children. Having one is probably too intense. She's noticed that people with lots of children, like Leonora, are inclined to spread their concern thin, as though being a mother only equips you with so much maternal balm, no matter how many children you have. And Leonora doesn't worry much about physical safety. Probably in your DNA or somewhere you are able to accept the possibility of loss if you have plenty of children. It was a mystery why they could have only one child. There was technically nothing wrong with either of them, but her ovaries simply wouldn't function.

Anthony and Mike are very late. But she knows that with Mike anything can happen. He's chaotic, although Anthony is more than ready to find excuses for him. There's a certain conspiracy there: it helps to have a completely clueless friend because it paints you in a good light. She remembers her plain friend, Sarah, who was always useful because she could talk to boys, although they never really fancied her. God, girls can be cruel. Watching Fergus grow up has given her an understanding of the way men behave. Boys are floundering around looking for a personality to inhabit, but girls seem to come with one ready-made.

Sometimes she thinks that Anthony has forgotten that she loved Mike before she even knew him. In marriage this is what happens: you create competing versions of events and friendships. In her class they have been studying perception and she finds it extraordinary, a revolution even, to be shown how we make up a picture of the world. There is no real picture of the world, although Mr Freedman told them a lovely story about Dr Johnson kicking a large stone and saying, *I refute it thus*, to disprove Berkeley's theory about the non-existence of matter. Mr Freedman has been particularly kind to her and suggested that they might go together to the Mind and Body exhibition at Olympia next week. Although he's a psychologist, he has problems at home. Sometimes he quotes Freud: *The great question which has never been answered and which I have never been able to answer in thirty years is, what does a woman want?*

The college is very correct in its prospectus and its code of conduct, but it is clear that Mr Freedman has his reservations.

The phone rings. She closes Fergus's door quickly, although he is never woken by noises, not even by the crashing thunderstorm which ripped up hundreds of trees, and hurries to their bedroom. It's Anthony's mother.

– *Is Anthony there?*

– *No, he's on his way home, I think.*

– *It's very late.*

– *It is. Things are tough at the office. He may be in his car, have you got that number?*

– *I can never make it work. The other day I found myself talking to a sex line. Is that what you call it? Sex line?*

– *I don't know.*

– *How is Fergus?*

– *He's asleep. He has such a busy day that he goes out like a light.*

– *I think you young try to cram too much in the day. But perhaps I'm old-fashioned.*

– Can I give Ant a message?

– Ask him to ring me. The builder has put in for planning permission for an Olympic swimming pool.

– Is that going to be a nuisance?

– Five lorries an hour for five weeks. Or perhaps five lorries a week. I forget. Anyway, I didn't come here to live in the middle of a building site. That man's always fiddling with something. As soon as he's finished the garden lights he starts on an ornamental pond and then a fountain and then a new garage and now an Olympic swimming pool.

– Are you sure it's Olympic? I mean, that's absolutely huge.

– Well, it's big anyway. Anthony has to stop him.

– I'll tell him.

– I'm not a complete fool, you know. Don't be ironical.

She puts the phone down. Geraldine hopes she hasn't upset her. It's hard to tell. She phones with these rushes of indignation, demanding action, more and more often. It's as though she wants to leave this world with some reminders of her principles. Geraldine wonders if she contemplates death. Do old people lie awake at night guessing how long they've got? Eleanor, Anthony's mother, gives the impression, during daylight hours anyway, of a brisk accommodation with the idea of death. She sometimes mentions old friends who have died recently in short, quick sentences, as if not to dwell on what it means to stop existing: *– Did I tell you that Peggy Granville died last week? Heart.*

Sometimes there is a qualifying sentence which might be taken to mean that the circumstances did not apply widely: *– Smoked like a chimney for years. So did Ted, of course.*

Geraldine's father died quite young. His death was strangely colourless. He had a heart attack at work, before he was aware of old age.

She goes in once more to look at Fergus. He's lying with his arms flung out as though he is practising to fly. She did his room in blue with a duvet decorated with blue rabbits, but now he's beginning to get ideas of his own. He's put up some Arnold Schwarzenegger posters and skateboard stickers. He also has a pile of Amiga computer magazines which are completely unintelligible to her. These childen seem to know instantly how to play very complex games. When Geraldine was a schoolgirl playing her music, her mother used to say to her, *I don't know how you can listen to rubbish like this. What's the point of someone singing 'Yeah, yeah, yeah' over and over?*

She thinks that maybe Fergus and his friends are tuned into computer rhythms just as keenly as she was to every nuance of 'Honky Tonk Woman' and 'The Ballad of John and Yoko'. She warms in the gloom as she thinks of Anthony doing his Mick Jagger. He still does it at parties, given any encouragement. The parties they go to these days involve eating and drinking and standing around. She used to love dancing and now she hardly ever gets a chance. Not even at the Christmas party, since that was moved.

She twitches the bunny duvet straight. Fergus wants something more manly. It saddens her that Anthony doesn't have a closer rapport with him. There's just an element of restraint, a few inches of distance, which neither of them can overcome. It's not Fergus's responsibility, at nine, but it's true that he resists Anthony. The space between them is like an ill-fitting door. Anthony, of course, suspects that she is over-mothering him and unconsciously creating the rift.

She goes downstairs. It is very quiet: there are none of the creaks and groans of an older house like her parents'. Anthony and Mike must be here soon. She's left the curtain open so that she can keep an eye out, as if that will hurry them along. It's like being left waiting in a restaurant: the uneasy feeling grows. You are dying for the other one to arrive, and yet there is no reason why you shouldn't read a paper or eat olives or scan the menu and have a good time. Mr Freedman wants to have lunch with her in a Polish restaurant he knows in Earl's Court. It stocks many flavours of vodka. Earl's Court has some personal resonances for him. Maybe she will go.

Outside the window, beyond the cherry trees, she sees a fox flaring briefly in the light from her windows. The country people, the few of them left, hate foxes, but she thinks it's just a ritual. They are harmless enough. The fox moves with an anxious lope and sideways glances back at the house.

14 $\int$

Mike says that he is dog-tired. And it's true that violence is exhausting. They pull the rear seat forward – it splits in two – and he climbs right into the back to lie down. He covers himself in Anthony's muddy waxed coat which always lies in the back, and a bit of dust sheet. He is six foot three but he makes himself instantly comfortable, just as he is able to sleep on an old sofa and unmade beds.

Anthony rings Geraldine, but the phone is busy. She spends a lot of time talking to her fellow students and remedial teachers. He switches on the radio. The news is that the Iranians have confirmed their death threat against Salman Rushdie. In Geneva agreement has been reached between the Soviet Union and America on inspecting each other's nuclear weapons. He fiddles with the dial, and finds football. Although he watches occasionally he believes that football contributes in some way to the deteriorating condition of the country. The faces of the kids in the streets are sullen, angry and resentful, just like the soccer players'. Sometimes the faces he sees of boys, even quite young boys, are haunted by longing. They want something but they have lost the connection between what they want and the means of getting it. They long to be in those video games, where the world is free of consequences, except for the possibility of being eaten by an alien. And he hates the way the players are angry and swearing as though football was always disappointing them. He went to watch a match at Wembley with a client and the fans were violently possessed with hatred against the inoffensive Dutch.

At rugby matches, even England–Wales, there is a warmth, a

communion, a love of rugby. Sometimes players throw punches and lose their tempers, like the French on Saturday, but it's accepted that in a rugby game this happens. What the crowd hate is not the wild punches which seldom land, but the deliberate maiming or injuring of a helpless player. When they see it, the crowd reverberates with the shame, the dishonour of it. But at football matches the violence and the hatred sustain the crowd. Many of them come, like the spectators at a Hitler rally, to air their loathings.

The French at Parc des Princes lost their control and lost the game. It's become a mental game, a test of control. He read in some paper that the forwards have to be like the *corps de ballet*, expressing themselves by carrying out perfectly the wishes of the choreographer. They must all dance to the same tune in order to create the conditions for the soloists to perform.

He finds his way back to the South London he knows. Anthony thinks of this road as a tapeworm, burrowing, winding, flapping through South London, as if this part of town came first and the road then attacked it, forcing its way through where the resistance was weakest. When he was a boy he was advised to wash his hands before eating: tapeworms were very long, ribbon-like things, which grew phenomenally quickly. If he was hungry it was speculated that he might have a tapeworm. The thought of playing host to this immensely long, wraith-like worm frightened him. It was common knowledge that the natives routinely evacuated sixteen-foot tapeworms.

It is certainly not a road that anybody planned, threading its way mindlessly through the former villages and suburbs and industries of London, most of them blurred now by the years. He went, reluctantly at first, to the Post-Impressionists with Geraldine, and he was amazed to find that Pissarro had painted scenes in Norwood and Forest Hill. They are places now so lost in the anonymous sprawl that there would be nothing to paint.

Anthony always takes an interest in the road. As he drives by he notes the traffic schemes, the garden centres, the herbal clinics, the fast food outlets, the tree planting and felling, the cheery new Tescos and Texas Home Stores, the plumbers and DIY merchants, the churches and mosques, the schools, the pubs. One week he tried to work out how many businesses there were fronting the road on his forty-minute drive. The radio says that there have been record business failures, almost three thousand, in the past year. But on this road alone there are two or three thousand enterprises ranging from the crazy to the stately. He has a good idea of which businesses will last: video shops are flourishing, sex shops have vanished, home decorating is collapsing. That's how he passes some of the time, in a dream where he is an urban inspector without power or responsibility. He switches to Capital Gold. Sometimes he listens to a play or a tape. He used to worry about spending a hundred minutes a day in his car, but he finds the time passing almost unnoticed, as if it were another form of sleep or coma. He glances round: Mike is visible only as a mound, like a fresh grave.

He rings Geraldine again. He feels nervous as the phone rings.

– *Hello.*

– *Where are you?*

– *Mike had to see Babette. We'll be about forty minutes.*

– *Is he with you?*

– *Yes. He's asleep.*

– *What is that on the radio?*

– *Capital Gold.*

– *No, I mean the song?*

– *It's Tim Hardin, 'Don't Make Promises You Can't Keep'.*

– *Like you. I haven't heard it for years.*

– *Fergus all right?*

– *Sound asleep. I've got chili for you. Your mother called.*

– *What does she want.*

– *A hit man.*

– *Fine, no problem. See you in thirty, forty minutes.*

– *Bye.*

And now he longs to be home, as though this day will resolve itself in the familiar outlines and scents of High Woods; the loop of cherry trees, the pastel furnishings, the crystal glasses (put out for Mike), the fresh towels and the pine cleaner in the downstairs toilet. He looks forward to the things which sometimes drive him mad: the quiet orderliness, the familiar objects. And he looks forward to being greeted by Geraldine, wearing a little extra make-up for Mike's sake, still girlish if not sexy, and looking in on Fergus, asleep, like Mike. He feels a fizzing pain in his gut now because he has spent the day indulging himself while she has been performing the real business of life. She has helped people. She has readied the house. She has fed Fergus. She has cooked. And he? He's dreamed of flight and encouraged his friend in his folly.

The car swings up the hill out of Brixton. It passes the town hall which advertises itself as an equal opportunities employer on a large banner. The press love this council, because it is full of Trotskyites and utopians who think it's not too late for the revolution to start right here. But Anthony sees that if you give councillors the intoxicant of money, of budgets, they will inevitably try to change the world because they are not the sort of people for whom power and money were ever envisaged. They are minor people whom the world has treated with disdain, moaners and complainers, who have found by accident the access to money. And by chance, they have found a forum for their opinions in the council chamber.

Tonight when they go to bed, with Mike tucked up in the spare room, he will tell Geraldine about Nelson Mandela. But not about Babette's mortgage. He will tell her about his promotion, with the warning that the company is in poor health. He will transfer the house into her name. It's their only asset. He commends himself for this foresight and gives thanks to Basil for his warning.

Now there is a long, curving section of road where the buildings thin out. If you didn't know better you would imagine you were approaching the outskirts of town, but there's plenty more to come before you break free. The radio's playing 'Jumping Jack Flash'. Mick Jagger comes from somewhere not far from here. These mean streets, these seeping, blind streets have produced famous figures in rock and roll who sing as if they were born in Tennessee and play the guitar as if they were raised on a bayou. *Jumping Jack Flash, it's a gas, gas, gas* – just as he's passing the South East Thames gasworks. Rock and roll, like boxing in the ghetto, has provided an escape from these dreary places. Anthony knows nothing of what goes on one block from the A23. He sees the road as a façade, behind which there may be nothing at all. Occasionally, of course, he can see tower blocks where people, surprisingly, consent to live, but it is a blank, unknown landscape.

He turns down towards Streatham High Road which becomes glitzier each month, although the glitz seems to be too much for the area. The nightclubs and restaurants glow and burn out. There is something wrong with the area, not supplying enough wattage to keep them alight. In the back, Mike groans in his sleep, a painful, anguished noise. It's a toned-down version of the noise the bull made when the Swazi warriors had it down and were smothering it, watched by their king with the smiling, gentle face. He sees in this slaughter the renewal of life.

Anthony's father the banker-ethnographer says: *It's the renewal of life, the first fruits. Every year the king must be reborn. He must perform exactly the same rituals and eat exactly the same fruits.* Under 'fruits' his father included, but did not specify, intimate organs of the bull, which the king would eat naked, wearing only a penis cap of ivory. Anthony discovered this many years later by reading a book called *African Aristocracy* which he bought from a stall. This was probably what his father meant when he said they got down to business after the whites had left. Anthony imagines that Nelson will have been thinking about the meaning of this sort of ritual on the island. He is himself a Temba prince, an African aristocrat, and he will be in a position to update King Sobhuza's beliefs. Renewal is a popular idea. It seems to be the basis of all religions and maybe of politics too. The Swazis weren't so far from the mark in believing that their king had to be renewed every year.

The road narrows by the old police station before it swings down towards the railway bridge. Something's going on at the police station. The place is glowing from within. He slows. Down a side street he sees film trucks and now he sees that the police station is brightly lit by arc lights, so that the excess light is blue and exciting, like the glow from the spaceship in *ET*, as it spills out on to the moist, monochrome pavement. The tapeworm road is now strangely empty. He accelerates down past the railway towards the common and stops at the lights, which have just turned red. He sometimes tries to anticipate lights; you develop a knowledge of their span on a familiar journey. It's one of the myriad things which he has felt accumulating, falling on him like snowflakes, things which have little meaning but nonetheless you are powerless to avoid as they bury you. When he gets home he will try to explain to Geraldine how Nelson is going to reveal, to his satisfaction anyway, that human beings – what strange words – have no choice but to measure themselves against some ideal. And what's more, it is an ideal which has nothing to do with God (or Marx, as Nelson probably believed when he was young):

Birds fly, fish swim, humans . . . but before he can compose the thought there is a crashing on the roof of the car, followed by an urgent banging on the less resonant glass of the passenger side. It takes him, because he is thinking about Nelson and why fishes swim nonstop, completely by surprise, like being woken in the middle of the night by an alarm. He looks around in time to see the door open and a young girl climb in. He knows instantly: she has been raped. Her dark blonde hair is dishevelled, her blouse is torn (he can see her breasts in a white bra) and she has a bruise on her cheek, shading towards her ear.

– *Quick, quick, you gotta help me. Please. I been raped. I gotta get outta here. Please.*

She is gulping for air. It reminds him, quite inappropriately, of when his mother swallowed a chicken bone at their barbecue after they moved to High Woods. The girl seems to be having difficulty breathing, as if the air itself is lumpy. She looks fearfully up at the common, stretching away beside them. Her voice is choked.

– *Okay*, he says. *I'll take you to the police.*

– *I don't want to go to the police, I want to go to me mum's. She lives just along there. I don't want nothing to do with them. I know 'im, the bloke. If I go to the police 'e'll kill me. Honest.*

Although there is no traffic coming down the hill, Anthony feels compelled to wait for the light to change. The car is filling with her scent. There's no mistaking this heavy musk; it's the smell of fear, of semen, of rape. She is dabbing at her face with a dirty Kleenex now, and trying to pull her blouse together.

Her skin is not too good, not exactly acned but rough, as though it is covered in a rash. She looks out of the window again, sniffing.

– *C'mon. C'mon. Can we go?*

– *Lock your door*, he says, hoping to sound reassuring. When he gets his new car it is sure to have central locking.

The light changes. He accelerates, but misses a gear now that he's thinking about driving and the car stalls. He restarts the engine. Even as he does so he feels fear. It's the fear which rises when a tramp lurches towards you in Soho, the fear of the unpredictable, the vortex. He knows that the rape business is unlikely to be a simple matter.

– *Straight on. You turn just up there by the newsagent.*

She's stopped gulping for air, thank God. She rubs her eyes and crosses her legs, probably because of the pain.

– *I could take you to hospital, to casualty.*

– *No, if I do that they'll only call the police. I've got a little boy at me mum's. I gotta go home. He's not well.*

She's so young. Rape is one of the things which happen, almost routinely, never reported, that Geraldine mentions. Not that Geraldine herself has seen much abuse, but she has studied it at college: – *It's just the tip of the iceberg apparently.* He didn't want to believe then that the country had sunk in this way. And now he desperately wants to get home, to make some small offering to the household gods which he has been neglecting for too long.

– *What's your name?* he asks as gently as he can, but very aware how stiff the question is.

– *Chanelle, and what's yours?*

– *Anthony.*

He hasn't been expecting to be asked his name. He sees himself in the role of counsellor, not participant.

– *Just turn here, Anthony*, she says. *Left, and right. Me mum lives in that estate over there.*

Her blouse has come open again and he can see her breasts as he swings the car round. But he catches them briefly in the corner of his eye, guiltily, as if he has seen a woman breast-feeding or watched a doctor examining a patient. He wants to help this girl, but he doesn't want to get involved. He doesn't want to know if she has been buggered or if the man was her boyfriend's best friend or her stepfather or a casual acquaintance. He isn't able to think about rape in its details. It's beyond him, not out of fastidiousness but because of a fear of diminishing himself. (Just as Mike was diminished by hitting Babette.)

– Turn 'ere.

She's crouched and shivering now, like the survivors of accidents you see on television, hunched against further disasters. Catatonic. She rubs her nose, just as Fergus sometimes does, compulsively. They have turned into one of those short, dreadful roads of square, low, crude shops leading to a huge tower block, which he can see rising grey above. Beyond that, put there with playful symmetry, are two more towers. There is always a battered launderette, a betting shop, a chip shop, a shabby supermarket and a hairdresser's. These are the basics which the people in the tower blocks need.

– Turn 'ere.

He turns and finds the car going down a ramp, under the tower block.

– It's better. There's a lift straight up. It's safe. I don't want to go in the front. Not like this, I don't.

It was once a car park. Now it seems to be a junkyard, workshop and motor repair shop as well. There are a few cars, some of them stripped down or up on bricks. One is burnt out. He pulls up near the lifts, where she indicates.

– Do you want me to come up with you?

– Nah. I'll be all right. Me mum'll look after me.

She doesn't move. She's too frightened to get out, and he can't blame her. The place is frightening. It's vast and the roof is low so that it's like being in a mine working. The walls, as far as he can see, have been sprayed on every available inch with slogans like 'Motherfuckers', 'Palace', 'NWA', 'Cool 2' and 'Wanker'. All the usual things, as well as that illegible script which they use like Sanskrit or Cyrillic for the names of gangs. Also, an errant thought, he has seen so many underground car parks used in gangster movies as places where terrible things happen, anonymous battlegrounds, standing in for urban hell. He keeps the engine running and the lights on. They bounce back off the lift doors and make the girl look very pale, a cholera victim.

– Anthony, she says.

– Yes?

– I need some money. Can you lend me some?

– I'll give you some. I've got about fifty. You can have half.

– *Ta.*

As he reaches for his wallet her hand finds his unready balls and his sleeping cock and rummages there.

– *Wait a minute.*

– *Don't you like it?*

He takes her hand and removes it.

She opens the front of her blouse and pulls her bra down below her breasts, which rest on it lifeless.

– *Come on. You give me the money and you can do what you like. How much you got. You got more than fifty, ain'tcher?*

The rash extends down her chest to her breasts, which are waxy and white, like Luigi's mozzarella. Now she pulls up her skirt and opens her legs. He can see her dark bush.

– *I bet you got a big one. Go on, stick it in. Fuck me.*

She pushes her hips forwards. Horrified, he feels an erection swelling.

– *No, look. I thought I was helping you. Take this money, you can have the lot, here, it's fifty or sixty quid, and get out. I won't say anything or go to the police.*

She snatches the keys and throws them out of the window into the filthy dark. Then she grabs his cock and pulls it roughly and tries to undo his trousers. He pushes her strong, blotchy arm away.

– *I'll give you French. C'mon.*

She's wildly agitated and her breath falls on him heavily, as though she has already been having sex. It doesn't smell natural. Now he realises that she has a whore's face. It's got that battered look, battered from the inside. She lunges for his cock again, partly unzipping his fly. But he grabs her wrist and holds it. It's not easy. With the other hand she is trying to get at his face. He holds her off.

– *No, don't do that. Just get out now, okay?*

Maybe she's on drugs, or maybe it's street toughness, but she is surprisingly strong, the muscles in her arm convulsing. He pushes her, not too hard, but she comes back at him and gets one leg over his legs so that her breasts are almost in his face.

– *What the fuck you doing with my girlfren'?*

A man is standing by the window. He is wearing a baseball cap, dark glasses and a huge, black, shiny jacket. He is holding a gun which he points straight at Anthony's head. His face is brown, but it's hard to tell in this light just how brown.

– *Get out of the car. Get the phone, Chanelle.*

When he gets out of the car, he finds that he is a foot taller than the other man.

– *Look. You can have the money. Take it.*

– *You're going to have to pay for this. You haven't shown my girlfriend any respeck.*

He has a high, edgy voice and a strange accent.

– *I beg your pardon?*

– *You kind of people think you can do anything you like. You can rape my girlfren', you can stand there with your pants open, you can do any fucking thing you want. You don't have no respect. Stand over here in the light.*

– *What do you want? I've said you can have the money.*

– *What do I want? What I want and what Chanelle want is for you to apologise for trying to rape her and to pay for your disrespeck.*

– *Come on, you know what happened. Let's not piss about.*

– *I can see what happened, don't worry. You can't go round behaving like this. I'm gonna have to call the police. You're under arrest, citizen's arrest. Open his wallet.*

The girl opens the wallet and counts the money.

– *Sixty-five quid, Jace.*

– *Cash card?*

– *Yeah, he's got all sorts in 'ere, Jace.*

– *Visa?*

– *Yeah, and Switch and Access and somefink else.*

– *Right. We're going to the bank. Behave yourself or I'll shoot you.*

Anthony hopes that Mike is awake, but he can't be sure. If he wakes now, God knows what might happen. Jason stands just a few feet from him. At times the gun is almost touching him, nosing him. He is unable to keep still. He looks to Anthony like one of those schoolboys he sees, rolling, slouching, sauntering out of the school gates. The pistol is waving about. He is wearing an ANC amulet around his neck, the map of Africa in green, black and gold. Anthony wonders wildly if he can tell him about Cape Town.

– *Okay. Now you take everything out of your pockets and put it on the front of the car.*

Anthony's hands are shaking. He removes the plane tickets, his chequebook, a pen, his Travelcard. A memo he should have read, a pamphlet from the Swedenborg Society, a tube of peppermints, some change, Fergus's report. (He hasn't read it because he finds schoolteachers' judgements disturbing. They're a judgement on him too.)

– *And your watch. Chanelle, get his watch.*

Anthony hopes they don't go to the car looking for his briefcase.

– *Right. You gonna pay for this. You gonna walk with Chanelle just ahead of me. You go where she says. When we come to the bank, there's two banks there, you gonna draw all the money you can on all your cards. Right? And when we've done that we gonna let you go. If you been good. You go to the police, Chanelle gonna tell 'em you brought her down here to fuck her. And then you start to beat her up and wouldn't pay and that's where I come along. To help her. You get the idea. You gonna have to explain to your wife and your boss what you were doing with this girl down here? Or I could just shoot you. Unnerstan'? You paying for your lack of respect.*

– *I understand. I can probably draw out two fifty on each card.*

– *That's good. But you better be'ave. Orright?*

His voice has come down from the high, nervous register. He's from Birmingham, judging by the way he says 'all right'. Anthony's mind is veering and lurching.

The girl starts to walk and he falls in beside her. They walk past the lifts, which he can see now are derelict, the doors bent and fused, the call buttons like blind eyes or cracked marbles. The place is almost silent, except for a deep hum as though there are giant electric turbines somewhere behind the concrete. Chanelle opens a heavy door, faced in sheets of metal, and leads the way up some stairs. Anthony has to follow behind her as there is not room for them to walk side by side. Her backside is broad, too big for her flabby, shapeless legs. He is painfully knotted with expectation, worse, far worse, than before a match. His stomach and his breathing apparatus and his neck are locked in a spasm. It must be shock. He should be frightened, but he feels instead a sort of crazy excitement. He glances behind him. Jason is close, with the gun out of sight, but his right hand is in the voluminous pocket of his jacket, presumably still pointing the gun at him.

The stairway is lit by one bulkhead light buried in the concrete somewhere above them. At the top of the stairs the girl pushes open another metal door. They are in the hallway of the tower block, where stairways and ramps and rubbish chutes converge. The walls are crazed with graffiti. There are other doorways leading off this hall but they are all metal-shuttered and bolted. A long walkway leads off to another tower where there are many hutch doors, each with a small barred window. The girl walks across the hall and out of the front door which leads to an area of concrete terraces with neatly arranged concrete slabs, presumably for sitting on, and huge tubs which once contained plants, but are now full of bottles and lager cans. He notices all these things without an idea of why he is logging them.

    – *Walk next to Chanelle.*

These terraces are blearily yellow from the sodium lights overhead, out of reach, on poles. An old woman passes, with that curly perm the old favour, and she is muttering under her breath. Anthony thinks she is saying, *I dunno, I dunno, I really dunno, I dunno, I really dunno.*

Jason comes up behind them as the girl stops.

    – *Where is it now? Which way, Jace?*

    – *Jesus. Don't be a stupid cunt. Turn left here, follow that path. Jesus.*

    – *Oh yeah. I forgot wha' you said. I remember.*

They walk down the steps across a piazza designed for pedestrians who would stroll this way to the high street, pausing to greet one another. Anthony thinks of that moment when you break free of the clutching hands, which happens occasionally, after the quick break or outside swerve or dummy frees you from the constraints of the game and releases you, and there you are running upfield, free, exhilarated but lonely. Your lungs are bursting and your legs are beginning to drain, as much from the knowledge of sudden freedom as the endless yards still to be covered. He thinks of Rory, and how a sight of the open spaces electrifies him. And now Anthony decides to escape; it can't be difficult. He will push the girl suddenly and run, weaving as he used to when the cover was after him The boy may fire, or he may not. Even if he does, he's unlikely to hit him.

    – *Stop*, says Jason.

From his pocket he pulls out some cable ties, already looped together. He looks round quickly, his back to the exit from the pathway.

– *Chanelle, hold these. Put your hand in here. Chanelle, put your hand there. The other one. Pull tight.*

With a quick tug, Chanelle locks them together.

– *Okay, let's go. Just in case you was thinking of getting clever.*

The pathway leads to the main road, down which Anthony drives every day. It's a part of his worm trail home. But the familiarity makes him afraid now. Before, down in the clanking dungeon of the garage and through the echoing, barely inhabited tower block, he had a feeling of being in somebody else's story. Survivors always say, *You don't believe it's really happening,* and he now understands the irresistible force of the cliché. The agitated little Jason and the lumpy Chanelle have now become very real in the familiar high street. He farts. Yes, his bowels are loosening too.

– *Right, straight over to Barclays and draw the whole lot. Okay, unnerstan' me?*

– *Yes.*

He hopes to see a police car, but he's not sure what he can do, bound to the girl.

– *If you try anyfing I'll shoot you.*

It's more likely the boy will run if there is trouble, leaving him and the girl awkwardly yoked together. Cars go by. Nobody takes any notice of them and he has no way of signalling to them. No mental powers strong enough to stop them and attract their human concern.

15

Geraldine eats a small amount of chili and rice. She closed the curtains some time ago.

She leaves a note for them on the table: *I'm tired. Had to go to bed. Long day. Welcome Mike. There's some chili on the stove. Just heat through. Night, night. G.*

She leaves the best silver and glasses on the table to show that she made an effort and goes upstairs. Nowadays she likes more classic clothes; the parents and the support committee see her differently since she qualified and it's affected the way she dresses. She takes off the new skirt and matching jacket, not so new that she looks dressed up. She put on the Nicole Farhi suit for Mike, and now she's hanging it up unseen. She goes to find her nightie. Naked, she feels weighed down, although she is in pretty good trim, with her feet too flat on the ground and her hips too heavy. All her friends, except Leonora, are becoming more earthbound. Perhaps they should go skiing, if they can afford it. She's got some money in a deposit account. She skis far better than Anthony, although they have only been twice. In the morning she'll ring Cowgate Travel and see what they've got. She slips on the nightie. She won't be able to sleep. She walks through to Fergus's room. Now he's lying on his back with one arm flung across his body, the rabbit duvet on the floor. She picks it up. In these countless small actions she sees her life being painted, the way the Impressionists used dots of colour. She believes that the picture will emerge fully some day. Anthony seems to be looking for more sudden revelation, although he wouldn't put it that way. He hides his feelings. She sees that as a mother you simply get on with the tasks, the unavoidable things, which cover such a range from the near-spiritual to picking up the duvet, because the blood dictates it.

She admires Anthony all the same, for the reason he admires Mike, because he has tried to keep himself intact, unalloyed. He has some strange enthusiasms: like his almost religious belief in Nelson Mandela. Her classes suggest – although she doesn't accept everything by any means – that there are personality types who are burying early traumas. Anthony's mother once said that the death of his brother affected them all badly; Freddie never really recovered, but Anthony appeared to escape untouched. That's the way people used to think, unaware of how dissociation works. There's obviously some connection between Clive's death in Africa and Anthony's hopes of redemption through Mandela. It's interesting how religious themes recur in people's minds. Mr Freedman believes that religion corresponds to a map of the unconscious, although she hasn't quite followed him along that track. Nor has she agreed to follow him along the track to Mind and Body at Olympia. As she said to Leonora, it's the body he seems most interested in.

She sits on the edge of Fergus's bed. And she begins to weep softly. For Mike, for Anthony, for the gently undulating Fergus.

16 ∫

– Okay, let's go.

They cross the road, he and Chanelle together and Jason right behind his shoulder, like three friends. People will imagine he and Chanelle are holding hands. She's frightened of Jason. Tying them together incapacitates her as well. He glances at her. With her free hand she is still rubbing her face. Her face is empty. His chest is tight: he is still sucking in the air, making an effort. They are at the cash dispenser. Jason looks around.

– Okay, now here's your Visa card.

He gives it to Anthony from behind. With his right hand, Anthony feeds the card into the machine. He punches in his pin number. Eight one one eight, which is his mother's birthday. Jason writes it on the palm of his hand. The screen registers the pin number with a row of four stars. Anthony is offered a choice: cash, cash with receipt, statement, or other service. He punches the button marked 'cash'. Jason is standing so close that he can feel his breath. The screen offers him a choice of amount. It goes in multiples to two hundred, or he can opt for 'other amount'. He chooses 'other amount'.

– It will give me two fifty.

– Try five hundred.

He types five hundred, but the response is 'Exceeds daily limit' in green letters.

– Okay. Get two fifty.

He types the numbers. The transaction is accepted. His card emerges, followed by the tightly packed money. Jason takes it. Anthony has always wondered where the cash is stored back there. It is one of the trivial mysteries of everyday life. Jason is agitated; he's hopping from leg to leg.

– *Try another hundred.*

He goes through the whole process, until the machine says 'Exceeds daily limit' again.

– *Okay. Give me that card. You try this one.*

– *That's not a cash card.*

It's a card which says that Mr Dingle is his new account executive at the bank.

– *Try it. I want to see.*

Anthony tries, but it is rejected instantly.

– *Okay, back across the road.*

They cross to the Halifax Building Society. Anthony is not familiar with these Link machines, but Jason seems to know. He hands him his Access card, which he seldom uses. The procedure is different. Anthony has difficulty reading the instructions. He finds it impossible to read the words. They seem to fall in no order. He is offered a choice of languages. He presses 'Italian'.

– *Hurry up. Orright? We haven't got all fucking night, orright.*

Jason is jumpy. A small window slides back. After each request, you have to press 'enter' on the keypad; his pin number is 7881, Fergus's birthday. Jason writes it down on his hand. Anthony becomes angry. Why should this little, barrel-chested bastard use his son's birthday for his drug habit? The anger rises from some deep level; it feels as though it is originating in his stomach and flying outwards. His lungs ease. He sees the dispenser more clearly. The instructions are simple. He punches the buttons. I'm going to kill the bastard, he thinks. He's breathing easily now. Two hundred comes out of the machine and the window closes. He hands it to Chanelle. She drops it and falls to one knee, forgetting they are tied together, so that his wrist is pulled downwards sharply.

– *Jesus H. Christ*, says Jason. *Try again for another hundred.*

He goes through it again, and finds he can get another hundred which he hands over.

– *That's it, that's the limit. It says so on the back of the card.*

– *Now we go back to your car. You wait there for half an hour before you look for the keys. And don't go to the police, like I said, or I'll tell them you tried to beat up Chanelle. They know Chanelle. She's never been in no serious trouble. Let's go.*

Anthony wonders if it's true. He thinks Jason may shoot him when they get back to the garage.

– Okay, now when we get into the lane, I'll take off the cuffs. When we go through the estate, you just act natural, like you was walking along, orright?

– I understand.

They turn into the pathway to the estate. Jason takes a small pair of cutters out of his pocket, and turns his back on the High Street so no one can see what he's doing. He hands it to Anthony.

– Cut through them. Hers too.

Anthony snips through the nylon ties although his hand is still trembling. The skin of his wrist rubs against Chanelle's for a moment. Then a strange thing happens. He looks up, and there, above Jason's head, framed in the entrance to the pathway to the estate, he sees Mike passing slowly. He is whistling 'Swing low sweet chariot, comin' for to carry me home'. He looks like a drunk, a tall, unsteady drunk, as he walks down the High Street and out of sight.

– Right, same as before. You go with Chanelle. Be'ave or I'll shoot you.

They start to walk in their formation towards the piazza in front of the tower block, which rises into the impure air above them.

It is a short sprint for Mike, from the High Street. He rounds the corner into the pathway at full speed. Anthony hears his feet slapping and turns before Jason or Chanelle. Mike is huge. He seems to fill the whole footpath. Anthony sees him just as he was on a rugby field, filled with unthinking joy. Before Jason is fully turned towards him, trying to get the gun out, Mike hits him with his shoulder right in the chest. Jason goes over backwards and his head strikes the soiled paving slabs.

– He's got a gun, shouts Anthony. It's a strangely familiar cry.

Mike is on top of Jason, and Anthony grabs his arm as the gun comes up. Mike smashes him in the face with his forearm. Jason's wrist escapes from Anthony. It is full of panicky strength. His cap has come off and his hair stands up in a quiff on the top of his head. Anthony grabs his arm again, trying to point the gun away from Mike.

Anthony feels the burning sensation, a terrible burning as though something hot has been pushed into his chest, before he hears the report, which is deafening. He has no sense of the speed of the bullet at all, only this slow, igniting pain.

Three

People work much in order to secure the future; I gave my mind much work and trouble trying to secure the past.

Karen Blixen

The mountains are hazy at this time of day. They are violet, shading to black in their many valleys and rifts. Although they are blurred, the sky above them is clear, so that the blue is both a flat surface and an infinite sea of blueness, like a picture from space. As he looks at the mountains they are changing colour. They change as if paint were running down from the tops and gathering in the folds. He recognises the mountains. They are the mountains that he saw out of his bedroom window in Swaziland. He feels drawn to them: he is back in their force-field as he was when he was a boy. He sees now that the mountains are the cathedrals that tower over the plains. They have a massive surplus of mystery over the flatlands.

The pain in his chest is spreading up into his jaw. It seems to be travelling up his bones, the way heat travels up the metal handle of a frying pan. But the pain has become softer; by moving outwards from his chest, it has lost some of its intensity.

The mountains are not subject to the same physical laws as the plains. It can be raining up there while down here the earth is gasping for moisture. Up there, sun can fall on the rocks, making them richly golden or red, while the plains are already subdued and drab. The mountains are as familiar to him, and they cause him the same tremulousness, as when he was seven or eight. Perhaps this is what Geraldine is talking about, with her memories. People say that aromas are more evocative of childhood than any other sense. It could be true, he thinks, because now he can smell the mountains; the scent is so strong and so familiar that he wonders how he could have forgotten it. It's a smell of tough plants and implacable minerals. It's a scent which used to waft down to the house to remind him of Clive who was buried up there. It's Clive's smell.

There is something warm on his cheeks; he can't lift his hand to wipe it away, but he knows that it must be tears. They seem to be flowing very freely, almost gushing, like that statue of a saint in Italy which cries blood once a year for believers.

Now he can hear voices but he can't see anybody. He can only see the sky, a sky, his father would say, as clear as gin, and beneath the sky the familiar mountains. He closes his eyes to staunch the tears. The voices are louder now, a great crowd incomprehensible but thrilling, like the noise of a rugby crowd in the distance when you are approaching the stadium. He tries to open his eyes, but they appear to have become glued shut as though his tears are gummy.

But he is still bathed in the aromatic gusts off the mountains. When he was a boy the guardians of the graves used to sit in the forest directly below the rockface all day. They were like the guards in the British Museum, pointedly doing nothing for hours on end. The forest they inhabited was not large, perhaps thirty acres, one of the forests which grew only in the clefts of the mountains and provided a home for monkeys and bushpigs. Bushpigs could be unpredictable, his father said, although he never met a victim of their moods. The guardians were old men. They had a faraway, stoned look in their yellowing eyes. Their actions were very deliberate, like those of chameleons. Before the sun set they would come down from the forest and head back to their village, which was sending smoke spirals into the sky inviting them home for porridge and tea.

Now his eyes are open again. He doesn't realise it immediately. The pain in his chest and jaw is bubbling, it's effervescent. It's prickling behind his eyes so that he feels the light like the spray of a waterfall, inside his eyes. His eyes clear. Where he could see only the mountains and the sky, he can now see the plain. He sees a road and on the road crowds of people whose voices reach him. The voices enter his thorax and make it tingle. He tries to move but he cannot; he can't make out where he is or whether he is standing, sitting or lying down. Now he sees some gates and a surge of people at the gates. They are walking through the gates and towards him. He thinks they may have walked down from the mountain behind, although he cannot remember these gates. They're probably new; things move on. And as they come closer, he sees that there is a knot of people in the middle of the crowds, which is stirring them into movement. But before he can see what's going on, his eyes close again and he is tumbling about uncontrolled. The light and the pain and the noise have all become one. The sensation makes him feel sick, like reaching the highest point on a roller-coaster or slowing too fast in a lift.

When he can see again after a time – he doesn't know how long he's been asleep, or away – the knot of people is right upon him. In the middle is an old man with greying hair. His face is smiling. Anthony recognises him instantly. He's wearing a suit and he's lost weight, but there's no question who it is. And the old man walks towards him: he detaches himself from his group and walks with that near smile towards Anthony.

He stops in front of him and says, *Hello, my boy. Are you ready to join the regiments this time?*

– *Yes sir, I'm ready now.*

– *Good, that's the ticket.*

And then he has to go. Of course. But it is amazing that he should remember.

– *Mike*, he says, *Mike, can you see him?*

His eyes close. He feels the tears flowing again. He has no say at all in whether or not he stays awake. He drifts off now, wondering where Mike could be. It would be typical of him to miss it.

When he wakes again, if he has been asleep, he can no longer see the mountains or anything else, but he can hear a voice calling his name quietly.

– *Hello*, he says. *Where have you been?*

– *Oh God, Anthony. Oh, Ant.*

He can't say any more and he can't see her, but he's pleased Geraldine's there and a little guilty for having been away.

Anthony's eyes close again and when they open he can see her, although dimly.

– *Hello*, he says again.

– *Oh, Anthony.*

– *Where's Mike?*

She doesn't answer. She can't find the words. From this he knows that something terrible has happened. And now he can see that he is attached to plastic tubes which enter his nose and his arm. Geraldine is leaving. She is hurrying towards the door. He's frightened her. He must be dying.

But no, she soon returns with someone in a white coat.

– *Hello Mr Northleach. How do you feel?*

– *A bit sore.*

Four ∫

Someone must have been telling lies about Joseph K, for without having done anything wrong, he was arrested one morning.

Franz Kafka

∫

November 1990

– Court rise.

The freelance writer Julian Capper rises, standing among the diffident little herd which is the jury. He's had a poor night. He likes to start each day fresh. There's a Carpathian proverb which he treasures: *The wise farmer keeps his chickens in the roost at night, so that his wife may enjoy omelettes.* There is a second version, which concludes, *so that his wife may prosper at the market.* He likes to think of his mental resources as chickens. He likes to see them early to bed, fed, watered, et cetera, so that they may produce eggs in the morning.

But he has been worrying about whether or not his fellow jurors will elect him foreman. It's a small thing, he knows, even petty, but he feels that it is essential he should guide them in reaching a verdict, which will be more difficult if they do not recognise him as their natural leader. In fact, because he has already been too vocal in their early, informal discussions in the canteen over a cup of coffee, and because he has had a run-in with Keith, the personal fitness trainer, and because he has seen a group of the other members of the jury taking lunch together, as if by some unexpressed conviviality which does not include him: he fears, for all these reasons, that they have already lined up against him. If this is so it will be doubly difficult to make his views count. And his views are likely to be unpopular at first, because he has divined that his fellow jurors are inclined to believe that a black pimp who goes out to rob armed with a gun doesn't deserve sympathy.

These concerns have kept him awake.

They stand until the judge has found his seat. Joyce, their bailiff, smiles at them to indicate that they may sit down. She has other duties, apart from marshalling them, like handing round the evidence. She passed around the gun, in its plastic envelope, to verify what it was. Exactly what was it? A .45 Webley which the police said was the gun which fired the four shots, one of which had been recovered from Anthony Northleach's upper right sternocleidomastoid, after having passed through the lung and broken a rib en route and having passed through Michael Frame's body before that. Two of the other three bullets had been recovered from the footpath and the third from Jason Parchment's skull itself. The last three bullets had killed Jason Parchment. There has been plenty of discussion about the path of the bullets. The jury have been shown diagrams. The accepted version now is that the first bullet first passed through Michael Frame, wounding him fatally, and then struck Anthony Northleach.

The circumstances in which Jason Parchment came to be killed are the subject of the trial. But the purpose of handing around the gun is to bring the jury to their senses. Look, this is the sort of thing you are dealing with. This is the sort of person we are talking about, the sort of person who could go out with something like this in his pocket.

While Jason Parchment's criminal proclivities have been mentioned often, the character of the other deceased, Michael Frame, has not been fully explored, not to Julian Capper's satisfaction anyway, although both the prosecution and the defence seem to be content to leave his character unexplained. They don't agree on anything else. They don't agree on how Northleach's car came to be in a garage of one of the most crime-ridden, drug-raddled, burned-out housing estates in London, a place so notorious that it had been featured in a weekend supplement as the most dangerous place in Britain, with a mortality rate only slightly better than the slums of Kingston, Jamaica. (That's how they slip in the racial quotient.) What's more, a place which was tolerated by the police and the local authorities as the last resort of the criminal, the drug-addicted and the socially dysfunctional. If you wanted to find a place that symbolised both the decay of the inner city and – in Julian Capper's view, more importantly – the decay of the human spirit, you would choose the Bevan North estate. You would have to be wilfully blind not to know it and not to know that the area around Bevan North was crawling with prostitutes and drug dealers day and night. Elderly women have been raped there. Asian shopkeepers have been knifed for a can of Coke. There had been newspaper articles about that too.

And also, of course, which the prosecution seems to have forgotten, but which Julian Capper proposes to bring up in the jury's deliberations, Mr Northleach, the ex-rugby player and 'company director' (also ex) passed down this road five days a week for seven years, presumably asleep or driving with a blindfold or trying to tune in to sports programmes on his flashy, five-band car radio, or perhaps calling his mistress on his car phone to arrange their little meetings, while his wife (alas, now also ex) sat at home teaching children with learning difficulties. Northleach's mistress has recounted her story to the newspapers: their affair started many years ago when his wife was in hospital with complications after the birth of their first and only child. It resumed when she returned to England. He was an insatiable lover. On the day of the killings he had offered to take her to Cape Town.

It's all too easy for Keith to say that these are matters they should ignore, that they are not evidence, but Julian Capper will be pointing out to them that the evidence is not as clear-cut as they think. For instance, can you rely on the evidence of a man who was unconscious for six days and believed he was in Cape Town when he woke up in Guy's Hospital? A fact which the defence seems to think entitles him to special treatment. Some of these barristers act as though they only have to turn up, unprepared, to collect the fee. The defence has tried to suggest, although not in so many words, that Jason Parchment was not quite British. They can't say that, of course, but there was an elaborate pantomime to establish that his father was believed to live in Sierra Leone, and that his name on the birth certificate is Ndongo, and that he had been brought up, entirely at the state's expense, in a children's home in Hanley, Birmingham and at various young offenders' institutions. Northleach, by contrast, was once selected for a trial for the England B rugby team. He is the son of a bank manager. The defence has also insisted on passing around, via Joyce, pictures of Jason Parchment's clothes placed on a dummy without a face. These are supposed to make it easier to understand the sequence of events, but they are obviously largely designed to make him look sinister. In the pictures he is wearing a capacious hooded jacket, voluminous trousers, dark glasses and a baseball cap with 'Los Angeles Raiders' written on it. Round his neck is an ANC badge. He is wearing giant black Nike trainers. Also part of the evidence in the photos is a portable phone and some credit cards – allegedly belonging to Northleach – ammunition, a bundle of nylon wire ties and a balaclava, which were all found in Parchment's many pockets. He looks, in short, like a dangerous black pimp. Of course, the photographs do not reveal that he was only five foot five inches tall and barely twenty years old. Julian Capper has made a note to remind his colleagues of this in his summing up. He feels that he should point out these glaringly obvious, even insultingly obvious, ploys to his fellow jurors. He will also tell them, in case they are unaware of it, that this is how young black men habitually dress. But because of his hasty comments earlier and the prickly atmosphere between him and Keith and the subsequent pained reaction to him on the part of some of the others, he fears that his views may be brushed aside.

The judge, Mr Justice Applethwaite, who wears a red gown with a black sash, is looking at his papers. When he begins to speak, it is with the clearly enunciated diction of someone who is used to talking to simple people.

– *I am going to repeat what I said to you at the start of this trial: it is for you and nobody else to determine the facts in this case. You will make the decisions. My job is to direct you on matters of law. You are obliged to follow my directions. I will now sum up for you the evidence and I will, where necessary, tell you what questions of law arise and which you must take into consideration in a case like this, involving the loss of life and serious injury.*

The jurors sit in two rows looking across the lawyers to the defendant. The judge is to their left. Julian Capper is sitting in the front row, as near to the judge as possible.

– *The point of fact which you will have to decide is this: did Anthony Northleach, the defendant, act in self-defence, legitimate self-defence, using only that much force as was necessary, or as any reasonable person would have considered necessary under the circumstances, in killing Mr Parchment? You have heard the prosecution claim, and you have heard the evidence of Miss Carole Smith, that Mr Frame tackled Mr Parchment, Mr Northleach joined in, the gun went off. Mr Northleach, in his evidence, did not dispute this version of events. The prosecution then say that Mr Frame punched Mr Parchment who was lying on the ground. They say that Mr Northleach, who had wrestled the gun from Mr Parchment, and was himself severely wounded, as you have heard, then shot Mr Parchment three times in the head. This is what the prosecution say happened. The crucial difference in these accounts is that the prosecution say that Mr Parchment was knocked unconscious before the shots were fired. Either from the force of the blow or from the fact that his head had struck the ground, Mr Parchment was inert, they say, when Mr Northleach fired, and no threat was presented to him or Mr Frame. The defence say that Mr Parchment fired first. They say that you cannot be sure that there was any intention to kill Mr Parchment or that his death was anything but an accident and, second, even if you are sure that it was deliberate, that Mr Northleach was acting in self-defence, believing that Mr Parchment intended to kill one or both of them. The forensic evidence certainly confirms that Mr Parchment was shot three times in the head at close range. The defence say that there was a scuffle after Mr Frame bravely tackled Mr Parchment, the gun went off in the confusion four times, and three of these shots killed Mr Parchment. The defence say that there was no intention to kill Mr Parchment, and furthermore, they say that Mr Northleach was acting in self-defence, believing that Mr Parchment intended to kill one or both of them. Mr Northleach has told you, and you must decide whether or not you believe him, that he has only the haziest recollection of what went on after the moment of being shot himself. It certainly appears that the whole event took place in a few, confused seconds. So what you have to decide is how Mr Parchment came to be killed. Are you sure that he was intentionally killed by Mr Northleach using more force than was necessary under the circumstances, or was Mr Northleach, or may he have been, justified in killing Mr Parchment on the grounds of self-defence? Remember, if you are to convict the defendant, you must be satisfied beyond a reasonable doubt. The prosecution must prove every aspect of their case; the defence is not obliged to prove anything.*

Things have not gone well for Northleach since the shooting. He and his wife are living apart, his mother has died and the company for which he worked has failed. Julian Capper imagines some justice in this. Northleach was a director of one of those fly-by-night companies which burgeoned under Mrs Thatcher. And now, just eight months later, Mrs Thatcher has been replaced and the company, like so many others, has gone into liquidation. Northleach has sat in the dock motionless, except for a gentle swaying at key moments. Occasionally he beckons the solicitors in the benches in front of him to whisper something to them. Sometimes he smiles in a pained manner at a large, square-rigged young woman in the public gallery, who is said to have been his secretary. He has had surgery to repair the nerves to his lower jaw and is very thin. His face, once probably beefy, is now drawn and lopsided. His suit, a double-breasted junior executive suit, looks as though it belongs to a man considerably larger. Julian is reminded of how he looked when he had to wear his brother's cast-offs.

The defence has made much of his injuries. There has been a lot of medical evidence rich with long words: *Damage to the sternocleidomastoid muscles . . . severing of the mandibular ganglia . . . rupturing of the trapezius . . .* The truth is, he is standing proxy for his friend who was killed. But his relationship to Michael Frame, a bankrupt, a wife-beater and a man who was unable to hold down a job, has been given the most cursory treatment. They were friends. We must understand that. They were two ordinary men who had played rugby and suffered a few of life's vicissitudes and enjoyed some of its rewards. They were from that unassertive, rootless – to Julian Capper, somewhat sinister – group of people who inhabit southern England, which the defence has called – pretending to quote – 'the bedrock of society'. Jason Parchment (born Ndongo) is not from the bedrock of society. He is a product of society's institutions. The defence has told the court of his many convictions and his slide into criminality, feigning some sorrow about the inevitability of the process. They have failed, however, to uncover any convictions for armed robbery or possession of a firearm.

The judge claims to be dealing with points of law, but he has the power to decide which points of law he gives weight to. The jury is straining to give the judge their fullest attention, although Julian Capper in his preliminary, informal discussions, has found that one or two of them have a very short attention span.

– So it will be for you to decide how Mr Parchment came to be killed. Those are the points of law, the issues, if you like. Before I begin a more detailed summary of the evidence, may I remind you that the fact that the defence has painted a picture of Mr Parchment as a drug dealer and a pimp, and that they have pointed out that Mr Parchment had fourteen convictions, that is not in itself proof of anything.

This is how they do it. Just in case you have forgotten who the real villain in this matter is, Mr Justice Applethwaite is there to remind you. The wrong defendant is on trial. Anthony Northleach sits directly across in the dock, the decent man caught up in this urban nightmare (although, of course he is a suburbanite, living until his separation in an estate of 'executive homes', as the defence put it.) Caught up in this dreadful chain of events, his only crime was to help a woman he thought was in trouble. What the defence are saying is that if it were not for all these prostitutes and pushers and pimps, none of this would have happened to a decent man. There has been an invasion of dear old leafy England by a new, and unwelcome, culture which cares nothing and knows less about the tolerance and respect which once, not that long ago as a matter of fact, prevailed in our country. This seems to be a second line of defence: if, on some technicality, you are thinking of finding him guilty, bear in mind who is really to blame.

– You will have to decide not if Mr Parchment was a pimp, but if, as Miss Carole Smith has told the court, Mr Northleach seized the gun after Mr Parchment was already helpless, possibly even unconscious, and fired deliberately three times. You have heard the ballistics expert say that the last three shots fired were the ones which struck Mr Parchment. In order to reach a verdict, you will have to decide if these three shots were, or may have been, part of a scuffle for the gun as the defence maintains, or a deliberate act by Mr Northleach. If you are sure they were a deliberate act,

then you must decide whether they may have been in legitimate self-defence.

Miss Smith has told the court that Mr Northleach was screaming, 'I am going to kill you, you bastard.' You will have to decide whether you can believe her evidence. You have heard evidence that Miss Smith is a crack cocaine addict, and you have heard at some length from experts the effects that addiction is likely to have. You have heard that Miss Smith has numerous convictions for soliciting. She is, in the old-fashioned and possibly pejorative terms which our law still employs, a common prostitute. She also has various other convictions for shoplifting and malicious damage. Of course this does not necessarily mean, as the defence has said, that you must disregard her evidence entirely. You may believe all of it, some of it, or none of it. She may have lied about some aspects of the matter and spoken the truth in others.

But you must also ask yourself this question: in the horrifying circumstances of the night of February fifth earlier this year, whatever Mr Northleach did, is it possible for you to be sure that he acted in deliberate cold blood when pulling the trigger, or may it have been self-defence? You will have to decide if there were two distinct phases in this ten- or fifteen-second sequence of events which led to two deaths. The first phase, undisputed, is that Mr Frame rugby-tackled, as the defence put it, Mr Parchment and that Mr Northleach tried to seize the gun which the deceased, Mr Parchment, had removed from his pocket. A shot was fired which resulted in the death of Mr Frame and the wounding of Mr Northleach. All that was a matter of seconds. Phase two, in the prosecution's case, then commences. Mr Frame, despite being fatally injured, punches Mr Parchment who is lying on the ground senseless, Mr Northleach seizes the gun and turns it on Mr Parchment, firing three times. You will have to decide whether it is possible so to divide the overall incident into these two phases. You will also have to decide the significance of the fact that these three shots were undoubtedly fired at very close range and that there is no sign of Mr Parchment having been moving at the time. All three bullets entered his head from the front. You have heard evidence that Mr Parchment was declared dead when the ambulance arrived and that Mr Frame died in hospital about forty minutes later and that Mr Northleach later lapsed into unconsciousness. You will have to decide whether you can draw any conclusion from the evidence of the police officer first on the scene, Police Constable Blakely, that Mr Northleach was holding the gun, kneeling beside Mr Frame, when he arrived. Is it or may it be right to describe Mr Northleach's actions as brave, instinctive reactions to a very real threat – after all, Mr Parchment was in possession of a gun – and which led to the act of self-defence, or did Mr Northleach go on to carry out an unnecessary act of revenge?

The defence have invited you to consider what would have happened if Mr Parchment had retained possession of the gun. The defence have also described Mr Northleach's character and you have heard a very different account of his character from the prosecution. These are not facts. They are designed to sway you to believe one or other account of what happened. But on a point of law I must instruct you, and you are obliged to follow my instruction, to ignore anything you may have read in the newspapers that was not produced as evidence in this court. In particular I refer to the story which appeared in the People newspaper regarding a Mrs Francine Batt, who claimed that Mr Northleach appeared desperate on the day of the incident and that Mr Northleach was her lover and that Mr Northleach was proposing to leave the country that week for good, to escape his wife and failing business career. Mrs Batt received money for her story from the newspaper in question. She has not been a witness in this case and there has been no opportunity for the court to hear her evidence – if evidence it be – or to cross-examine her. You must disregard anything you have read absolutely.

Julian Capper sees the way this is going. He's some distance ahead of the judge. Under the pretence of being helpful and judicial, the judge is clearly establishing the difficulty of being absolutely certain of what happened. He has virtually said that Northleach could not have formulated the intent to kill Parchment in the available time. He has undermined the evidence of Carole Smith too, without pointing out that she could have no obvious reason for lying, that she saw Northleach deliberately fire the gun three times shouting, *I'm going to kill you, you bastard*, while Parchment was lying on the ground unconscious with Frame slumped on top of him. Julian Capper has noted the tone of his remarks. *You may decide whether or not you can believe her evidence . . . a crack cocaine addict . . . you have heard from experts the effects of this addiction . . .*

He is choosing to ignore the fact that two large men, former rugby players, jumped on a petty thief, a would-be mugger and small-time hash dealer, a five-foot-five-inch boy, knocked him unconscious and shot him dead. He has ignored the evidence that it may have been Northleach who inadvertently shot his friend in the scuffle. This theory, put to Northleach by Kirsty Badenoch, QC, was ruled out but not before Northleach said haltingly, *God, I hope not. It has crossed my mind.* The judge stepped in, forbidding such speculation. He knew that the prosecution wanted to draw Northleach into admitting that he was angry. But the judge has allowed the defence to make a meal of his friendship with Frame, although this is just as speculative.

In Julian Capper's opinion it was a strangely destructive friendship. The two friends were able to justify their weaknesses, particularly their ambivalence towards women, by appeals to their friendship. No doubt before too long the judge will be reminding them of the long duration and manliness of their friendship. Julian Capper remembers Carole Smith's tears as she described her affection for Jason and his love for her child Bradley. No mention of that, of course.

And then there was the hokum about Nelson Mandela. The two men, according to the defence, were going to Cape Town to witness Mandela's release. What a marvellously convenient excuse for the fact that they had bought plane tickets to Cape Town where, as the rather wild-eyed Mrs Babette Frame had testified, Frame had a 'few friends' including some women. The attempt by the defence to link their client to the euphoria and idealism surrounding Mandela's release, rather than to the 'rugby-club type jolly', as Mrs Badenoch phrased it, was transparently bogus. Even some of the members of the jury whom Julian Capper has been able to canvass had seen that. But they hadn't been aware that there was another motive: to free Northleach from any suggestion of racism by pretending that Mandela was his hero. (It was while he was making this point in the canteen that the run-in with Keith took place. Keith used the phrase 'boring fart'.) And the judge, having explained to them the relative weight they should attach to the evidence of the witnesses, will now be asking them as a logical consequence which segment of society they are backing: the vicious underclass or the decent (if flawed) majority. But instead he says, *I will continue my summing up this afternoon. We will break now for lunch. Please be back at two o'clock. And*

members of the jury, do not talk to anyone about the case during your lunch break.
– Court rise.

They rise and stand transfixed not by the judge himself, Julian Capper thinks, but out of deference to the idea that the courts are a bastion against moral disorder. Of course the courts are only dealing with the results of social changes, changes in the climate which have been brought about by people at a level way above that of Jason Parchment or Carole Smith. Or the jury, for that matter. The judge – he can just see a flash of his red robe as his personal door closes – is trying to enlist them against the seething menace from the lawless. But the truth is the menace from that quarter is greatly exaggerated because it suits those in power. They need the notion of threat to lend some urgency to their prescriptions for society.

The defendant in turn disappears from sight, down his staircase. He looks dazed.

The jury room is predominantly brown, a version of the prevailing colour of the court itself, but of cheaper materials. The carpet, the chairs and the wall are autumnal.

Julian Capper tries to detain Lynne with an anodyne remark: *– Gets more interesting by the minute.* But she smiles very briefly and says, *Yeah,* before hurrying after the main body of the jurors led by Keith towards the canteen.

There are many jurors in the building, waiting in a large holding area to be called. He remembers a book he has read in which two jurors become lovers. It was in Chicago. It doesn't seem very likely here. But Keith has attracted admirers with his muscular definition and, who knows, perhaps they go back to his house at the end of the day. Julian Capper sometimes wonders if, by trying to inhabit the intellectual landscape, he isn't missing out on the easy friendship that the less burdened people seem to be able to strike up. Friendship is a prized asset, as the defence has kept reminding them. The friendship between Carole Smith and Jason Parchment has had to be downgraded to a business relationship. She sold her body and he took the money. But Carole Smith described Jason Parchment as her boyfriend without any ambiguity. Kirsty Badenoch, with her Scots accent in moments of stress as harsh as furniture moving, has tried to cast some doubts on the friendship between Northleach and Frame.

– *Would you describe yourself as having been a very close friend of Mr Frame?*

– *I think that is obvious.*

– *Through thick and thin?*

– *If you mean, did I support him in hard times, yes, I did.*

– *Did you, as you say, support him even when he was in the wrong?*

– *What do you mean?*

– *Well, for example, we have heard Mrs Babette Frame's evidence that earlier in the evening you were called to Mrs Frame's house in Greenwich to prevent Mr Frame doing Mrs Frame further violence.*

– *It wasn't quite like that.*

– *It wasn't? Well, let me ask you a specific question. Had Mr Frame hit his wife?*

– *It was a matrimonial dispute.*

– *Could you answer the question.*

– *Yes, he had hit Babette, but it wasn't that simple.*

– *He had hit his wife. And another specific question. Was she bleeding?*

– *Yes, from a minor cut on her lip. What we would call a fat lip.*

– *A fat lip. What do you mean, 'What we would call a fat lip'?*

– *I was thinking in terms of rugby. It's common in rugby.*

– *Oh, it's common in rugby. But her mouth was bleeding?*

– *Yes.*

– *And was she threatening to call the police?*

– *Yes.*

– *And did you give her a cheque for one thousand pounds?*

– *Yes, I did. It was for her mortgage. Mike was broke.*

– *So it wasn't, as we have heard in evidence to prevent her from calling the police, because you were both drunk?*

– *No, I was trying to be helpful,*

– *Her words under oath were, 'He tried to buy me off.'*

– *No, I tried to be helpful.*

– *You tried to be helpful. To whom?*

– *To Mike and Babette.*

– *And what was your attitude to this – as you call it – matrimonial dispute?*

– I was shocked and saddened.

– You were shocked and saddened?

– Yes.

– But is it true that you were so shocked and saddened that you took Mr Frame away with you to a pub where you had a few drinks with your old friend, leaving Mrs Frame to call an ambulance to have her injury – her fat lip – stitched up at Greenwich Hospital?

– I was shocked and saddened that the marriage had come to this.

– But your sympathy seems to have been directed entirely towards Mr Frame. You left Mrs Frame bleeding from a blow, possibly a number of blows, as we have heard in Mrs Frame's evidence, from Mr Frame, who was, may I remind the jury, six feet two inches tall, alone and bleeding to call an ambulance.

– I didn't know at the time. She said she was all right.

– You went to a pub with your old friend and what did you do there?

– We had a drink.

– This was at about nine thirty?

– I think so.

– And what else did you do?

– We talked. Naturally.

– What did you talk about?

– About Mike's future and about Nelson Mandela, as I remember, and about Babette of course.

– Was this while you were watching the show?

– What?

– Was this while you were watching a show?

– Yes.

– And what kind of show was it?

– It was a strip show.

– Involving how many acts?

– Three or four.

– And so, just let me get this straight, while Mrs Babette Frame was trying to summon an ambulance at number 7 Jellicoe Terrace, and your wife was waiting for you at number 4 High Woods, South Godstone, Surrey, you were in the pub watching women strip naked?

– Believe me, it wasn't quite like that.

– Just answer yes or no.

– Yes.

– *Does this, in your opinion, demonstrate a contempt for women, a suggestion that friendship, male friendship, comes above mere domestic considerations?*

– *I don't think so.*

– *Is this leading anywhere, Mrs Badenoch?* asked the judge.

– *I believe it is, my lord. I believe it is enabling the jury to see the background to this terrible incident and it is enabling them to determine the state of mind, not to mention the state of intoxication, of Mr Northleach, both of which the jury may think have some bearing on what happened later.*

– *All right, I'll allow it, but don't be too long.*

– *No, my lord. So, Mr Northleach, after you had left the public house, after a number of drinks, on top of the amount of alcohol you had consumed earlier in the day, estimated by Mr Ludovico Moro of the Trattoria d'Ischia – I believe, yes, that is correct – estimated by Mr Moro to be two bottles of Pinot Grigio and three-quarters of a bottle of Barolo, very alcoholic wines, and at least a couple of liquers . . . am I correct so far?*

– *Yes, but I was not drinking as much as Mike.*

– *You were just keeping him company, as the saying goes, so let's suppose he was drinking twice as much as you. You might not have had much more than half a bottle of white wine and half a bottle of red and one liqueur. Which was sensible, as you were driving home.*

– *Not after lunch.*

– *No, not after lunch, but in the evening. Alcohol, as I am sure I don't need to remind you, is not dispersed from the bloodstream for twelve hours or more. You were driving home, so you were exercising moderation. After the meal at the restaurant it was approximately four p.m. Mr Frame disappeared. Did he say where he was going?*

– *Yes, he said he had to go and see Babette to sort out some financial things.*

– *He didn't say, as Mrs Frame has testified, that he was going to sort her out?*

– *If you mean he was going to beat her up, no.*

– *That's what I do mean. To sort someone out is a common enough term, used in rugby, I believe, quite frequently.*

– *I must object.*

– *Sustained. Mrs Badenoch, what is the purpose of this speculation?*

– *My lord, I'm simply trying to establish the nature of this friendship, because I believe it has considerable bearing on what happened later. As we said in our opening statement, the prosecution believes that there is clear and incontrovertible evidence that Mr Northleach shot and killed Mr Parchment long after he posed any threat, if he had ever posed a threat, and the reason for this may lie in the nature of the relationship between Mr Frame and Mr Northleach.*

– I am going to allow you to continue, Mrs Badenoch, on the condition that I don't want to hear any more conjecture about the nature of the friendship. Stick to the facts as far as you are able.

– Thank you, my lord.

Julian Capper has excellent powers of recall. He is sitting in the jury room alone, eating a sandwich which he made himself at home. Before leaving the house he also sent off a proposal for a monthly column to *The Grocer*. He had not planned to write for trade papers when he became a writer, but they are now the staple of his existence. It is surprisingly easy to familiarise yourself with the language of any trade. He also writes occasionally for *Travel Trade Gazette* on conference facilities, and for *Software User* on new games.

Mrs Badenoch, for the prosecution, painted a wonderfully vivid picture of two drunken, violent, misogynist ex-rugby players. Her purpose – when the judge would allow her – was to demonstrate that they were quite capable of picking up a prostitute. Northleach had covered Frame, who was slumped drunk in the back – perhaps he was just pretending to be asleep – with some old coats because prostitutes will not get into a car with two men. They were picking up a prostitute for a harmless bit of fun, as Mrs Badenoch put it. The striptease in juxtaposition to the violence at Mrs Frame's (a good-looking woman with an imposing bust) was a stroke of genius. He makes a note, between bites, to remember this point in his own, informal summing-up, because the judge won't.

The key to this whole matter is whether or not Northleach asked Carole Smith to get into his car, as Julian Capper has tried to tell his fellow jurors.

– Look before you leap, chum, said Keith somewhat menacingly.

– I have got a mind of me own, you know, said Lynne.

Northleach says that she ran up to his car saying she had been raped and that out of the goodness of his heart he let her in. She says – and the police have confirmed it – that she is a regular on Mount Royal Road, a well-known haunt of prostitutes, that she was there that night and that Northleach stopped to pick her up. She has no record of being involved in blackmail. Jason Parchment was hiding in the garage to keep an eye on her – she was after all his girlfriend – because earlier in the evening a client had hit her and she had refused to go out again unless he drove to the garage first. She was afraid. She is only nineteen and has a child she loves despite the dreadful life she leads. As he finishes his sandwich – York ham on multi-seeded batch loaf – he sees that this is a case which has important resonances. But there is a sense – he wipes his fingers to write down some bullet points – in which the case is symbolic.

The shucking off of responsibility for the weak and defenceless.

The contempt for the unsuccessful and under-privileged.

The promotion of business and market values above individualism.

The attempt to preserve the status quo.

The nostalgic belief in an earlier golden age.

Racial innuendo.

Mr Richard Simmonds, QC, for the defence, implies, without actually saying it, that Jason Parchment comes from a racial group inevitably sucked into drugs, prostitution and crime:

– *Unfortunately, Mr Parchment, after his father returned to Africa, was drawn into juvenile crime in Hanley, Birmingham. When he first arrived in South London he soon became involved in a world, as members of the jury know, where crack cocaine and increasing use of firearms have resulted in a frightening disregard for human life. Members of the jury may think that this life was bound to lead to tragedy. But the tragedy in this case is compounded by the fact that my client, Mr Northleach, was wounded and his friend, Mr Frame, was killed trying to save his life. For this entirely innocent man to be in court charged with murder only serves to underline the unacceptable consequences of this contempt for life in certain sections of our great capital city.*

The black sections. This was followed by a quick reminder of the Mandela fairy story. Northleach had said that he was expecting some sort of revelation from Mandela.

– *Could you describe what it was that you were looking for?* asked his barrister.

— Is this relevant, Mr Simmonds?

— It has some bearing on the question of the aeroplane tickets, my lord.

— In what way?

— In that the prosecution has suggested that Mr Northleach and Mr Frame were leaving the country for other, less exalted reasons.

— All right.

— Could you describe to the court what you were expecting from Mr Mandela?

— I have come to believe over the last few years that Mr Mandela would offer the world some vision, I'm not exactly sure what. But I wanted to be there and I suggested to Mike that he came with me. I saw it as historical, like the Berlin Wall coming down. And of course, I was brought up in Africa.

— Just a minute. Did Mr Frame share your interest?

— Mr Frame said that he thought I was naïve, but that he would like to come.

— Was there any suggestion of girlfriends in Cape Town?

— None at all.

— So it wasn't, as the prosecution has said, 'a rugby-club type jolly', whatever the precise meaning of that may be?

— No. Far from it. It was deadly serious.

— And in the event you didn't see Mr Mandela, did you?

— No, I was in hospital unconscious, although I believe I saw the release on television.

— And why did you not tell your wife of your plans?

— It was a spur-of-the-moment thing. I just didn't have an opportunity to tell her.

Julian Capper looks at his notes. He feels compelled to point out to his fellow jurors the artifice, the rehearsal, the duplicity of this exchange. He must deconstruct it for them, without, of course, appearing pompous or overbearing. ('A boring fart.') He must explain to them once again the significance of trying to enlist to the cause Nelson Mandela, the single most powerful symbol of our times.

Joyce appears at the head of the rest of the jurors. They are animated and giggling, but they quieten when they see him sitting alone with his notes and sandwich box. He feels as he sometimes did at school, on the periphery of the fun, but unable to break through, as though the others are surrounded by a clear, impenetrable membrane. He remembers when the rugby teams set off to matches leaving the bookish in uneasy, unmerited possession of the school.

Joyce tells them that the judge is hearing legal argument and that they will probably be called quite soon. But she can't be sure. She confides that this judge is known for the speed of his thought and the conciseness of his summing-up. To her, all the judges are distinct characters. Julian Capper is sure that his own summing-up will be both concise and decisive. He is, after all, the only one among them who has to marshal his thoughts systematically, almost daily, even if these thoughts, for example on whether the new popularity of mozzarella is consumer- or trade-led, are not in the same category as arguments about society and its instruments of control. The apparent reluctance to admit him to the circle of bonhomie suggests to Julian Capper that it is increasingly unlikely that they will elect him foreman. But that will not prevent him putting the case decisively. He sees it as a duty. From the entrance of the court you can see across Parliament Square to Winston Churchill's broad, overcoated back and beyond that to Big Ben and the Palace of Westminster. The location of the court is a gift to a wordsmith.

But they are not called back to court immediately. They are told that there is some hold-up in the legal argument, probably documents delayed. They may return to the canteen for half an hour for a coffee. Julian Capper elects to stay in the jury room to work on his notes, although its windowless brownness is beginning to get on his nerves. Perhaps in the judge's comfy chambers they are preparing some sort of deal. After an hour or so, Joyce calls them into court. They follow her glossy hair and strong behind. The defendant is already there, flanked by two officers.

– *Court rise.*

They rise and sit. Mr Justice Applethwaite plumps himself up. He arranges his robes. His face, under the wig, is ruddy and grave.

– *Members of the jury, the prosecution has withdrawn its case. I must direct you, and you must follow my direction, to find the defendant not guilty. Before I do that, I will outline the legal reasons for this decision.*

You will remember the witness you heard earlier on Tuesday, Carole Smith, who is in Pentonville prison on related charges. This morning she made a further statement, which has been duly sworn. She has said, and I will be brief, that she was threatened by Mr Parchment into trying to entrap Mr Northleach, that she approached Mr Northleach when his car stopped at the war memorial at Norwood Road, as the defence said, claiming to have been raped. It was Jason Parchment's idea. He needed money urgently. She has given evidence that this was the third extortion attempt of the evening. She ran away the moment Mr Frame appeared and she was extremely unhappy about the prospect of robbery with a firearm. She had explicitly asked Mr Parchment not to use a firearm. She went along with the scheme because she was frightened of Mr Parchment who had hit her earlier in the evening. She lied to the police about the shooting, which she did not witness at all, because she was frightened that she would be locked up when her young son was ill. She had no idea who Mr Frame was when he appeared and thought he might be a policeman. She has made this new statement because last night, tragically, her young son was killed in a fire at her mother's house.

The prosecution has accepted that it no longer has a case. Before I instruct you to find the defendant not guilty, I would like to make a few remarks. Firstly, I would like to thank you, members of the jury, for your patience and diligent attention over the nine days of the trial. And secondly, I would like to put on record the fact that I do not think this case should ever have been brought to court. To you, Mr Northleach, I can only say that you have the court's greatest sympathy for the ordeal you have undergone and the tragic loss you have suffered. Now you, sir – he points to Julian Capper – *could you stand up? The clerk will ask you to find the defendant not guilty so that this case may be brought to an end.*

Julian Capper stands up. The clerk stands in front of him.

– Do you find the defendant Anthony Preston Northleach not guilty in accordance with the judge's directions?

There is a short, but perceptible, pause.

– We do.

The defendant leaves his box. He walks towards the back of the court where his former secretary is waiting, in tears. As he passes Julian Capper he smiles a lopsided smile of gratitude, between mates.

*   *   *

The writer Julian Capper leaves the building after signing his attendance and travel sheets. He passes through the metal detector out into Parliament Square, with its emblematic red buses, black taxis and Big Ben. He walks towards the Underground, past Abraham Lincoln, past General Smuts and past Winston Churchill. He sees an *Evening Standard* banner: 'Major to welcome Mandela'.

As he is making his way down the escalator to the station, he at last realises what happened. He should have seen it earlier. When Northleach was questioned and told that he was accused of killing Jason Parchment, he was not able to tell the truth. The truth is that his old friend, Michael Frame, pulled the trigger.

That's how it is with friends: you don't dishonour their memory.